"Hey, Mollie." Paul stood and crossed the room in two giant steps. "Don't you look all bright-eyed after your nap." He tickled her under her chin and smiled when she smiled at him.

"You sure are at ease with little ones for having none in your house."

"I guess I inherited that from Mamm."

"Would you like to hold her while I prepare her bottle?"

"Sure." He expertly lifted Mollie from Rosanna's arms as if he'd been handling infants regularly.

Rosanna scooped powdered formula into a bottle, added water and a nipple, and shook the bottle to mix the ingredients. Paul sure would make a great *daed* one day. How many times had that thought run through her head? When she turned back around, she found Paul had dropped onto a chair and cuddled Mollie in his arms.

"Can I feed her? Do you think she'll take the bottle from me?"

"I don't see why she wouldn't. She certainly seems to like you." Rosanna gave the bottle a final shake before handing it to Paul.

When Mollie opened her mouth and started sucking the bottle, Rosanna plunked down on a nearby chair. The scene in front of her looked so natural that it nearly stole her breath away . . .

Books by Susan Lantz Simpson

THE PROMISE

THE MENDING

THE RECONCILIATION

ROSANNA'S GIFT

Published by Kensington Publishing Corporation

ROSANNA'S GIFT

WITHDRAWN

Susan Lantz Simpson

ZEBRA BOOKS
KENSINGTON PUBLISHING CORP.
www.kensingtonbooks.com

ZEBRA BOOKS are published by

Kensington Publishing Corp.
119 West 40th Street
New York, NY 10018

All Kensington titles, imprints, and distributed lines are available at special quantity discounts for bulk purchases for sales promotion, premiums, fund-raising, educational, or institutional use.

Special book excerpts or customized printings can also be created to fit specific needs. For details, write or phone the office of the Kensington Sales Manager: Attn.: Sales Department. Kensington Publishing Corp., 119 West 40th Street, New York, NY 10018. Phone: 1-800-221-2647.

Zebra and the Z logo Reg. U.S. Pat. & TM Off.
BOUQUET Reg. U.S. Pat. & TM Off.

First Printing: January 2020
ISBN-13: 978-1-4201-4980-7
ISBN-10: 1-4201-4980-6

ISBN-13: 978-1-4201-4981-4 (eBook)
ISBN-10: 1-4201-4981-4 (eBook)

10 9 8 7 6 5 4 3 2 1

Printed in the United States of America

For all those who have welcomed children into their hearts and homes

ACKNOWLEDGMENTS

Thank you to my family and friends for your continuous love and support.

Thank you to my daughters, Rachel and Holly, for believing in me and dreaming along with me. (Rachel, you patiently listened to my ideas and ramblings, and Holly, I couldn't have done any of the tech work without your skills!)

Thank you to my mother, who encouraged me from the time I was able to write. I know you are rejoicing in heaven.

Thank you to Dana Russell and friends at Mt. Zion United Methodist Church for all your enthusiasm and support.

Thank you to Mennonite friends Greta and Ida for all your information.

Thank you to my wonderful agent, Julie Gwinn, for believing in me from the beginning and for all your tireless work.

Thank you to John Scognamiglio, editor in chief, and the entire staff at Kensington Publishing for all your efforts in turning my dream into reality.

Thank you most of all to God, giver of dreams and abilities and bestower of all blessings.

Prologue

Rosanna wavered. She wanted to stay right where she was and talk to Henry. Maybe he'd mention something about taking a ride with him if she gave him enough time. But Mamm needed her. "I'm sorry, but I can't talk right now, Henry. I need to help my *mamm.*"

"With that *Englischer*?" Henry had stopped his horse near the back door of the big two-story house and stood beside his gray buggy.

"You saw the girl who came to our door?"

"*Jah*, I was just driving up. You have to help with her?"

"From the way things looked, she definitely needs our help."

"Why doesn't your *mamm* just call the rescue squad and send her to the *Englischers'* hospital?"

Rosanna stomped her black athletic shoe–clad foot and looked Henry straight in his small brown eyes. Since he stood only a hair's breadth taller, looking him in the eye was not a challenge. "Henry Zook, you know *gut* and well Mamm would never turn away a woman who needed her help—Amish or *Englisch*. What's gotten into you?"

"Nothing. It just seems to me that girl should seek out help from her own kind."

Rosanna's exasperation mounted. She'd heard from her older *bruders* that Henry wanted little or nothing to do with *Englischers*. That she could accept, she supposed, but not his lack of compassion for a fellow human being in need. Disappointment crept in with the exasperation. This was the fellow she wanted to step out with?

She'd secretly watched him at school and had felt a huge void when he finished two years before she did. At the young people's singings, she stole glances at him and, once or twice, caught him looking back. That proved he was interested, didn't it? But this attitude was a little hard to swallow. Maybe Henry was just having a bad day. Everyone had one of those days now and again.

Henry dropped his gaze under Rosanna's scrutiny and stared at his toe drawing circles in the dirt. "Do you always help your *mamm* with, uh, with these things?"

"Of course. I love helping her with—"

"I see."

Henry had interrupted her before she could complete her sentence. Honestly! Childbirth was a natural occurrence, a blessed event. Men could be so squeamish about such things.

"Rosanna!" Mamm's voice carried right outside to where Rosanna was wasting time with Henry. That's what Mamm would think she was doing. How many times had Mamm asked her why she wasted her time and dreams on Henry Zook? "I have to go, Henry. Maybe we can talk later?" Could her hint be any more blatant? If he didn't catch on that she wanted to step out with him, then that head under the mud brown hair must be pretty dense.

Henry shrugged. "I really came here to see your *bruder* Tobias anyway."

Rosanna flounced off without a backward glance and kicked the heavy wood door closed behind her. That was not the response she'd hoped for.

All thoughts of Henry and everything else flew from Rosanna's mind as she and Mamm worked in sync to help this stranger who had shown up at their door ready to bring her infant into the world. The air outside may have had a bite, but here in the spare bedroom that used to belong to her two married *bruders*, Rosanna fanned the girl on the bed. She mopped the girl's brow in between contractions and encouraged her to push when Mamm deemed it time to do so. The thin wisp of a girl nearly crushed the bones in Rosanna's hands but never cried out. In fact, she didn't speak at all until after the birth.

Chapter One

"She's yours." The voice came out as a mere gasp. The young woman raised a trembling hand to flick the matted light brown hair off her forehead but dropped it back onto the mattress as if the effort was too great.

Rosanna Mast pulled her gaze from the hazel eyes boring into her own to send a silent plea of help to her *mamm*. Amish midwife Sarah Mast, shrugged her shoulders and continued drying the mewling, rooting infant. Rosanna sponged the young woman's face with a cool, damp cloth. She looked more a girl than a woman, younger even than Rosanna's twenty-one years. She'd told them her name was Jane after Sarah had asked repeatedly what they should call her.

Sarah expertly cradled the newborn in the crook of one arm. She raised the other arm to wipe her forehead along the sleeve of her blue dress. She stepped closer to the bed and held the infant out to the woman who had just given birth to her. "You have a perfect little girl."

"No!" If the voice hadn't been so raspy, Rosanna felt sure the sound would have been an earsplitting shriek. The girl shook her head so hard, Rosanna expected to see brain matter fly out of her ears. She made no move to reach for the bundle in Sarah's arms. Instead, she kept her arms on the bed with the edges of the cotton sheet bunched tightly in her fists. "Yours," she croaked, looking Rosanna straight in the eye. "I. Want. You. To. Have. Her." The words were uttered as if with great effort, but the piercing gaze never wavered from Rosanna's eyes.

Rosanna felt her mouth drop open to her knees. The girl must be delirious. She must have a fever. Rosanna had assisted her *mamm* with births more times than she could count. Never had she seen a new *mudder* refuse to cuddle her *boppli*. Never had she heard a woman say she wanted to give away her newborn. And to her of all people!

Sarah again offered the infant to the panting girl. She leaned down to give her the opportunity to better see the little one. "Look at your *dochder*. What will her name be?" Sarah's voice was soft, soothing.

"Ask her!" The young woman jerked her head toward Rosanna.

"I-I-I . . ." Rosanna couldn't seem to form a coherent sentence. She tried again. "Sh-she's your *boppli*." Rosanna looked to Sarah. What in the world was going on here? Mamm would make it right. She always knew what to do.

"She *is* yours." The exhausted-looking girl let go of the sheet she clutched so tightly and pushed against the mattress to raise herself. Two seconds later she flopped back onto the bed, totally spent. She gasped for breath. "I want you to have her." The voice might have been ragged, but it was forceful at the same time.

"Why me? You must be confused." Rosanna glanced from the girl to her own wringing hands to her *mamm*, and finally to the helpless newborn.

"Not confused."

"Here, why don't you nurse your *boppli* and then we'll talk. She's hungry."

"No! I-I can't." She panted after her outburst. Her eyes widened in panic or fear or desperation. Rosanna couldn't be sure which.

"Calm yourself, dear. We'll help you." If Sarah's soothing voice and serene manner didn't settle the young woman, nothing would, though Rosanna felt far from settled herself. Sarah shifted the infant to one side and patted the thin arm lying limp on the bed with her free hand. She turned to Rosanna. "Here, Dochder. Hold the *boppli*. I have to find something to feed her."

Rosanna automatically reached for the bundle Sarah passed to her. At least her arms weren't numb like her brain. She looked down into the sweet little face and smiled. The miracle of birth never ceased to thrill her. She'd been ever so glad Mamm had let her start assisting with births. Every newborn was a gift. This precious one somehow seemed even more special. She felt right in Rosanna's arms. A perfect fit. Rosanna snuck a peek at the girl in the bed. Her eyes were closed tightly, and she didn't show any sign whatsoever of wanting to bond with her infant. How was Mamm going to fix this?

Well, first off, she'd prepare a bottle of store-bought formula for this wee one, who would soon be wailing in hunger. Most Amish women nursed their newborns, but occasionally someone needed a bit of help. Mamm always kept a little formula around for emergencies. That would take care of this *boppli*'s physical needs. But what about her emotional needs?

"You are such a beauty," Rosanna crooned. The infant focused on her face. Rosanna knew better, but she thought for sure the little bow-shaped mouth curved up in a tiny smile. She knew she was not supposed to pay attention to outward appearances, but this little girl was gorgeous. She wasn't at all red and wrinkly like most newborns. Her head was not misshapen from squeezing through the birth canal. It was totally perfect and even sported a shock of honey-gold hair.

"Are you ready to see your *boppli* now, Jane?"

"I don't want to look at her." Jane turned her face in the opposite direction.

"I know the whole childbirth experience can be overwhelming, but you need to at least look at your little girl."

"No! The *boppy* or whatever you called her belongs to you." Jane pointed a shaking finger in Rosanna's direction.

"Why do you keep saying that? You can't simply give your *boppli* away." Rosanna had never been more confused in her life.

"I already have."

"What?" The word slid out of Rosanna's mouth on a gasp.

"Look in my bag." Jane nodded toward the over-sized purse on a nearby chair. At Rosanna's hesitation, Jane spoke louder. "Go ahead. Look in my bag."

Rosanna shuffled to the chair, holding the poor unwanted infant closer. She lifted the bag and carried it to the bed. "You can search for what you need." She wasn't about to prowl through someone's personal belongings.

The weary young woman pushed against the mattress to hoist herself up in the bed. She plunged a hand into the deep recesses of the bag and fumbled around.

"Aha! Here it is." She pulled a slightly dog-eared paper from her bag and waved it in the air. "Read this."

Rosanna wasn't entirely sure she wanted to read the paper fluttering in Jane's hand. She wished Mamm would hurry back into the room. What was taking her so long to mix a bottle of formula?

"Read it!" The voice from the bed came out stronger, more forcefully this time. The paper shook violently in Jane's hand.

Rosanna jumped, startled by the sudden command. She cradled the newborn with her right hand and reached for the paper with her left one. She squinted to focus in the waning daylight. She should have lit a lamp earlier. At least the print was in bold, black letters. "I-I don't understand." Now she was more confused than ever.

"You are Rosanna Mast, correct?" The voice had taken on a slightly sharp tone.

"*Jah*, but why is my name on this paper?"

An exaggerated sigh filled the room. "You are the baby's mother."

"Don't be ridiculous. You just gave birth to her." Rosanna stretched out a hand to lay across Jane's forehead. The girl must have a raging fever. Rosanna felt a sting when her hand was batted away.

"I do not have a fever. I am of sound mind. You are the *adoptive* mother then. How's that?"

Rosanna could only stare. What in the world was this obviously mixed-up young woman talking about?

"You have heard of adoption, haven't you?"

"Of course." Rosanna dropped her eyes for a quick glance at the infant, who obviously had grown too tired to be hungry and dropped off to sleep. Rosanna's body swayed to and fro in a slight rocking motion all of its own volition.

"I chose *you* to be my baby's mother."

"Why? Why would you give her up? Just look at her. She's precious."

Jane turned her head away to avoid looking at the bundle in Rosanna's arms. "I'm only nineteen. I can't take care of a baby. And I'm sick. She needs a good home."

"Why me? And how did you know my name to put it on this paper?"

"I've watched you at the market the past few weeks. I can tell you're a good person. I've seen you with other people's children. Besides I want her to be raised Amish. My world certainly hasn't been very kind to me. I want her raised right. You can do that."

Rosanna shivered and snuggled the newborn closer. It was all so creepy that someone had been watching her, even if it had been a young, very pregnant girl. "My name? You put my name on this paper, but I've never met you."

"I felt like I knew you as well as I've ever known anyone. It wasn't hard to get your name. I simply asked around. Oh, and I asked *about* you, too. Everyone said you were a *wunderbaar* person. I assumed that meant wonderful."

Rosanna nodded.

"Well, I've always heard the Amish were honest and trustworthy. Wonderful is just the kind of mother this baby needs."

"But you are the *mudder*."

"Did you read that paper? It says I give all parental rights to you. It's all signed, official, and legal. The baby is yours."

Chapter Two

Rosanna gasped. She looked into the precious, innocent face. Long eyelashes brushed the rounded cheeks. Little wisps of honey hair curled near the forehead. The pink lips almost smiled in sleep. *My* boppli. She tried the words on. Immediately a fierce protective instinct grabbed hold of her and wouldn't turn loose. The image of a mother bear with her cub took over her brain. *My* boppli!

Rosanna nearly leaped from her shoes at the touch of a hand on her arm. She had never even heard her *mamm* reenter the room. All her focus had been on the tiny being snuggled in her arms.

"Dochder, are you all right?"

"I-I don't know." All she could think of was the fact that she was a *mudder*. Something inside her wanted this *boppli* more than anything in the world. Yet a niggling little voice begging to be heard uttered, *What about Henry?* Henry Zook. The fellow she'd hoped would ask her to marry him. How would he feel about a ready-made family? How would he feel about raising an *Englisch boppli* as his own? He barely tolerated *Englischers.* Though he was always polite, Henry never wanted much dealing with folks who weren't Amish.

Well, if he cared about her at all, he'd have to care about her *boppli*, too. Her *boppli*?

"Rosanna?" Sarah shook the arm not curved around the swaddled infant. "What is it?"

"Here, Mamm. You'd better read this paper."

"Just a minute. First let's see if this little one will wake to eat. I've got a bottle warmed." Sarah held up the bottle as if to prove her point.

"What is your *boppli*'s name?" She smiled at Jane, who had pulled the covers up to her chin and lay observing mother and daughter.

"Ask her." The young woman nodded at Rosanna.

Sarah turned raised eyebrows toward her *dochder*, who shrugged her shoulders and jiggled the piece of paper in her free hand. "Hand the infant to her *mamm*, Rosanna, and we can talk while she eats."

"No!" Jane's voice bounced off the stark walls.

This time, Sarah jumped in surprise. "You don't want to feed your *boppli*? Are you in pain?" Sarah started for the bed.

"No to both questions. And you don't have to come over here to feel my forehead. Ask her." Jane nodded at Rosanna again.

"*Kumm*, Dochder." Sarah moved to take the infant, obviously intending to hand her to Jane.

"Take the baby with you." Jane turned on her side and pulled the covers over her head.

"I've never seen anything like it," Sarah mumbled as she and Rosanna filed out of the room. She pulled the door closed behind them. "I've never seen a woman not eager to hold her newborn. I know this girl is young, but I've attended many young Amish girls' births, and none have acted like this. Could it be post-partum depression?"

12   *Susan Lantz Simpson*

"Mamm." Rosanna nudged the older woman, breaking into her monologue. "You need to read this paper Jane handed me."

"What kind of paper could be more important than her own *boppli*? She didn't want to feed her or even hold her. I really should make sure she isn't feverish or hemorrhaging or . . ."

"Mamm, read the paper." Rosanna thrust the sheet of paper into her *mamm*'s hand.

Sarah gave an exasperated sigh and shook the paper open. Rosanna studied her face as she swayed to and fro to rock the infant whose long-lashed eyes were still closed in innocent slumber. She watched the color fade from her *mamm*'s cheeks.

"What is this?" Sarah's voice rose a little on each word.

"Shhh!" Rosanna dared to hush the obviously astonished woman. "I couldn't believe it at first, either."

"How do you know this girl, Rosanna? I thought she was a stranger to you, too, when she showed up at our door asking for help."

"She was, Mamm. Truly, she was. Apparently she'd been watching me for, well, I don't know how long, at the market or wherever. She said she felt like she could trust me. She asked people about me and got my name from someone she spoke with."

"Well, this is absolutely ridiculous! Women don't just hand their *kinner* over to total strangers. This-this paper . . ."

"Is a legal document. There's a seal at the bottom. I don't think adoption is too foreign in the *Englisch* world."

"Let me talk to that girl. She simply has some

strange postpartum thing going on, that's all. I'll clear up this whole confusion quick."

Before Sarah could move, Rosanna laid a hand on her arm. "I asked her all the questions I'm sure you'll ask her. She said she was only nineteen, that she couldn't care for a *boppli*, and that she was sick. She said the infant was, uh, is mine."

"Yours! You aren't even married. You're young yourself."

"I'm twenty-one, Mamm. Lots of girls my age are going on their second pregnancy."

"What about Henry?"

Rosanna felt the heat rise from her toes to her scalp. Even if parents knew their *dochder* was interested in a fellow, they didn't mention it. Dating and court-ship weren't generally discussed. "I-I don't know." Rosanna's voice squeaked. She cleared her throat. "But if Jane truly doesn't want this precious little one, I will gladly accept full responsibility for her."

"You can't take on such a thing! You aren't ready for—"

"What first-time *mudder* is truly ready? They all have to learn, ain't so?" Rosanna suddenly felt the need to defend her case. "I'm probably more ready than most. I've taken care of my younger *bruders* and *schweschders*, sure, but I've cared for newborns fresh from the womb. I'm comfortable with them." She glanced down at the sweet infant in her arms and smiled.

"You've already fallen in *leib* with this one, ain't so?"

Rosanna nodded. A tear slipped down her cheek. "If Jane doesn't want this *boppli*, then I do."

Sarah wrapped an arm around her *dochder*'s shoul-ders. "You've always had a tender heart. I don't have any doubt you would make a fine *mudder*. I just don't want you to get attached to this wee one until we check this all out. I don't want you to ruin your chances at a happy marriage. And I don't want you to get hurt if this is all some kind of sham."

Rosanna nodded. "I know, Mamm. I truly think this paper is for real. Widows with *kinner* remarry all the time, and their new husbands willingly take on a ready-made family. I'm not worried about the whole marriage thing." Much.

"That's different."

"Well, if any man cares about me, he'll have to care about my *boppli*, too."

"Let's not put the cart before the horse, Dochder. Let's check this out more before you let your enthusiasm run away with you."

Thoughts spun through Rosanna's mind as fast as the windmill spun on a blustery day. Would Mamm and Daed forbid her to keep the *boppli*? Surely they wouldn't turn away a helpless little one. Would they say she belonged in the *Englisch* world? Jane wanted her raised in the Amish faith. The Lord Gott must have led Jane to their door. Wasn't it His will Jane sought her out to raise the infant?

If Jane was befuddled, as Mamm insisted, she stayed that way for the next day and a half that she dozed or pretended to doze in the Masts' spare bedroom. Rosanna had taken over care of the infant, as Jane had requested, but tried repeatedly to get the girl to hold or even look at her precious newborn.

"That girl has rested and recuperated and eaten every morsel of food we've taken her. I'd say she was ready to talk sensibly about her decision now." Sarah stood in the upstairs hallway with hands balled into fists on her hips.

"I've tried, Mamm, over and over again. I haven't gotten anywhere."

Sarah squeezed Rosanna's arm before marching into the bedroom. "Well, I'll straighten this whole business out," she muttered. "That girl is simply confused. That's all."

Rosanna followed on Sarah's heels. She didn't want to miss a single word exchanged between Mamm and Jane. Her heart hammered. What if Jane had changed her mind after all? What if she said she'd made a mistake and wanted to raise the infant herself? Mamm would tear that paper to bits, and Rosanna would have to relinquish this precious little one she already thought of as hers.

"Jane, let's talk about this." Sarah pushed the door open and then stopped so abruptly Rosanna nearly crashed into her. "Jane? Where is she?"

Rosanna scooted around her *mamm*. The rumpled bed stood empty of its patient. "Where could she be?"

"We would have seen her leave the room. We were right there in the hallway."

"The window." Rosanna pointed to the almost fully opened window.

"The girl just recently gave birth. She couldn't have leaped from the window. We're on the second floor."

Rosanna beat Sarah to the window and stared outside. Jane could have easily climbed down by way of the old oak tree, just like her older *bruders* bragged of doing years ago. Since the tree had already shed its leaves, Jane's climb would have been a little easier than that of the *buwe*, who generally only made this escape when the foliage hid them. Only Jane had to be exhausted and more than a little weak so soon after delivery, especially if she was as sick as she said. "I don't see her. Could she have run off that fast?"

"Certainly not. Not in her condition. She's probably hiding somewhere."

"Hello!" a deep voice called up the stairs.

"*Ach!* I forgot." Sarah smacked her forehead. "Paul Hertzler was stopping by to pick up the quilt I finished up for his *mamm*. She ran into a problem with it, and I helped her out. Her arthritis has been acting up something fierce lately." Sarah turned toward the door and spoke louder. "Be right there, Paul."

"If you're busy, you can just tell me where the quilt is, and I'll get it." A thump sounded on the step.

"I'll go." Rosanna whirled away from the window and started down the stairs, still cradling the infant. She heard Sarah descending behind her.

"Hello, Rosanna." Paul's handsome face crinkled into a smile. "Hey, who's this?" He nodded at the newborn who Rosanna now felt was a part of her.

"It-it's Mollie." Where did that thought come from? She did like the name, though, and it seemed to fit this golden-haired little angel. It certainly beat calling her "Boppli."

"She's a beauty." Paul leaned close to look into the little face. He reached one large finger out to gently stroke the little cheek. Would Henry do such a thing? Not many young men would pay much attention to a *boppli*. "Who does she belong to?"

Rosanna looked up and up. My, but Paul was tall. He must be at least six feet, so at least a good seven inches or so taller than her. Henry was barely her own height. Maybe only a whisper taller. Now, why on earth was she comparing the two? At last her eyes reached Paul's. Hazel, they were. Not quite green and not quite brown, with flecks of gold. If eyes could smile, his did. "She's m—"

"How is your *mudder* doing?" Sarah interrupted before Rosanna could lay claim to the infant.

"She's had right many bad days here lately. I know it's frustrating for her when her hands hurt too much to do her usual activities." Paul gave a little chuckle. "You know how stubborn Mamm is, though. She hates to ask for help."

"We all need help now and then." Sarah flew off in the direction of the living room but turned to throw a warning look over her shoulder at Rosanna.

Rosanna ventured a look at Paul and caught his raised eyebrows. So Mamm's cautionary expression hadn't escaped him. She shrugged her shoulders and opened her mouth to finish answering his earlier question.

"Here's Mary's quilt. Tell her I was happy to finish it for her. That's what *freinden* are for, ain't so? To help one another?"

"That's exactly what I keep telling her." Paul grabbed the folded quilt Sarah thrust into his arms.

"Say, Paul, you didn't see an *Englisch* girl on your way in, did you?" Even if Mamm believed Jane was hiding and couldn't get very far, Rosanna thought differently. She had seen how determined the girl was to give up her *boppli*. She was convinced the girl could have outrun their fastest horse if she put her mind to it.

"As a matter of fact, I did. I saw a girl run down your driveway like she was being chased by a pack of wild dogs. I had almost made it to your driveway when a car came along. The girl flagged it down and hopped into the back seat when it stopped. I could see the driver's surprised look even from my buggy."

"She's gone, then," Sarah muttered.

"Was she someone you knew?"

"Uh, sort of." Rosanna gazed at the infant and smiled. *I will love you, protect you, and care for you, little Mollie. Don't you fret one single bit.*

Paul shook his head. "I don't think I've ever seen anyone in such a hurry."

"I suppose she was." Sarah spoke more to herself than to the young man in front of her.

"*Danki* for the quilt, Sarah. Mamm will be ever so pleased." Paul plopped his straw hat back on his head, covering much of his pale blond hair. "You know, there's a change in the air, a nip, for sure and for certain. I think winter is upon us."

When Paul pulled open the door, a cold gust of air rushed in as if on cue to confirm his pronouncement. Rosanna snuggled the newborn closer.

"Say, she looks very content in your arms, Rosanna." Paul smiled. "Almost like she belongs there."

Rosanna jerked her gaze up to Paul's face. A little thrill shot through her heart. "Do you think so?"

"*Jah.*" Paul smiled again. This one caused little crinkles to fan out around his eyes.

Rosanna smiled back. She would almost have danced a little jig, if that had been permitted. Could Paul's words have been a message from the Lord Gott?

Chapter Three

"Such a nice *bu*," Sarah mumbled as she closed the heavy wooden door behind Paul. She turned to look squarely into Rosanna's face and crossed her arms over her chest. "Don't you go getting any crazy ideas just because someone said the *boppli* looks like she belongs in your arms." Her stern expression softened when she shifted her gaze to take in the swaddled infant.

Rosanna hadn't needed to hear those words from Paul Hertzler, but his opinion bolstered her own resolve. She didn't know how it *looked*, but she knew how it *felt*. And it felt right to claim this little one as her own. She had seen Mamm's tender expression, fleeting though it was. Now Sarah's demeanor returned to seriousness. Rosanna rocked the baby a teensy bit faster, keeping pace with her rapid heartbeat. What would Mamm's next words be?

"This is not a stray puppy you can simply keep as your own. This is a little human being, Rosanna."

"I know that perfectly well, Mamm. I also know Jane wanted me to have this little human being. She wrote it on that legal paper. She chose *me* to take her *boppli*."

Sarah clucked her tongue. "We have to check about that."

"Don't you think maybe it's the Lord Gott's will, Mamm? That girl showed up out of the blue. She found out about me and picked me to be her little one's *mudder*. I actually feel honored and blessed."

"How honored and blessed are you going to feel at two in the morning, *every* morning, when she wakes up screaming and wants to nurse?"

"I remember when Katie, James, and Sadie were little. I know they wake up often to eat."

"And I nursed them all."

"It's true I can't nurse Mollie, but I can feed her a bottle of formula like I've been doing."

"Do you know how expensive that stuff is to buy in the grocery store?"

"Well, I've picked up a can or two for you to have on hand, so I know it's not cheap, but the Lord will provide. I have faith."

Sarah grunted.

"Mamm, you wouldn't turn away a helpless newborn, would you?"

Sarah sighed loud and long. "Of course not, Dochder. I just don't want you getting too attached to the notion that you are this little one's *mudder*. I don't want to see you hurt if things don't turn out as you've built up in your head."

Too late. Rosanna already felt attached to and totally in love with the precious infant she cradled in her arms.

"You do understand we have to check out that paper. We have to make sure we aren't doing anything we can get in trouble for."

Rosanna nodded. Her nose burned and her eyes

watered at the very thought of giving up the *boppli*. How had she become attached so quickly? She'd assisted in dozens of births. She'd oohed and aahed over each newborn but had never felt the infant belonged to her. This little one was completely different. "H-how are you going to check things out? We don't know any lawyers." Whatever would she do if the paper was a fake and the authorities took her *boppli* away?

"I'll visit Amy Rogers after we clean up."

"How can she help?" Amy was the *Englisch* neighbor who often drove the Amish to destinations too far to travel by horse and buggy.

"I'm sure she or her husband will know a lawyer. They seem to know everyone. If they can't help us, they will know who can."

"Do you have to clomp through like an elephant?" Rosanna had finally coaxed Mollie to accept an ounce of formula and sat rocking her to sleep near the woodstove in the living room.

"Yikes! I didn't know we still had a guest." Tobias tried to lower his voice.

"We don't," Rosanna whispered.

"Are you rocking a baby doll?"

Rosanna heard a muffled snort behind her big *bruder.*

"Very funny, smarty-pants. *Ach*, Henry! I didn't know you were here." Tobias was so tall and broadshouldered Rosanna hadn't seen the smaller man behind him. She attempted to straighten up in the chair but didn't want to disturb the *boppli,* who had finally closed her eyes.

"Why do you have her downstairs? What is her name

anyway?" Tobias tiptoed closer. Living with a *mudder* who helped women give birth made her *bruders* more comfortable around expectant women and newborns.

"This is Mollie."

"Isn't Mollie's *mamm* upstairs?"

"Uh, *nee*, uh . . ." Rosanna tried to give Tobias a look that said to drop the subject. She hoped he was astute enough to pick up on her cue. She wanted to twirl about and shout that the infant was hers, but she didn't dare until Mamm returned and, hopefully, brought favorable news. Rosanna had a distinct feeling that what she considered *gut* news might not be so *gut* to her *mamm*.

"Is . . . ?"

Rosanna threw another quick frown at Tobias and softened her features into a smile when she glanced in Henry's direction. She had to redirect their attention elsewhere before Tobias asked more questions. "Would you like to stay for supper, Henry? Mamm has a big pot of stew simmering on the stove, and I'm going to make corn muffins in a few minutes."

"I should probably get home, but I appreciate the offer."

She tried not to let her disappointment show. How could Henry sometimes seem interested in her and other times look at her like she was a two-headed monster to be avoided at all costs? What would he say if he knew Mollie was hers? Would that scare him off for sure and for certain? That was a chance she'd simply have to take. If that paper was completely legal, Mollie would be hers forever. A little tingle of excitement raced up her spine. *Please let it be legal.* "Maybe another time?" She smiled at Henry again. Why was he making this all so hard?

"Sure. Maybe. I'll see you, Tobias." Henry turned and disappeared through the door he'd entered only moments before.

"You certainly seem to have a way with fellows. They're running away from here like a mad bull is behind them."

"You are just too funny for words. And who is 'they'? I only saw Henry tear out of here."

"Didn't I see Paul Hertzler leave earlier?"

"*Ach*, Paul." Rosanna waved a hand in the air but kept her rocking steady. "He was here to pick up a quilt from Mamm."

Tobias dropped to one knee beside the rocking chair. "So why were you giving me the evil eye? What's the story with this one?" He nodded at the bundle in Rosanna's arms.

"I wasn't giving you the evil eye."

"It sure looked like it to me."

"I didn't want to say anything in front of Henry—yet."

"I thought you were sweet on Henry."

"Tobias!"

"Okay. Okay. What's the story with, uh, Mollie? Isn't that what you called her?"

"*Jah*. Mollie. And she might be here to stay."

Tobias whistled. The infant startled at the sound.

"Shhh, it's okay, little one." Rosanna gently patted the bundle and continued rocking.

"Why might she be here to stay? Where's her *mudder*? Isn't she still upstairs?"

"She's gone, I told you."

"Gone as in flew the coop or had to go to the hospital or what?"

"As in disappeared."

Tobias pursed his lips to whistle again but caught himself before any sound came out. "What happened?"

"I should know more later." Rosanna smiled down at the infant. "I wonder if Henry is afraid to be around little ones," she mused aloud.

"Why would he be?"

Oops! She hadn't meant to voice that thought. "He sure hightailed it out of here." She paused in mid-rock. "Unless it's me he doesn't want to be around." That thought made her stomach slide south. She reached out a hand to snag her *bruder*'s arm. "You're his *freind*, Tobias. Is he, um, interested in another girl?"

Tobias shook off her hand. "I wouldn't know about that, Rosanna. We fellows don't talk about such things like you girls do."

"Right."

"Honest. I don't know, but I don't think Henry is interested in anyone. I've never seen him leave a singing with anyone, not for a long time anyway. I haven't seen him out and about with anyone."

He hasn't left a singing with me, either. "Who did he leave with before?" Rosanna's curiosity got the best of her. Was that a long, long time ago, before she started attending the singings, or a shorter time ago and she didn't notice? She didn't know how she wouldn't have noticed. She normally paid strict attention to Henry's whereabouts during singings. And he usually planted himself near the refreshment table with a couple of other fellows. Still, she could have been momentarily distracted by one of the girls and missed a stealthy departure.

"Just leave it alone, Rosanna. Henry will do whatever he wants to do."

That's exactly what she was afraid of—that Henry

would continue to do nothing. Perhaps he needed a nudge in the right direction, her direction. Who had captured his attention before, and how had she done it? "Tell me who, Tobias. Pretty please?" Rosanna hated the little whine that crept into her voice. "I'll make surprise muffins instead of corn muffins." She knew Tobias' favorites were the muffins with strawberry, peach, or cherry jam in the centers. She could tell he was wavering. "I think there might be some blueberry jam, too." Tobias' favorite.

"Nancy Glick."

"Oh." Nancy's hair was as fair as Rosanna's was dark. She had big, green eyes. Maybe Henry preferred blondes. "But Nancy's family moved away."

"Only to Pennsylvania. That's not too far. And letters can travel anywhere."

"Are you trying to tell me Henry writes to Nancy Glick?"

"I wouldn't know, but he hasn't really taken an interest in anyone since she moved."

"In me, you mean. But the Glicks moved a couple years ago, ain't so?"

"Something like that."

"Tobias Mast, you aren't a very *gut* informant."

"I'm not an informant at all. I'm simply having a conversation with my nosy little *schweschder*. Now about those muffins."

Rosanna heaved an exaggerated sigh. "If you'll bring that cradle downstairs from the spare room, I'll lay Mollie down and see what kind of surprise I can *kumm* up with."

"It better be a *gut* surprise. I don't want any muffins with onions or peppers or anything else disgusting."

"Would I do such a thing to you?"

"Probably, but I'll get the cradle anyway. You'd better look hard for some blueberry jam."

"I'll see." Rosanna stopped rocking. She stood with the infant in her arms. "Your *onkle* is fetching a cradle for you," she whispered. She carried Mollie into the kitchen. "I'll have him put the cradle in here so I can keep an eye on you." She shifted the *boppli* to one arm so she could pull out the canisters of flour and sugar. What could be keeping Mamm? It seemed she'd been gone for ages.

"Here you go!" Tobias' booming voice bounced off the kitchen walls.

"Shhh!" Rosanna peeked at the infant, who slumbered on, oblivious to her surroundings.

"Aren't you a *mudder* hen? If this little one is going to live here, she'll have to get used to noise. This house is anything but quiet."

"I know." And Rosanna did know that Mollie would have to get used to a house full of boisterous *kinner*, but she was a newborn. Surely she deserved a little peace for a few days.

"Do you want this by the stove? It's not exactly lightweight, you know."

"Against the wall near the stove will be fine. *Danki*, Tobias."

Daed had made the solid cherry cradle years and years ago when Rosanna's oldest *bruder*, Adam, had been born. The seven *kinner* who followed Adam all took their turns sleeping in the cradle. Now Mamm used it for any infant who happened to be born at their house. Usually women gave birth in their own homes and Rosanna and Sarah traveled to them, but occasionally someone showed up at the Mast house, like Jane had.

Rosanna tiptoed to the shadowed corner and eased Mollie into the cradle. Bless Tobias. He'd even thought to bring an extra blanket.

"Now about those muffins." Tobias' attempt to speak in a hushed tone was almost comical. "Did you find blueberry jam?"

Rosanna couldn't hold back a giggle. Her towering *bruder* looked and acted like an overgrown little *bu*. "It wouldn't be a surprise if I told you, would it? There's a reason they're called surprise muffins."

Tobias' shoulders slumped. "I hope there will be some blueberry ones."

Rosanna laughed. She half expected to see Tobias' lower lip poke out in a pout. "I can always make corn muffins instead."

"*Nee. Nee.* Any surprise will be a *gut* one." Under his breath, he added, "I hope."

Rosanna pulled out the other ingredients after shooing Tobias away. "It also won't be a surprise if you watch me."

"All right. I'm sure Daed is ready to start the evening chores anyway. His last furniture customer must be gone by now."

Samuel Mast, their father, operated a furniture shop in addition to farming. Of course, at this time of year the corn, hay, and soybean crops had been harvested. The land was ready for its winter rest, but the horses and black-faced sheep still needed tending. All three of her older *bruders*—Adam, Roman, and Tobias— worked in the shop. Adam and Roman were both married and had their own places to look after as well.

Fifteen-year-old Joseph helped out now and again in the furniture shop, but he showed a keener interest in farming. He tended the greenhouses and planned to sell plants in the spring. Katie, James, and Sadie still attended school.

Rosanna loved her big, boisterous family and would surely miss them when she married, but lately her thoughts had been filled with a home and family of her own. Some of her *freinden* had already gotten married. But with Mollie's arrival, Rosanna's own plans might be drastically altered. She now had someone else who depended on her for her every need. It would be a monumental task, but she found herself eager to take it on.

Rosanna's glance kept sliding to the cradle in the corner as she stirred the batter and filled two muffin pans. She smiled as she spooned Tobias' favorite blueberry jam into the center of half the muffins. If she didn't watch him, Tobias would poke a little hole in every muffin to find whichever ones might contain the blueberry filling. She spooned strawberry and peach jam into the centers of the other muffins.

While the muffins baked, Rosanna flitted from the stove to stir the stew, to the cradle where Mollie slept soundly, to the window to look for Mamm. Darkness descended earlier and earlier these days. She had expected Mamm home way before now. She pulled bowls and plates from the cupboard and set the big oak table herself instead of calling Katie and Sadie to help. She needed to keep herself occupied. Even though she loved her little *schweschders* beyond belief, her nerves would not handle the chattering of a ten-year-old and an eight-year-old right now.

Rosanna had just tapped the big wooden spoon against the side of the pot and laid it in the ceramic spoon rest when she heard a commotion at the door. Either Mamm had finally made it home or twelve-year-old James had raced to the house after chores, hoping to pilfer a little snack before dinner. He tried that most evenings and was always turned away empty-handed by Mamm. Rosanna didn't know why he continued the daily ritual. *Buwe!*

"*Gut*, you've got supper ready."

"Mamm! What took so long? What did Amy say? Is the paper legal?"

"Let me get my cloak and bonnet off, please." Sarah untied her black bonnet and hung it with her black cloak on a peg near the door. She reached to reposition her white *kapp* before crossing the room to wash her hands. "You brought the cradle in here." It was more a statement than a question.

"I had Tobias carry it down for me. I couldn't bear to leave her all alone. Please, Mamm, don't make me wait until Daed wanders inside. Please tell me what you found out." Rosanna crossed the room to stand beside the cradle. Mollie slept peacefully. Every now and then the edges of her pink, bow-shaped mouth curved upward as if she was enjoying some pleasant dream. What thoughts and dreams filled a newborn's brain? Did they dream of floating in the womb, or were their little heads filled with dreams of the Lord Gott, heaven, and angels? Rosanna lifted her eyes to find her *mamm* staring at her.

"Amy's husband called a lawyer *freind* to *kumm* over. That's what took so long, but I figured it would be best to wait to hear what he said. I knew I could count on you to finish fixing supper."

Rosanna's heart pounded hard enough to shake the rafters. She clasped her hands together in front of her to still their trembling. "Wh-what did he say?"

"I really don't want to tell the story twice. Your *daed* will be in soon."

"Please, Mamm. I have to know. It's my life we're talking about here. Mine and that precious little girl's."

Sarah sighed. "*Jah*, it is your life." She sucked in a huge, audible gulp of air. "This lawyer man said the paper was perfectly legal. In fact, Jane went to his office. His partner wrote up the paper. He called the partner while he was at Amy's house. The partner said he remembered Jane. He said she seemed of sound mind and was absolutely insistent that you be named her infant's guardian. She gave up all parental rights so you can adopt the *boppli*." Sarah collapsed onto a kitchen chair like a sail collapses on a suddenly windless day. The transfer of information appeared to have robbed her of all her energy.

Rosanna couldn't resist a little squeal and jump. It was all she could do to keep from racing over to the cradle, snatching Mollie up, and hugging her close.

"I don't believe you've thought this through, Dochder."

Sarah's words brought Rosanna back to earth. "What is there to think about? Mollie is mine. Jane didn't give me any choice, but if she had, I would have chosen to take her newborn in a heartbeat."

"I know it seems exciting, but an infant is hard work."

"I know that, Mamm." Rosanna had to make her *mamm* see that she was a responsible adult.

"It's a hard task for two parents to raise a little one. It will be even harder for a single woman."

"I understand. But I'll have all of you for support. Mollie will have the love of a bunch of *aentis* and *onkles*, as well as a *grossmammi* and *grossdaddi*."

"What about a *daed*?"

Rosanna's heart skipped a beat. "Sh-she can have that in time. Couldn't she?"

"I don't want you to sacrifice your own happiness and chance to marry."

"Having Mollie makes me happy. If a man should want to marry me, he'll have to accept my *boppli* as well." Could Henry do that? Would he?

"I hope so, Dochder. I hope so. This is all such a mess. What will Samuel say?"

The last words were spoken so softly Rosanna barely heard them. She knelt beside Sarah's chair. "Everything will work out. Isn't that what you always say, Mamm? Who knows? The Lord Gott may have planned this special gift all along."

"I hope you feel this way later on."

"I will, Mamm. I've been around *kinner* enough to know there will be trying times. I know I'm young, but I'm not so naive to think everything will always be rosy. But everyone has ups and downs and trying times, ain't so?"

Sarah grabbed Rosanna's hand and squeezed it gently. "My little girl has grown up. I guess this makes me a *grossmammi*." Adam and Roman had both been married for more than a year, but neither had been blessed with *bopplin* yet. Mollie would be Sarah's first *grossdochder*. She wiped her eyes with the edge of her black apron.

Rosanna threw her arms around her *mamm* and

held on tightly for a moment. "*Danki*, Mamm." She sniffed and pulled away. "*Ach!* My muffins!" She jumped to her feet and ran to the oven. "Tobias will have a fit if I've ruined his surprise muffins."

"I hope Samuel doesn't have a fit."

Chapter Four

Thundering feet heralded the arrival of the rest of the family for supper. James' hands still glistened with water droplets, as though he couldn't take the time to thoroughly dry them. Katie's and Sadie's giggling ceased when they settled into their big oak chairs. At Samuel's signal, every head bowed for silent prayer.

Rosanna offered a quick thanks for the meal, but most of her prayer concerned the *boppli. Please, Gott, let Daed accept little Mollie. Please don't let him say I can't keep her. I don't know what I'll do then. Jane entrusted her to me.* She would have continued praying, but the tingly feeling that she was being stared at washed over her. She opened her eyes to find most of her family gazing at her. Her cheeks burned. She quickly grabbed the basket of muffins and passed it to her *daed.*

"Everything all right, Dochder?" Samuel chose two plump, golden-brown muffins and plopped them on his plate before passing the basket to Tobias, who studied the muffins intently, obviously trying to detect which ones were filled with blueberry jam.

"Pass the basket, Tobias." James drummed his fingers on the table.

"You can't tell from the outside," Rosanna said.

"That's what makes them a surprise. You could pass the basket along and take whatever is left if the decision is too great."

Joseph snickered. "*Jah*, Tobias. They're all *gut* anyway."

Tobias finally selected two muffins and passed the basket to Joseph. He broke into the first one. "Aha! It's blueberry!" He poked a finger into the second one. "This one, too!"

"I guess you'll go to bed happy tonight." Rosanna lifted a spoonful of stew toward her mouth.

"You didn't answer my question, Rosanna."

She had hoped the distraction would make Daed forget he asked her anything. Apparently that was not to be. "I, uh . . ." A soft whimper from the corner drew everyone's attention. Rosanna lowered the uneaten bite of food to the bowl and pushed away from the table.

"Is this the same *boppli*? Why isn't she with her *mudder*?" Samuel's voice hitched up a notch in volume.

Rosanna hurried to the cradle and lifted the swaddled infant into her arms. She returned to stand near her *daed*. "Th-this is Mollie."

Samuel's face softened when he glanced at the newborn. Rosanna prayed his great love for *kinner* would extend to this one.

"How much longer are we keeping her?"

"Sh-she belongs t-to me. Her *mamm* is gone, and we're keeping her forever."

"What?"

Mollie startled at Samuel's loud, deep voice. She whimpered again. Rosanna swayed to rock and calm her. "I think she's getting hungry."

"Explain, Rosanna. Tell me how you think this *boppli* is yours."

"I-I will, Daed. Let me get her bottle first, please." Rosanna scooted across to the counter to grab the bottle she'd placed in a pan of warm water earlier. She returned to her seat and placed the nipple between the perfectly shaped little lips. Immediately the infant began sucking. As Mollie ate, Rosanna tried to explain how she came to be Mollie's *mudder*.

Katie and Sadie squealed. "A *boppli*! We're *aentis*!"

"Absolutely not!" Samuel's declaration caused even James to stop eating, at least momentarily.

"It's all completely legal, Daed, and I accept full responsibility for her." Rosanna looked to her *mamm*, silently begging for help.

"It is legal, Samuel." Sarah's voice was as soft and smooth as the melted butter oozing from Tobias' muffin. "I asked a lawyer." She told her husband about her visit to the Rogers' house.

"We can't turn her away, Daed. It wouldn't be the Christian thing to do."

Samuel hedged. "We can keep her until we can find a couple to adopt her."

"*I* plan to adopt her, Daed. Jane chose me to raise her little girl."

"A *boppli* needs a *mamm* and a *daed*, a real family."

"We're a real family. Plenty of widowed people raise *kinner* alone. I'm fortunate to have all of you for support. Please, Daed." Rosanna silently forbade the tears pooling in her eyes to drip down her cheeks. She had to appear strong and confident even if her insides trembled so violently she feared her knees would buckle.

She looked down at the sweet, innocent infant, whose eyes grew heavy again now that her belly was satisfied. Rosanna felt her *daed*'s gaze and fought to muster the courage to look up into his face. When she did, her heart leaped. He was staring at Mollie. Little crinkles fanned out from his eyes, and his lips above his dark beard curved into the barest hint of a smile.

"Do you think you can properly raise this little one?" His voice wasn't nearly as loud or harsh as it had been a few moments ago.

"I'll do my best. That's all I can do. With Gott's help, I will be a *gut mudder*. Isn't that the way every new parent feels? It's new territory they're entering, but they vow to love their *kinner* and to raise them to know and honor the Lord." From the corner of her eye, she observed Sarah's nod.

Samuel continued to stare at Mollie. What seemed like eons later, he, too, nodded. "Well said, Dochder. We will all help you however we can."

A boulder lifted from Rosanna's shoulders. She sniffed and gazed into her *daed*'s dark eyes. "*Danki*, Daed." She shifted her glance to Sarah and raised her eyebrows.

"We will support you." She echoed her husband's sentiments. "And we will love this little one."

"Now, let me hold our newest family member." Samuel held out his arms.

"Yippee!" Sadie squealed again. "We can keep the *boppli*!"

"That means you aren't the *boppli* of the family anymore," Joseph pointed out.

Sadie looked thoughtful for a moment. "That's okay. It will be fun to have a real *boppli* in the house."

Rosanna set the nearly empty bottle on the table and raised the infant to her shoulder. She patted the little back as she stood. She rounded the table and placed Mollie in Samuel's waiting arms.

Immediately the burp Rosanna had been trying to coax out erupted, and Samuel laughed. "Do you feel better now, little one?" His smile broadened as he looked from Mollie to Sarah. "It's right nice to have a newborn in the house again, ain't so, Fraa?"

"I do hope you know what you're doing," Sarah whispered as she and Rosanna cleaned the kitchen. She'd sent Sadie and Katie into the living room after they had cleared the table.

"You'd do the same thing, wouldn't you, Mamm?"

Sarah sighed. "I would." She glanced toward the cradle where Mollie slept and then at the plate she'd nearly scrubbed the pattern from. "You're young—"

"Lots of girls my age already have a *boppli*," Rosanna jumped in to remind her *mamm*.

"I know, but they enjoyed their youth and had courtships before marriage. You are a *mudder* with responsibilities now, and you haven't had a chance to have a courtship yet."

"That could still happen." Couldn't it?

A real chill had settled over the house during the night. Rosanna had crawled out of her warm bed several times in between feedings to make sure Mollie was snug in the cradle. Maybe she should have left the cradle downstairs near the woodstove, but then she would have had to sleep on the couch. Every time she checked, though, Mollie felt warm. Tobias had been so *gut* about carrying the cradle up and down the stairs for the past week. She smiled into the darkness. Little Mollie was one week and one day old. Rosanna was exhausted but happy.

When the rooster crowed, she wanted nothing more than to pull the covers over her head and ignore his call, but since this was church Sunday, she would not have any time to spare. Last Sunday, an off day, she had stayed home with the newborn while her family visited others in the community. Today, though, she needed to get herself and Mollie ready and help get breakfast on the table. At least today she and Mamm would not be cooking their usual big morning meal. On Sundays, cold cereal and fruit were usually served. Of course, slices of bread could be smeared with jam or apple butter for anyone who didn't get filled up on cereal.

Rosanna almost drew her bare foot back under the covers when her toes first hit the cold floor. She felt around on the nightstand for the lamp and then danced across the room, hopping from one braided scatter rug to the other. She'd better get herself ready for the day while Mollie still slept.

She heard a faint stirring and a sucking sound from the cradle as she pinned her white *kapp* into place. Mollie would want her bottle any minute. She wished she could nurse the *boppli* like she would have had she given birth, but that was certainly something that couldn't be helped.

Rosanna quickly changed the infant's diaper and dressed her for the day. Assisting Mamm had given her confidence in handling newborns. She worked with deft fingers and hummed or cooed to Mollie the entire time. She still pinched herself to make sure Mollie wasn't a figment of her imagination. She also still feared any sound outside would be Jane returning to claim her *boppli*. So far that hadn't happened, but it had only been a little more than a week, even though it seemed Rosanna had been a *mudder* for much longer.

She swaddled Mollie in a warm blanket, extinguished the lamp, and tiptoed across the room. If Mamm wasn't up yet, she would have to stoke the fire and feed Mollie quickly so she could get the simple breakfast ready. Only necessary chores, like feeding the animals, would be done this morning, so Daed and her *bruders* wouldn't be outside long. And the *buwe* were always ravenous.

A glimmer of light streaming from the kitchen let Rosanna know Sarah was already bustling about. "*Gut mariye*, Mamm." Rosanna hoped her voice didn't give away how weary her body felt. "Let me feed Mollie, and then I'll help."

"I think I can set out bowls and cereal without help." Sarah peeked inside the blanket and smiled. "Go ahead and feed her so you can eat."

Rosanna scooped powdered formula into a bottle, added water, and screwed on the nipple. She shook the bottle vigorously to mix the contents. She had to send Tobias to the store yesterday to buy more formula since she didn't want to use up her *mamm*'s emergency supply. She'd tried to explain what to look for but ended up ripping the label off the can she was using so he wouldn't mess up his mission.

Sarah shuffled to the doorway and hollered for Katie and Sadie and James, who'd been allowed to sleep in since chores were few this morning. Rosanna listened to the thunder of feet overhead as she rocked and fed Mollie near the stove. It seemed her body always rocked now, even if she wasn't sitting in a rocking chair with an infant in her arms. She hoped she could sit still during the three-hour church service.

Gray buggies already lined the driveway of the Bylers' house by the time the Mast family arrived. Rosanna was glad the house was large enough to accommodate the congregation. Otherwise services would have been held in the big barn, which would have been much colder. Men in their black trousers and coats and black felt hats still stood in clumps outside, waiting to enter the house. Young people stamped around to keep warm as they chatted. Rosanna spotted many of her *freinden* huddled close together, their black bonnets nearly touching. *Mudders* kept little ones close to them to share their body heat.

Rosanna glanced from group to group. Where did she belong now? A few days ago there wouldn't have been any question. She would have hustled over to join the group of unmarried girls. Though still unmarried, she now had a *boppli*. Did she belong with her *freinden* or with the other *mudders*? It was too bad she hadn't thought that through before this very moment. And what about this evening's young folks' singing? Could she still attend? She couldn't very well show up with Mollie in her arms.

Her eyes traveled to the group of young men, instantly picking out Henry Zook. Rosanna was absolutely certain that news of her situation had spread along the Amish grapevine faster than the speed of light. Surely Henry had heard. What did he think?

She passed Mollie to Sarah while she climbed from the buggy and then held out her arms to take her back.

Maybe it was her imagination, but Rosanna sensed many pairs of eyes boring into her back. Hopefully, everyone would welcome her little one into their fold as she had. Mollie was an absolutely adorable newborn. Who wouldn't love her?

As Rosanna turned around, she caught Henry's eye. She offered her brightest smile, but he quickly averted his gaze. Maybe he was one person who would be reluctant to accept her *boppli*. Her smile evaporated. Katie and Sadie giggled as they raced to stand beside Rosanna. They rarely let Mollie out of their sight. They would be *gut* little *aentis*.

"Why don't you sit with us today?" Sarah said as she joined her *dochders*. The *buwe* and Daed hurried to join their appropriate groups. "That way these two won't be twisting and turning to keep an eye on Mollie."

Rosanna exhaled the breath she'd been holding. She nodded. Leave it to Mamm to offer a solution. Would she ever be as wise as her *mamm*?

Another gray buggy stopped, and the Hertzler family piled out. Mary Hertzler, whose *kinner* were all over the age of sixteen, couldn't exit the buggy fast enough. She called out a greeting as she approached. "I heard about your newest family member, and I couldn't wait to meet her."

Rosanna moved the blanket aside for a moment so Mary could peek at the *boppli*. "This is Mollie."

"*Ach!* What a beautiful little girl. Rosanna, I think you are doing a *wunderbaar* thing taking this little one on as your own. The Lord Gott has favored you with a special gift."

Rosanna smiled, and her heart warmed. Here was someone who felt the exact same way as she did. She pulled the blanket back over Mollie so she wouldn't become chilled.

"If ever you need someone to watch her—you know, if you and Sarah have a birth to attend or you simply need a little break—I would be more than happy to babysit. Any time of the day or night. I had all *buwe*, you know, so caring for a little girl would be pure delight."

"*Danki*, Mary. That is so kind."

"Maybe I could hold her later, *jah*?"

"Of course."

"I can't wait to hold a little one in my arms again. My *kinner* grew up much too fast."

As if on cue, four *buwe* ranging in age from nearly seventeen to twenty-four filed past. The last one, the tallest, stopped beside his *mudder* for a moment. "*Gut mariye*, Sarah and Rosanna. Hello there, girls. How is the *boppli*, Rosanna?" Paul leaned down to look at the bundle in Rosanna's arms.

She was surprised a young man would inquire about an infant. She raised the little flap on the blanket again, since Paul wanted a glimpse.

"*Jah*, she is a beauty. I can see Mamm is already besotted." Paul gave a low chuckle and squeezed Mary's arm.

"Go on with you." Mary swatted at her oldest son but beamed at him. Mary's love for her son was nearly palpable.

"See you later." Paul made a general statement, but he looked straight at Rosanna when he spoke.

She felt her cheeks grow warm. What a nice fellow. He even spoke to Katie and Sadie. If her cheeks glowed as red as they felt, she'd have to blame it on the wind if asked. Just the same, she kept her head down as they proceeded into the house, group by group.

Chapter Five

Little Mollie had slept throughout the entire service. The singing and preaching had not caused her to stir one bit. Rosanna figured if the infant could sleep during the ruckus in her busy household, sleeping in church should be a piece of cake. There were moments during the past three hours when Rosanna had nearly joined Mollie in slumber. The occasional wiggling of Katie or Sadie, who sat on either side of her, kept her from giving in to the almost overwhelming urge to nap.

Ordinarily she would have helped set food on the benches-turned-tables for the common meal after church. Today, though, she sat in the Bylers' spare bedroom to feed Mollie. Even though she could sleep through assorted noises, hunger was an entirely different matter. The *boppli* definitely awoke to eat. Two other young *mudders* sat in the room with her to nurse their infants. Rosanna was pretty sure she looked as tired as the other women, even though she hadn't physically given birth.

The men had been served and had already donned their black coats and hats to escape to the barn by the time Mollie had finished her bottle. Rosanna would rather sleep right now than eat, but since that wasn't an option, she shifted the infant to one arm while she plopped a slice of bread, a sliver of ham, and a piece of cheese onto a plate. Half of a sandwich would do just fine. She added a scoop of creamy coleslaw and a few bread-and-butter pickles to the plate before settling on the end of a bench.

She supposed she could have put Mollie down to nap with the other young *kinner*, but Rosanna couldn't bear to let Mollie out of her sight. What if the *boppli* wasn't there when she returned for her? What if Jane crept into the house to steal her back?

Rosanna shook her head. She had to relinquish her fears. Jane was not returning. The girl had made it clear she didn't have any intention of being a *mamm*. How she had escaped from the community without being seen was a mystery to Rosanna. And they'd never heard a word from her. Rosanna had already contacted authorities about the adoption proceedings. Mollie was hers! As soon as she could make that completely legal, she'd breathe much easier. She hoped so, anyway. She nibbled at the corner of the sandwich she really didn't have any interest in.

"Let me hold the *boppli* while you finish eating. Then go join the youngies for a while. You need a little break, ain't so?" Mary Hertzler smiled down at Rosanna.

"I'm fine, Mary. You go ahead and eat."

"I've already eaten, and I'm itching to cuddle that little one."

Rosanna knew she could trust Mary but still felt reluctant to hand Mollie over. Besides, did she fit in with her peers? She was still unmarried, for sure and for certain, but she now was an unmarried *mudder*.

The other girls didn't have her responsibilities, and she didn't want to appear to be shirking hers.

"Here." Mary held out her arms. "I'd be more than happy to relieve you for a spell. I promise that my hands are feeling much better, and I won't drop her."

Rosanna couldn't disappoint Mary, one of the sweetest souls on earth. She laid her sandwich on the plate and raised the sleeping infant to Mary's waiting arms. "She just ate . . ."

"Then she'll be fine for a few hours. You eat and catch up with *freinden*."

"I won't be long."

"Take your time. I'll enjoy every minute of holding this sweet girl." Mary's face fairly glowed as soon as she settled Mollie in her arms.

She might not have given birth, but Rosanna's innate nurturing instincts had kicked in immediately. Her eyes followed Mary as the older woman walked and cooed to Mollie. She forced herself to take one bite of coleslaw and to eat two pickles before giving up the attempt to eat. Should she approach the other girls, who had disappeared outside? From across the room, Mary smiled at her and made shooing motions with one hand. Maybe a tiny visit with the others would be all right.

Reluctantly, Rosanna slipped into her black cloak and tied the black bonnet over her white *kapp*. She was torn between the desire to remain with her *boppli* and the urge to catch up with her *freinden*. She cast a final glance at Mollie, who still slept in Mary's gently rocking arms.

Some of the young people were already playing volleyball. They swatted at the ball and shouted at each other good-naturedly. Henry, she noticed, hadn't joined in the game. Maybe he would *kumm* over to talk to her.

"*Gut* shot!" a strong male voice encouraged.

Rosanna turned toward the voice. Paul Hertzler, who stood at least a head taller than the *bu* in front of him, congratulated the other fellow on his play. The younger *bu* panted hard but beamed his appreciation. Paul probably could have knocked the ball over the net with very little effort, but he let the younger fellow shine. What a nice guy!

Movement in her periphery shifted Rosanna's focus. Henry shuffled along, but he was moving away from her rather than toward her. She sighed. He'd probably ignore her at the singing, too, so there wasn't any use in thinking about attending. Besides, she had Mollie now and couldn't be traipsing off on a whim.

"Hi, Rosanna."

She had been so preoccupied with thoughts of Henry she hadn't heard anyone approach. She whirled around. "*Ach*, Emma. Hi. It's *gut* to see you."

"You've been busy, I hear."

"That's for sure and for certain."

"Tell me about it. I can't believe you have a *boppli* now."

"Sometimes I don't believe it yet myself." Rosanna laughed. Emma Kurtz had been one of her closest *freinden* all during their growing-up years. "I'm sure you heard all the details from the grapevine."

"*Jah*, word does get around. The *Englisch* girl just vanished and left you with her little one?"

Rosanna nodded.

"How odd. I don't know how any woman could give up her newborn."

"She was more of a girl than a woman. She said she

wasn't able to properly care for an infant. At least she didn't leave her *boppli* in a basket on a stranger's doorstep."

"It sounds like she chose you even before she gave birth. That's what I heard anyway."

"You heard right. It was a total shock, but how could I refuse? I was there at her birth. I couldn't let Mollie go to strangers, especially since Jane specifically chose me, though I'm not sure why."

"You are a kind, compassionate, caring person. Jane must have picked up on that."

Rosanna shrugged. Her eyes flicked over the young people milling about. Was that Henry disappearing around the corner of the barn with some other fellows? All the guys wore black pants, coats, and hats, so it was a little difficult to be absolutely certain from this distance. Her gut told her Henry was one of those fellows, though.

"Where are you, Rosanna?" Emma nudged her, bringing her back to their conversation.

"Huh?"

"I asked if you were planning to attend the singing tonight. It will be here at the Bylers."

"I-I'm not sure. I have Mollie to care for now."

"Surely your *mamm* would watch her for a few hours, ain't so?"

"Probably, but I hate to ask her. Mollie is my responsibility. I can't just pass her off when I want to go out and have fun."

"But this is the time for you to do exactly that." Frannie Hostetler horned in on the conversation. A stray strand of light brown hair flew across her face. She grabbed at it as she pushed her silver wire-rimmed glasses up her nose. "How are you going to get a fellow to court you if you don't make yourself available?"

"I suppose if someone really wanted to court me, he'd do it even if I didn't attend singings." Rosanna couldn't seem to infuse her words with a whole lot of conviction. At one time, she had thought Henry might have done that, but now he always seemed to be running the opposite way from her. She had difficulty imagining him tossing pebbles at her window late one night, since they hadn't already been riding home together after singings. He could surprise her, though, couldn't he?

"I don't know, Rosanna. You may have doomed yourself to being an old *maedel* when you took on the little one." Again Frannie fiddled with the glasses that made her small brown eyes appear even smaller. "I think I'll go see if there were any cookies left." She patted Rosanna's arm as if in pity before taking off toward the house.

"If she keeps eating cookies and growing plumper, she'll be the old *maedel*," Emma muttered.

Rosanna giggled. "Emma Kurtz! I can't believe you said that."

"Well, it's true. I haven't seen the fellows stumbling over each other to ask her to ride home."

Rosanna laughed again. She looked at her tall, willowy *freind* with a mock stern look but burst out laughing again at the smirk on Emma's face.

"*Ach!* You're right, Rosanna. I'm being mean. The fellows haven't exactly been flocking around me, either. I guess they don't want either a beanpole or a plump girl."

"You are just fine. You can't help it that you're tall

and thin. You have the loveliest blonde hair and blue eyes."

"You say that because you're my *freind*."

"I say it because it's true."

"Maybe I should go hunt down some cookies."

Rosanna chuckled. "At least you can eat as many of them as you want, and they won't make you fat."

"*Gut* point."

Rosanna turned thoughtful. "Frannie might have been right about me ending up an old *maedel*. If that happens, then so be it. Mollie is worth it. I might be willing to leave her with Mamm sometime, but not yet."

"You do what's best for you. I want you to *kumm* to the singings, but I understand your feelings. We'll get together to do other things, like frolics and such, ain't so?"

"Sure."

Emma squeezed Rosanna's arm. "And you're right. If a fellow is interested, he'll seek you out."

"Maybe," Rosanna whispered.

"The game must be over." Emma nodded toward the volleyball players, who were cheering and clapping.

"I guess." Rosanna hadn't been paying much attention. When she hadn't been looking at Emma, her gaze had wandered to the barn where Henry had disappeared earlier.

"Let me guess. My *mamm* has Mollie."

The deep voice wrapped around a laugh snapped Rosanna's attention to the very tall fellow who'd trotted over to where she and Emma stood. "You guessed right. Mary couldn't wait to hold her."

"Mamm sure loves the little ones. You may have to pry your *boppli* out of her arms."

Rosanna laughed. "I didn't want to leave her, but

Mary convinced me to take a break and let her dote on Mollie for a while."

"I'm sure she's doing exactly that."

"Oops! I've got to run. I'll see you two." Emma sprinted off to join a group of girls who'd been playing volleyball.

"Wait!" Rosanna swallowed the rest of her comment. Emma was already out of earshot. Now, why on earth did Emma leave her alone with Paul Hertzler? Not that he wasn't kind and terribly *gut*-looking, but she had never given the slightest indication that she was interested in him as anything other than a *freind*.

"Rosanna!"

"Huh?"

"I asked how Mollie is doing."

"She's fine. She's a little mixed-up on the night and day still, but that's pretty normal."

"How are *you* doing?"

Rosanna laughed. "I'm sure the dark circles under my eyes prove I haven't slept much, but that's also normal when there's a new *boppli* in the house." How many fellows would think to ask about her or even inquire about an infant? Would Henry?

"You look fine, Rosanna."

A red stain crept up Paul's neck and onto his cheeks. Rosanna thought it was cute. She also believed it matched the color that most likely tinted her own face. Somehow she managed to croak out a *danki*. She grappled to find a neutral topic of conversation to put them both at ease. "How was the volleyball game?"

"Invigorating. It's always *gut* to work off a little energy—and some of the cookies I scarfed down."

"I saw what you did."

"You saw me eat a handful of cookies?"

"*Nee*, silly. I saw you let the younger *bu* make that play. That was so, uh, nice of you." Rosanna caught her tongue right before the word "sweet" rolled off it. It would never do for her to tell Paul she thought he was sweet.

"I wanted him to have a chance. I'm so much taller that I could have swatted every ball. That wouldn't have been fair."

"It was a thoughtful thing to do." If it was possible, Paul's cheeks glowed even brighter. In an instant they went from rosy red to scarlet. Even the tips of his ears blushed. Rosanna smiled.

"I think it was pretty *wunderbaar* for you to take on a *boppli* single-handedly."

Now Rosanna's face was about to burst into flames. "My family is around for support."

"True, but not every girl would be so bold or so compassionate."

"I couldn't let that innocent little girl be taken away. Somehow I seemed to bond with her from the beginning."

"It must have been Gott's will that the *Englisch* girl picked you and showed up at your house for the birth."

"I think so, too, Paul."

"You know my *mudder* will babysit whenever you want."

Rosanna smiled. "So she told me. I guess I should relieve her now and check on Mollie."

"I'm sure Mamm is enjoying every minute of holding her. You chose a *gut* name for her. She looks like a Mollie."

"You only saw her briefly."

"*Jah*, but I have a great memory." Paul tapped his head with an index finger.

Rosanna laughed.

"You think I'm kidding. The *boppli* has hair the color of honey and big blue eyes."

"Most newborns have blue eyes, so that would be an easy guess."

"But I'm right about the hair, ain't so?"

"You are."

"See. I told you." Paul's smile lit up his entire face.

"Maybe you just made a lucky guess." Why couldn't it be Henry who bantered with her? Rosanna glanced toward the barn again. No sign of Henry. He and those other fellows must have been swallowed up by the earth. Maybe her childhood crush should be left in the past. Smiling at her when they were scholars and helping her when she got hurt on the playground did not necessarily mean he was interested in her. It was entirely possible she misread, or worse yet, invented the cues she had gotten from the grown-up Henry. She slid her eyes back to Paul's smiling face and couldn't help but grin herself. "I'd better check on Mollie."

"I'll walk with you, if you don't mind."

"Are you looking for more cookies?"

"I was going to help you wrest your little one out of Mamm's arms, but if there happen to be any lonely cookies lying around waiting for someone to claim them, I'll be happy to oblige."

Rosanna laughed at Paul's impish expression. *My little one.* She sure did like the sound of those words.

As suspected, Rosanna found Mary in the same position as before with the infant snug in her arms. Her body gently swayed to and fro. An expression of pure contentment shone on her face like the sun's reflection on the Kurtzes' pond.

"What did I tell you?" Paul whispered behind Rosanna. "She's just as happy as a hound dog with a new bone."

Rosanna crossed the room to stand beside Mary. To her surprise, Paul stayed on her heels. She had thought sure he'd detour to search for cookies.

"Not a peep out of her." Mary smiled. "She's such a *gut boppli*."

"I'm afraid you have to give her back, Mamm."

"I'm well aware of that, son, but I certainly have enjoyed holding her." Mary lightly ran her finger along Mollie's cheek. "Such a precious little one."

"*Danki*, Mamm."

Rosanna burst out laughing.

Mary swatted at her son. "I wasn't talking about you."

"Do you mean I'm not precious?" Paul poked out his lower lip in a pretend pout.

"Of course you are. You'll always be my *boppli* no matter how old or big you get." Mary re-tucked the blanket and lifted Mollie up for Rosanna to take. "What brings you in the house, Paul?"

"Cookies, I think," Rosanna answered for him. "Apparently a vigorous volleyball game made him hungry all over again." She cuddled the infant in her arms.

"I thought I saw you grab several handfuls of cookies earlier." Mary wagged a finger at the young man who towered over both women.

"Not several, Mamm. It was only one handful. And I really don't need more cookies, at least not right now. I was teasing. But I might need a little snack for the ride home when you're ready to leave. I came in to peek at Rosanna's *boppli*."

Paul's warm breath tickled the little hairs on the

back of Rosanna's neck as he bent to peer over her shoulder. It was not at all an unpleasant sensation.

"See?" he said. "Honey-colored hair. I knew my memory hadn't failed me."

Mary stood. "Is your *daed* ready to leave?"

Paul took a step backward. "I'm not sure, Mamm."

A chill like an icy blast of cold air assaulted Rosanna when Paul backed away from her. She had a sudden urge to rub her arms to restore warmth.

"I can go check on Daed, if you like."

"That's okay. I need to stretch a bit. I'll round up your *daed* and *bruders*." Mary gave Rosanna's arm a gentle squeeze. "I appreciate your letting me hold your little one. Remember, I'm available anytime to help you out. I know you have Sarah, but if you both get called out to a birth, send Tobias or Joseph to fetch me."

"It's so kind of you to offer to help, Mary. I'll surely keep that in mind."

Mollie wiggled ever so slightly and blinked her eyes. "See? They're blue. Told you so!"

"And I told you most infants are born with blue eyes. Often they change colors later."

"Did your eyes start out blue?"

"Mamm said they did."

"That's interesting." Paul bent slightly to stare into Rosanna's eyes. "There's absolutely *nee* trace of blue now. Your eyes are huge and dark like two big chocolate drops."

Rosanna's breath hitched under Paul's scrutiny. His face was so close to her own. She pulled back slightly and gave a nervous little laugh. "I don't think anyone has ever compared my eyes to chocolate drops. Maybe your hunger is making you see food everywhere."

"I'm actually not that hungry. And I meant what I said in a *gut* way. I think your eyes are beautiful. I meant they are as dark as chocolate. I mean . . ." Paul rubbed a hand over his face, obviously flustered.

Rosanna smiled to put him at ease. "I know what you meant. *Danki.*"

"I'd better help Mamm round up my *bruders.* Will you be at the singing this evening?"

"Probably not." Rosanna glanced down at the infant, who'd closed her eyes and returned to her slumber.

"That's too bad. You'll be missed. You *can* still attend, you know."

"I suppose."

"Sure you can. You're young and single. But I understand. Maybe you can attend the next one."

"Maybe."

"I'll see you and little Mollie later."

Rosanna smiled at Paul's rather endearing awkwardness. He looked like he wanted to touch Mollie but didn't know if he should. "See you, Paul. Don't forget your cookies for the trip home."

Paul winked before turning away. The simple little gesture made Rosanna's knees go all rubbery. Had Henry ever winked at her? She couldn't recall that he had. And Paul's deliberate inclusion of Mollie in his comments warmed her heart. With fatigue threatening to engulf her, Rosanna concluded the Hertzlers had the right idea. She hoped her family was ready to head home, too. If she could convince Katie and Sadie to leave, maybe Mamm would fetch Daed and the *buwe.* She'd check to make sure the girls weren't playing inside before poking her head outside to holler for them. Voices in the living room stopped her in the doorway.

"I thought she liked Henry, and there was Paul trotting behind her like an eager little puppy."

"Shhh, Frannie! Keep your voice down."

"Well, maybe that will free Henry up for someone else." Frannie's voice didn't drop in volume, despite Emma's admonition.

"For someone like you?" Emma asked.

"You never can tell."

Neither girl spied Rosanna in the doorway, but she could plainly see the smug look on Frannie's face. Should she clear her throat or somehow make her presence known? Before she could make a sound or a move, Frannie spoke again.

"I guess she won't be attending any more singings anyway, since she has a *boppli*."

"She can still go if she wants. She isn't married, the same as ever."

"Not quite the same as ever. She can't exactly bring a *boppli* to the singings. Besides, can you think of a single fellow who'd want to court a girl with an infant? Even Paul probably wouldn't want a ready-made family."

Rosanna saw a frown cross Emma's face as if she was thinking hard. "I'm sure the right *bu* wouldn't care one bit. Rosanna is the same girl. If a fellow cared about her, he'd care about her *boppli*, the same as if she was a widow."

Danki, Emma! Leave it to her best *freind* to defend her. She only hoped Emma was right.

"You certainly don't think Henry Zook would want a ready-made family, do you?" Frannie wiggled her glasses back into place.

"I can't speak for Henry, but he isn't the only available fellow, you know."

"But he's the one Rosanna has had her eye on for ages, ain't so?"

"I wouldn't know. Those things are private," Emma replied.

"Hmpf! If I could see that as plain as day, then I'm sure you could."

Rosanna couldn't stand being the subject of gossip any longer, but she couldn't charge into the room with steam pouring from her ears. She must have jostled Mollie enough to disturb her slumber, because she let out a little squeak.

"*Ach*, Rosanna. I didn't know you were there." Frannie's face turned at least three shades of red.

Obviously. "I-I was looking for Katie and Sadie."

"Well, they aren't in here," Frannie snapped.

"I can see that. I'll talk to you later, Emma." To Rosanna's horror, tears sprang into her eyes. She would not let Frannie see her cry. She spun away from the other two young women and crooned to Mollie.

"Wait, Rosanna!" Emma called after her.

"It's okay, Emma." Rosanna couldn't get any more words out, but she did hear Emma's comment as she fled from the room.

"Are you happy, Frannie? I'm sure Rosanna heard every word you said!"

Chapter Six

Sarah had offered to watch Mollie so Rosanna could attend the singing, but Rosanna declined the offer. Part of her wanted to go to prove Frannie was wrong, but a tiny part of her feared Frannie was right. She might not belong there anymore. Mostly, though, she didn't want to leave Mollie.

Rosanna bathed and fed the infant before tucking her into the cradle beside her own bed. She felt ready to drop into a dead sleep herself. She had struggled to stay awake as Daed read aloud from the Bible and nearly nodded off during prayers. A newborn's constant needs could sure wear a person out. She quickly exchanged her clothes for a nightgown and crawled beneath the covers to try to snatch a couple of hours of sleep before Mollie's next feeding.

When she closed her eyes, Rosanna saw Frannie's smirk and heard the girl's voice. Did Henry ask to take Frannie home after tonight's singing? It sure sounded like Frannie wanted that to happen. Rosanna squeezed her eyes tighter, hoping that would erase Frannie from her mind. She tried tensing and releasing various muscles from her toes to her forehead, a technique she and Mamm often encouraged during labor to help women relax.

The muscle relaxation must have finally worked, since Rosanna's next snippet of consciousness was a soft sucking noise emitting from the cradle. Mollie must have managed to raise her tiny fist to her mouth despite being swaddled in the blanket. Clever little one! Rosanna threw off the covers and bounced out of bed. She hurried to prepare a bottle of formula before the lip-smacking turned into an out-and-out wail of hunger.

Rosanna changed Mollie's diaper, swaddled her again in the soft pink blanket, and lifted her from the cradle. Daed, bless him, had insisted on carrying a small rocking chair upstairs to Rosanna's room. It was certainly colder in her room than near the living room woodstove, but it was ever so much more convenient to feed Mollie here. She pulled a heavy knit afghan around both of them once they were situated in the chair. That combined with their shared body heat should keep them warm enough.

Mollie slurped as Rosanna gently rocked the chair and softly crooned to her. Such a sweet *boppli*. She raised Mollie to her shoulder and patted her back to burp her. She continued to rock and pat even though Mollie had drifted back to sleep. She should do the same thing herself. Morning would arrive all too soon.

Rosanna heard a door open downstairs as she tucked Mollie back into the cradle. Tobias must be home from the singing. She had to know what had happened tonight. She cinched her robe tighter and flew down the stairs to waylay her *bruder* before he could escape to his room. He'd entered the back door, so she'd catch him in the kitchen.

"Psst!"

"*Ach*, Rosanna! You nearly scared the life out of me."

"I'm sorry."

"What are you doing up?"

"I just finished feeding Mollie and I heard you *kumm* in."

"Okay. I'm in. *Gut nacht*." Tobias headed out of the kitchen.

"Wait a minute!" Rosanna grabbed his arm, forcing him to stop.

"What do you want? I'm tired."

"Tell me about the singing."

"You've been to singings a zillion times."

"True, but tell me about this one."

"I sang. I ate three cookies. *Nee*, make that four cookies. And a brownie. A chocolate one with walnuts. I talked. I drove home and put the horse and buggy away. End of story."

"Tobias! You do that at every singing."

"Right. Tonight was the same as always."

"I'm not asking you who you took home—if you took a girl home . . ."

"*Gut*, because I wouldn't tell you."

Rosanna playfully punched her *bruder*'s arm. "Tell me who talked to whom, who left together, who—"

"You want me to gossip?"

"I want you to tell me what happened besides the fact that you gorged yourself on sweets."

"Is there anyone in particular you want details about?"

"Uh, just the general stuff."

"Right." Tobias again attempted to leave the room.

Rosanna quickly latched onto his arm and held it tighter this time. "Was Emma there?"

"*Jah.*"

"Was Henry there?"

"Aha! Now we're getting down to business."

"Tobias, you're making this a lot more difficult than it needs to be."

"Then why don't you spit out what you really want to know? Maybe I'll have an answer, and maybe I won't."

Rosanna rolled her eyes. *Bruders* could be so impossible. A girl would have told her who was there, what each person wore, who paired off, and who left first. With *buwe*, you had to drag every tidbit of information out of them inch by inch. How was she going to ask her questions without seeming too desperate? "Did Frannie leave with anyone?"

"Not that I noticed."

Rosanna sighed. Would Tobias have noticed if an elephant had stomped through the barn in the middle of the singing? "D-did Henry leave with anyone?"

"Let me think." Tobias tapped his head as if in deep thought.

Rosanna was about ready to tear her hair out—or Tobias'. "Well?"

"I'm thinking. If my memory serves me correctly, he left about the same time as Frannie, but they didn't walk out together."

"But they could have met up outside." Rosanna hadn't meant to give voice to her thought.

"That's possible, but I didn't leave then, so I don't know. What do you see in Henry Zook, anyway?"

"He's a nice *bu.*"

"I suppose. But there are lots of nice fellows, probably nicer ones than Henry."

"Maybe." Was Tobias trying to tell her something, or was she reading too much into his comment?

"Can I have my arm back now so I can go to bed?"

Rosanna released her grip on Tobias' upper arm. "Pleasant dreams."

"If I even have time to dream now." Tobias did his clumsy version of tiptoeing out of the room. At the doorway, he called over his shoulder. "I almost forgot. Someone asked about you."

"Who?"

"Paul Hertzler."

Paul shivered when he emerged from the barn. He glanced up at the stars gleaming in the inky sky. The absence of clouds allowed the temperature to drop quickly. It would definitely feel *gut* to get inside. He might have to stand by the stove for a minute or two to soak up some heat before heading upstairs to bed.

The evening had been a bit of a disappointment. Oh, he'd enjoyed the singing all right. And he'd talked and laughed with the other fellows afterward, but his heart wasn't really in it. When he looked across the barn at the girls and didn't see Rosanna's lovely, smiling face, he felt like a balloon that had sprung a leak. His joy seeped out the way the balloon's air hissed out of a tiny puncture.

He shouldn't have built up his hopes. Rosanna had told him she probably wouldn't attend. She had an infant to care for now. He understood. Really, he did. And he admired her. How many young women would take on such a responsibility? His opinion of her rose a notch—and he had thought it was already as high as it could go.

Paul slipped inside the dark, silent house. He hurried into the kitchen to stand beside the stove. His hands had grown cold even inside his heavy gloves. He rubbed them together to get the blood moving. A cup of hot chocolate might raise his body temperature and lift his spirits. That is, if he could find a little packet of the instant stuff around. He always tried to squirrel away a few packs, but his younger *bruders* were notorious scavengers, especially when it came to chocolate.

At several inches over six feet, Paul could easily reach the top cabinets without climbing onto a stool or chair. His fingers fumbled beneath the huge, heavy platter Mamm used at Thanksgiving or Christmas or whenever they had a large gathering. He was rewarded when two packets of cocoa mix fell to the counter. *Gut*, his secret hiding place was still safe. He tucked one packet back under the platter and reached for a mug on a lower shelf. The kettle of water Mamm always kept on the stove should be plenty hot enough.

Paul sipped the cocoa slowly, allowing the liquid to warm him from the inside out as his mind replayed the evening. Most of the youngies had attended the singing. The usual pairs slipped out together at the end. Most likely, several of those couples would be published at an upcoming church service. At twenty-four, he was more than ready to become one of those couples. The problem was "a couple" meant "two." He had yet to find the other half of his couple.

He supposed he could have asked to take Emma Kurtz home. She was nice enough, and pleasing to look at with her blonde hair and blue eyes, but he was rather partial to dark hair and chocolate eyes. Frannie Hostetler had brown hair and eyes, but they were light brown, not dark. He might as well face it. Only one person would do. And she didn't seem to know he existed. Her attention always seemed drawn to Henry Zook.

Paul had a sneaking suspicion that Frannie had her sights set on Henry, too. What was so appealing about Henry? He seemed like an average sort of fellow to Paul. Maybe he should be more observant of Henry and take note. Paul wasn't sure, but he thought Henry had followed Frannie outside tonight. That might be a point in his favor if Henry did that. Maybe if Henry showed an interest in Frannie, Paul would have a sliver of a chance to win Rosanna Mast's heart.

Paul had asked about her? He was such a thoughtful person. Rosanna refilled the kettle with water, since whichever of her siblings had snuck in for cocoa hadn't thought to do so. She rinsed the mug left on the counter and set it in the sink before the chocolate residue hardened. Whoever had drunk the cocoa could have easily done that. The culprit must have been Joseph. Tobias hadn't taken time for a drink, and there would have been two mugs if her *schweschders* had ventured downstairs in the dark. At least there wasn't a trail of chocolate on the counter to clean up.

She should return to bed. As it was, she'd only get an hour or two of sleep before Mollie awoke again. But now more confusing thoughts swirled around in her brain. Maybe she should prepare a cup of cocoa. *Nee*, she'd rather have tea.

Henry and Frannie. Rosanna wrapped her cold hands around the steaming mug. Did they meet up after leaving the singing separately? Had Henry never made any attempt to ask Rosanna to ride home because he was interested in Frannie? She plunked the mug down so hard that hot tea sloshed over the rim and splashed onto her hands. She blew on her fingers but scarcely registered the pain.

All this time she'd been waiting for Henry to make a move. She'd talked to him after singings. They'd laughed over a couple of the other *buwe*'s silly antics. He had even hinted that he was interested in her. At least she thought he had. Rosanna figured Henry was a little shy and that's why he hesitated to ask to take her home. Maybe he'd only been politely enduring their conversations when he really wanted to be spending time with Frannie. Or maybe the thought of becoming an instant *daed* scared him off. He certainly didn't show any interest in Mollie. Oooh! Why did things have to be so complicated?

Rosanna took a mental survey of the young men she knew. Would any of them want a girl who already had a *boppli*? Paul always seemed interested, and he often inquired about Mollie, but that was probably just his way. None of the other fellows had made any such gesture. It wasn't like she had done anything wrong and ended up with an infant. She sat back and crossed her arms across her chest. Well, Mollie was here to stay, even if none of the fellows wanted a package deal!

"Someone asked about you." Tobias' words echoed in Rosanna's head. Was Paul Hertzler simply being polite, as he always was? His interest in Mollie certainly seemed genuine.

She raised the mug to her lips. Yuck! The tea had grown cold while her mixed-up thoughts danced around in her brain. She threw a glance at the battery-operated wall clock. If she crawled back beneath her covers right now, she might be able to snatch a whole hour of sleep before Mollie stirred.

Chapter Seven

"Rosanna! Rosanna!"

Rosanna leaped from her bed. The room was still dark. She couldn't have missed the old rooster's crowing; she never slept that deeply. But she had been pretty sleep-deprived since Mollie arrived. Automatically she reached into the cradle to lay a hand on the *boppli*'s chest. The gentle rise and fall told her Mollie was fine. She stumbled to the door and stuck her head out into the hallway.

"Rosanna, get dressed."

"What's wrong, Mamm? What time is it?" Rosanna's heart thumped wildly. What tragedy had occurred to get her *mudder* out of bed in the middle of the night? She rubbed her eyes to clear away the sleep.

"It's three o'clock."

"Three? What's wrong?"

"Menno Troyer sent word. Becky is having her twins. I'll need your help."

"I thought she was delivering at the hospital."

"I thought that was the plan, too. Apparently the twins have other plans."

"Shouldn't they call the rescue squad and take her to the hospital?"

"Menno said she wanted to stay home. Hurry!"

"What about Mollie?"

"Bundle her up and bring her. We'll send word for Mary Hertzler to pick her up if we'll be a long time with Becky."

"Okay, Mamm, I'll hurry."

Rosanna raced back to her room, lit a kerosene lamp, and dressed as quickly as her shaky fingers would allow. She knew her *mamm* had told Becky she should go to the hospital for the birth. Becky's pregnancy had been progressing normally, but twins could present more challenges. Becky must have been so determined to have a home birth that she put off letting anyone know it was time until it was too late. The rescue squad could always be summoned if necessary, though. Rosanna prayed that wouldn't happen.

She threw diapers and clothes into the diaper bag. She'd grab a can of powdered formula from the kitchen. When all was ready, she eased Mollie from the cradle, extinguished the lamp, and juggled bag and *boppli* while trying to tiptoe downstairs.

"I've already got bottles and formula in a bag," Sarah announced as Rosanna entered the kitchen.

Daed, bleary-eyed from being aroused from his sleep earlier than usual, entered the kitchen from the mudroom. "The buggy is ready for you. Is there any *kaffi*?"

"Why don't you go back to bed, Samuel?" Sarah took a moment to pour a mug full of steaming *kaffi* after she filled a large metal thermos to take to the Troyers'. Even from Rosanna's position across the room, she could tell the dark brew would be as strong as a mule kick.

"I'd just have to get up in an hour, so I might as well

stay up." Samuel took the mug from his *fraa* and dropped onto a chair. He took a gulp and then set the mug down. He held out his arms to hold Mollie so Rosanna could fasten her cloak and tie her black bonnet over her *kapp*.

"Ready?" Sarah asked.

Rosanna nodded and retrieved Mollie. "Let's go."

She shivered as she settled on the buggy seat beside her *mudder*. She pulled the blanket tighter around Mollie and held her closer. "I can't understand why Menno didn't call the rescue squad, since you told them she should deliver at the hospital."

"Menno is a young husband who wants to please his *fraa*. If Becky said she wanted to give birth at home, Menno probably didn't even question it. If she said she wanted to give birth on the moon, he'd build a spaceship."

Rosanna laughed. Would she ever know such love and devotion? "You don't think there will be any problems, do you, Mamm?"

"I don't expect any. Becky's checkups have always been fine, but with twins, everything is a little trickier. I didn't want to have to transfer Becky halfway through the labor if a problem cropped up. That's why I urged her to go to the hospital."

"We'll pray everything goes well." Rosanna fell silent. If she wasn't so cold, she could easily drift off to sleep. She hoped the excitement of the twins' birth would keep her alert.

Three hours later, the sun had crept up the sky, the frost had vanished from the grass, and the twins had still not put in an appearance. Rosanna had fed Mollie and laid her in the little nest she had made for her in the corner of the room.

With each contraction Becky asked if the *bopplin* were almost here. Each time, Sarah replied, "Not yet," and Becky would flop back on her pillow and sigh.

"You can get up and walk around if you'd like. Sometimes that helps speed things up a bit," Sarah advised.

"I want to save my energy."

Sarah looked at Rosanna, rolled her eyes, and mouthed, "This could take a while."

Rosanna had to turn her back to the bed to keep Becky from seeing her shake with silent laughter.

"Maybe we should send Menno to fetch Mary before things get too busy here," Sarah said. "She can watch Mollie so you won't have to worry about interrupting your work for a feeding."

"*Nee!*" Becky sat up straight. "Menno has to stay here with me!"

"He's just pacing in the hallway right now, Becky." Sarah stepped over to the bed and patted her patient's arm. "It will give the poor *bu* something to do instead of wear a hole in the floor and worry about you."

"What if the twins *kumm* while he's gone?"

"I don't see any indication that birth is imminent. In fact, we probably have time to transfer you to the hospital." This wasn't the first attempt to persuade Becky to change her mind. So far all attempts had failed. Rosanna waited for this one to fail as well. Mentally she counted the seconds.

"*Nee!*"

Twelve seconds. Last time, it only took nine. Could she be wavering?

"Is there a reason you don't want to go to the hospital other than having your heart set on a home birth?"

Becky swiped a hand across her eyes. "My *mamm* died at a hospital."

Rosanna knew Becky's *mudder* had passed on but didn't know any details. Menno had gone to Ohio to stay with relatives for a while and had come back married to Becky.

"I'm sorry, dear." Sarah gave the girl a brief hug. "You know, hospitals really are *gut* places. They try to help people, but sometimes they just can't."

Becky bobbed her head and swiped at her eyes again. She grabbed Sarah's hand. "Please. I want to stay here. You can send Menno for Mary if that will make it easier for me to stay here."

"Okay, Becky. Remember to breathe, dear." Sarah nodded at Rosanna before snatching a tissue from the box on the bedside table to wipe Becky's tears.

Rosanna poked her head into the hallway to give poor Menno his instructions. She nearly chuckled at his eagerness to flee the house for a few minutes.

The twins, a boy and a girl, finally arrived shortly after noon. Most likely Menno was the most relieved person in the whole bunch. He had alternately paced, held his *fraa*'s hand, rubbed his stubbly brown beard that still hadn't filled in after a year of marriage, and paced some more. His pacing rankled Rosanna's nerves more than Becky's wailing had. She was used to women's sounds and actions during birth, but the bumbling, nervous fellows got to her after a while.

For all her weeping and wailing, Becky came through like a champ. She pushed when Sarah said to push and panted when Sarah said to pant. Now, holding two swaddled infants, she looked perfectly content. Rosanna couldn't help but wonder how the young parents, who were barely more than *kinner* themselves, would cope with two hungry, crying infants in the middle of the night. A single newborn was ever so much work. Becky would have that work times two.

"I've lined up some women to help you out, Becky, if that's okay with you," Sarah said.

The relief on the girl's face was almost comical. "That's fine with me." Menno immediately nodded in agreement.

"Since we've cleaned up here, Mamm, I think I'll walk over to check on Mollie. You can stay with Becky as long as you like. I can probably get Mary to take us home."

"It's awfully cold to walk, Rosanna. Look at how those trees are swaying. The wind must have picked up."

Rosanna followed her *mudder*'s gaze out the window, where big oak and maple trees scratched the sky with their naked branches.

"Why don't you take the buggy and pick me up later?"

Before Rosanna could answer, a voice called out from downstairs. "Hello! It's Mary. Is everything all right?"

Rosanna ran to the door and out into the hallway. "Hello, Mary. All is well. How is Mollie?"

"She's fine." A deep voice, definitely not Mary's, answered.

Maybe Reuben had taken a break and driven over with his *fraa*. But the voice, though quite similar, didn't sound exactly like Reuben's. Two sets of footsteps approached the stairs.

Mary paused at the bottom step with her hand on the banister as if unsure whether she should ascend. Three seconds later, Paul joined his *mudder* with a swaddled infant in his arms.

"*Ach*, Paul, you have Mollie?" Rosanna couldn't believe he was carrying the *boppli*. He looked perfectly calm and natural, not one bit nervous, like poor Menno, who held his own twins as if they were made of glass.

"I sure do. She's been as *gut* as gold. Well, that's what Mamm said. I only went inside the house to eat."

"And you stayed to play with the *boppli*, too. Tell the truth." Mary grinned up at the son towering over her.

"I couldn't really play with her, but I talked to her and held her. I hope that's okay, Rosanna."

"Of course." Rosanna couldn't have been more surprised. Well, maybe she would have been if it had been Henry holding Mollie instead of Paul. She had trouble imagining that scene at the moment. She returned Paul's smile.

"Mary," Sarah called from upstairs. "Becky asked if you would like to meet her twins."

"They're here already? I'd love to meet them." Mary scooted past Rosanna and hurried up the stairs.

"I was just on my way over to pick up Mollie," Rosanna said. Paul didn't look like he was in a rush to relinquish the infant.

"Great minds think alike. Isn't that what they say?" His smile lit his face and made his eyes sparkle. Today they looked green with flecks of gold. It was amazing how they changed colors.

"I-I guess so." Funny she hadn't taken much notice of his eyes until recently.

"Do you want to sit for a few minutes while our *mudders* are occupied? You must be tired."

"Sure, let's have a seat, but first I should check to see if the stove needs wood." Rosanna started for the kitchen.

"I thought you meant have a seat in the living room. I put wood in that stove when Mamm and I arrived."

Rosanna thumped her own head. She must be more exhausted than she realized. "I did, but I was also thinking of fixing some tea and cookies for Menno and Becky. The two thoughts sort of collided." She shook her head.

Paul chuckled. He shifted Mollie to one arm with the ease of someone who had been used to caring for infants. With his free hand, he grasped her upper arm. "The kitchen will probably be warmer since it's smaller than the living room." He led her into the room and to a big oak chair at the table. "Sit and rest a minute. You hold Mollie, and I'll check the stove."

Rosanna dropped onto the chair with a sigh. The strength left her legs, and her back ached with a vengeance. How *gut* it felt to sit! She reached out her arms for her *boppli.*

Paul gently lowered Mollie into her arms. "I'll add wood to this stove and check the other one again. Then I'll fix tea for everyone."

"You'll fix tea?"

"Don't look so shocked." He laughed at her raised eyebrows. "I know my way around a kitchen. Without any *schweschders*, my *bruders* and I took turns helping Mamm from time to time. I think I can brew tea and round up some cookies."

"That would be *wunderbaar!*" She almost told him he was *wunderbaar,* but that wouldn't have sounded right. Her cheeks warmed, so she quickly lowered her gaze to the infant in her arms. Immediately she began cooing to Mollie, who opened one blue eye. Rosanna rocked the infant and softly sang until the little eye closed again.

"You have a nice voice."

Rosanna hadn't heard Paul return to the kitchen. Her cheeks most likely glowed as bright as the neon sign outside of the Gas and Go. "*Danki*," she murmured.

"I, uh, we missed you at the last singing."

"I . . ."

"I understand you wanted to be with Mollie. If you want to attend sometime, I'm sure Mamm would be happy to watch Mollie if your *mudder* was busy."

"I'll keep that in mind. Mary sure loves *bopplin*."

"That she does. And they seem to take to her, too."

"She'll make a great *grossmammi* one day." Little prickles danced up and down Rosanna's arms. She knew Paul was staring at her. She didn't dare raise her eyes to meet his.

Chapter Eight

Paul opened cupboard doors until he found mugs. Then he searched for tea bags. Finally successful, he pulled out a box, removed tea bags, and plopped one into each mug he'd lined up on the counter. "It's just regular tea. Is that all right?"

"That's fine. I filled the kettle with water earlier, so it should be plenty hot, if it hasn't completely boiled away." Rosanna continued to sway even though Mollie had returned to a sound sleep. The rocking motion must be some innate trait of females that surfaced whenever they held an infant in their arms.

Steam rose from the mugs as Paul poured water over the tea bags. "Should I add honey or sugar or put them on a tray to take upstairs as they are?"

"You could take the honey and the sugar. I'm not sure which Becky and Menno would prefer. I'll take sugar in mine."

"I like sugar better, too." Paul added two teaspoons of sugar each to two of the mugs and set the sugar bowl, the honey jar, spoons, and the other mugs on a tray he found on the kitchen counter. "Now for some cookies. I'm guessing they would be in that cookie jar near the stove."

"That would be my guess." Rosanna smiled. Paul did seem at ease in the kitchen. She could just imagine Tobias preparing tea. He'd probably sustain a third-degree burn on his hand from boiling water that sloshed over the sides of the cup.

"*Gut* thing Mamm brought some extra cookies," Paul said after lifting the lid off the ceramic cookie jar. "And she brought enough supper to feed half the community, too."

"If there are oatmeal cookies in there, take those up to Becky." Rosanna knew oats were supposed to help nursing *mudders*. She wasn't sure if oatmeal cookies provided the same benefits, but it couldn't hurt to try.

"*Jah*, there are oatmeal raisin cookies in here—what's left of them, anyway. Menno must have had the munchies."

"That's entirely possible. The poor guy paced enough to work up a ferocious appetite."

Paul laughed. "Typical nervous new *daed*?"

"Most men are nervous when their *fraas* are giving birth, especially first-time *daeds*."

Paul plunked some cookies on a small plate and added it to the tray. "I'll take this upstairs. You rest." He was gone before Rosanna could protest.

A soft sigh escaped after Rosanna swallowed her first sip of tea. She closed her eyes as the liquid traveled down and warmed her from the inside. If she wasn't careful, she'd nod into slumber like Mollie. She needed to stay awake, though. She couldn't risk dropping the *boppli* on the floor. She opened her eyes when Paul reentered the kitchen.

"Here. I saved out a few cookies for you." He laid two fat cookies on a napkin and slid them over to Rosanna.

"I'll share." She held one out for Paul.

"Are you sure?"

"Absolutely. I'm more tired than hungry. Please, go ahead." She pinched off a bite of cookie and popped it into her mouth. She watched Paul take a big bite of his cookie.

"Ah! That hit the spot." Paul patted his stomach after swallowing his last bite. "I can take you home if your *mamm* needs to stay longer and then swing back by here to pick up my *mamm*."

Rosanna considered the offer. "Mamm and I usually stay until we're sure everything is okay, but we don't usually have a *boppli* of our own with us. With twins, though, she'll probably stay a bit longer." What should she do? Maybe she'd check with Mamm.

"I know my *mudder* would be happy to help out here—or she'll keep Mollie longer if you want to stay."

Rosanna still hesitated. She'd really like to get Mollie home. And to be completely truthful, she'd love to crawl into her own bed once she'd bathed and fed Mollie. But she always stayed after tending births to help the new parents or to tidy up the house or to prepare a meal. But Mary had brought supper, so she wouldn't have to prepare a meal. Other women would be dropping by with casseroles and vegetables and desserts for the next few days. Becky was going to need a lot of help, and the other women of the community would be more than willing to provide that.

"I'll check with Mamm and see what she'd prefer me to do." Rosanna scooted her chair back slowly so she wouldn't disturb Mollie.

"Finish your tea."

Rosanna took a gulp. "I'll need to wash the dishes when everyone else is done eating."

"I believe my *mamm* knows how to wash dishes, Rosanna. You look about done in."

"He's right."

Rosanna jumped, causing Mollie to startle but not awaken. She hadn't heard Mary's approach.

"I mean, you look fine, dear—tired, but fine. Paul is right that I certainly know how to clean up a kitchen." Mary crossed the room and slid the cookie jar forward. "That Menno could eat nonstop. He must have burned off a lot of nervous energy." Mary reached into the cookie jar and pulled out two cookies. "It's a *gut* thing I brought cookies."

"That's what I said," Paul mumbled.

"Is everything okay upstairs?" Rosanna couldn't help her concern.

"Becky nursed both *bopplin* with Sarah's help, and now all three are resting. Menno ate his food and half of Becky's. He seems to be a little more at ease now. At least he holds the twins with a firmer grip, so I guess he's not afraid he will break them anymore."

"I hope he won't be too nervous to help Becky. She is going to need lots of support with two infants to care for."

"I think he'll get the hang of it. They will learn together how to establish a routine. How is this precious little one doing?" Mary inched closer to the table to look at the *boppli* snuggled in Rosanna's arms.

"She's been sleeping."

"I'm sure you'd like to get her home. Or if you want me to keep her a while longer, I can certainly do that."

Paul quickly told Mary his idea for getting Rosanna and Mollie home.

"That's fine with me. I'll heat up supper here and

clean up afterward so you can go home, Rosanna. I don't mind one bit."

"That sounds like a fine idea." Sarah bustled into the kitchen, carrying the tray with empty mugs. "In fact, I can drop Mary off at home when we're through here so Paul won't have to circle back."

How did her *mamm* still look so energetic? Rosanna felt like she'd been run over by the workhorse and plow. Sarah looked as calm and collected as ever.

"Go ahead and take Mollie home, Rosanna. You did a fine job here, but you must be exhausted. You get up throughout the night for feedings while I'm sleeping, so I'm sure you are ready to drop. You know, you really should let me take turns with you at night so you can get some sleep."

"That's okay, Mamm, but if you're sure you don't need me here, I'll go on home."

"Mary and I can handle things here."

The late afternoon air seemed colder, or maybe it was because Rosanna had grown so warm in the kitchen that it seemed chillier than before. She shivered and hugged Mollie closer as she hurried to the Hertzler buggy. Paul gently lifted Mollie from her arms so she could climb in. He held her in one arm, as if he'd cared for infants all his life, and took Rosanna's arm with his free hand to help her.

"*Danki.*" What a gentleman! Rosanna reached out to retrieve Mollie.

Paul raced around to jump into the buggy and pulled out a blanket. He carefully spread it over Rosanna and the infant. "This should help warm you up a bit. Your teeth were starting to chatter."

"I think the temperature change from the house to outside gave me a chill. The blanket should definitely help."

"I think winter is settling in, for sure." Paul clucked to his horse and got them moving. "I'm glad I came with Mamm so I can get you and Mollie home. I happened to be at the right place at the right time, I'm thinking."

"I'm grateful for the ride home. It's been a long day." Rosanna sighed and smiled up at Paul.

"I'm glad I could help." He smiled back and patted Mollie in her little cocoon of blankets.

"They must be cold." Rosanna nodded at the approaching open buggy. The woman's black bonnet nearly touched the man's shoulder. They were probably huddled close together for warmth. She sucked in a breath and shrank back into the shadows as recognition dawned. Even though his black hat was pulled low, she knew beyond a shadow of a doubt who drove that buggy. If the woman would raise her head a tiny bit, she'd probably be able to identify her, too. Maybe it was Henry's *mudder*. Right!

"Henry Zook. Who has he got with him?" Paul spoke Rosanna's thoughts aloud.

She didn't want Henry to think she was with Paul. Well, she was with Paul, but not courting. Henry would never pay any attention to her if he thought she was stepping out with Paul. She gasped again when the waning sun glinted off something in Henry's buggy. Glasses. The person with him wore glasses.

"*Ach!* It's Frannie Hostetler." Paul waved as the buggies drew closer to each other. He read Rosanna's mind and voiced her thoughts, so she didn't need to say a word.

Rosanna's stomach lurched. It was a very *gut* thing she'd only had a few bites of a cookie and hot tea. Anything more would surely be traveling upward about now. Frannie certainly hadn't wasted any time worming her way into Henry's life. Rosanna hadn't so much as stepped a foot into Henry's buggy. She hadn't even been able to coax an invitation from his lips. And yet, there sat Frannie all snuggled up beside Henry as if she belonged there!

Rosanna didn't know if she felt more hurt or angry. What was wrong with her that Henry wouldn't ask her to ride home with him when she gave him opportunities galore? She always smiled and asked Henry about himself and tried to be as pleasant as she knew how to be. All for naught. She'd thrown out the bait, but Henry had never so much as nibbled at it. Maybe she should have been more direct, but that simply wasn't her way.

Frannie, on the other hand, must not have had any problem being direct. Either that, or she had turned on charm Rosanna hadn't been aware the other girl possessed. *Stop it, Rosanna. That wasn't nice.* Apparently something clicked between Henry and Frannie. Maybe by talking to him after singings she'd kept him from seeking out Frannie. A little dart pierced her heart. Seeing Frannie smiling and waving at Paul didn't help matters any.

Rosanna scrunched farther into the corner of the buggy and ducked her head. She hoped the occupants of the other buggy would not see her at all. Why did it take forever for them to pass by? She knew she should have stayed to help Mamm. Then she wouldn't have witnessed this painful event. Most likely, though, Frannie would accidentally on purpose mention her ride with Henry the next time she saw her. Oops! That wasn't nice, either. This whole situation was bringing out the worst in her.

"I'm sorry, Rosanna."

"Huh?" Paul had spoken so softly she wasn't sure he'd actually spoken.

"I mean, uh, I know, uh, well, I've seen you talking to Henry after singings. I thought, uh, you cared for him." The last few words tumbled over one another as if in a hurry to jump off his tongue. If his face flushed any brighter, it would burst into flames.

Gauging from the heat she felt in her own cheeks, they must be glowing nearly as red. "W-we weren't, uh, we haven't, uh, we're not a couple."

"Oh."

"From the looks of things, though, Henry and Frannie are getting along quite well."

"I'm sorry if that makes you sad."

Rosanna shrugged her shoulders and dragged in a deep breath. She forced a cheerfulness she didn't feel into her voice. "I'm not sad. I've got a beautiful *boppli* that I adore. I am truly blessed."

Chapter Nine

Paul could have gnawed his tongue completely off. Why in the world did he say anything about Rosanna and Henry? He should have left that topic alone. Now he'd made them both uncomfortable. He wished they hadn't passed another living soul on the way to Rosanna's house. But if they did have to meet someone, why did it have to be Henry Zook?

He slid a sideways glance in Rosanna's direction. Her face no longer glowed like the embers in the woodstove. His own face had cooled a bit, too. He needed to be more careful to keep both feet out of his mouth. Now he had to think of some neutral but pleasant topic of conversation. "Did Becky and Menno name the twins yet?" That seemed a safe enough question.

"They're still trying to decide. I think they were leaning toward Abigail and Jacob."

"Abigail is a different sort of name."

"I think Becky wants to call her Abby."

"Is Menno in agreement?"

Rosanna chuckled. "I think Menno would name the twins after planets if that's what Becky wanted."

Paul laughed. "Venus and Jupiter, maybe?"

"Now *those* would be different names."

Gut. Paul could practically see the tension ease from Rosanna's shoulders. "Little Mollie seems to be putting on weight."

"*Jah.* She's a great eater, for sure and for certain."

"And you're a great *mudder.*"

"I'm learning. I hope I can be a *gut* one."

"I think that *Englisch* girl picked exactly the right person to take her little one."

"It's all so strange, Paul. She could have picked a married couple, *Englisch* or Amish. I'm very glad she chose me, but why?"

"She wanted her *boppli* raised Amish, ain't so?"

"That's what she said, but I'm not sure how much she really knew about us."

"She must have been studying us for some time if she knew where you lived and that you and your *mamm* attended births." Paul ventured a direct look at Rosanna. "But she wouldn't have had to study you for too long to know what a kind, gentle, caring person you are and to know you'd love her *boppli* like your own."

A pink stain highlighted Rosanna's face again. She looked away, but not before Paul glimpsed tears in her eyes. "I-I didn't mean to upset you."

Rosanna sniffed. She reached out a hand to barely touch his arm, but even that whisper of a touch sent a jolt of lightning through his body. "You didn't upset me, Paul. I think that's the nicest thing anyone has ever said to me. And I do love Mollie like my own."

"She is yours, *jah*?"

"As far as I'm concerned. The papers from Jane were legal, and I've already started the proceedings to adopt her."

"That's *wunderbaar*!"

"Do you really think so? I know I'm delighted, but I don't know how everyone else feels about the whole thing."

"I'm convinced it's the best thing for Mollie. If there is anyone who doesn't think so, well, don't pay any attention to them. Mollie is a gift from Gott. He chose you to raise her."

Paul became a bit more alarmed when tears overflowed and coursed down Rosanna's cheeks. He wanted to wipe them away but settled for squeezing her hand. "Please tell me those are happy tears."

Rosanna sniffed and smiled. "Very happy tears. That was a beautiful thing to say. I believe Mollie is a gift, too. You're *gut* for my spirits, Paul Hertzler."

Rosanna sat up a little straighter. Paul was well aware that she had tried to hide in the shadows when Henry and Frannie had approached. He hoped it was because she didn't want anyone to think they were a couple, not that she simply didn't want to be seen with him, period. Would their becoming a couple be such a terrible thing? He didn't believe so.

In fact, for a long time he had harbored the hope that Rosanna would show the same interest in him that she did in Henry. If Henry truly was stepping out with Frannie, perhaps he'd have a chance now. He'd have to bide his time, though. He didn't want to scare her off. Talking about Mollie proved to be a safe subject, so he'd pursue the topic a little more.

"I'm sure your family loves having Mollie around."

"I-I think so. Mamm was hesitant at first."

"Your *mamm*? That's hard to imagine."

"*Ach!* She loves Mollie, that's for sure. But at first she was afraid having a baby would limit my chances for marriage."

"Really? Why?"

"Mamm figured most young fellows wouldn't want to be bothered with having a *boppli* right from the start."

"If a fellow cared for you, then he'd accept your *boppli*, too. Just look at her. Who couldn't love that sweet little girl?" Paul nodded at Mollie, whose lips were curved up in a slight smile in her sleep, as if she knew some delicious secret.

Rosanna smiled. "That's pretty much what I told Mamm. Any man that would be interested in me would have to accept Mollie, too. We're a package deal." A determined look crossed her lovely face. Paul imagined she would have folded her arms across her chest and huffed, *So there!* if she hadn't been cradling the infant.

"And what a great package!" Paul mumbled the words, but then bit his lip in horror that the thought had slipped out.

"What?"

"You're right. You do *kumm* together. But not all fellows would run from a *boppli*, you know." Did he really say that? What was wrong with his misbehaving tongue today? He reached over to gently pat the blanket surrounding the infant.

"Maybe not."

Out of the corner of his eye, Paul saw Rosanna frown and chew her bottom lip for a second. "I hope not."

He barely heard her whispered words. He gave her arm what he hoped was a reassuring squeeze. This time he managed to keep his tongue from betraying him again, because he almost said he'd like to be that fellow. If Rosanna could look past Henry Zook, she would see him ready and willing to *wilkom* her and Mollie into his heart and life.

"We're here."

"What?"

"My house. You're getting ready to drive past it."

"Right. I guess I was lost in thought." More like daydreaming. Paul pulled on the reins to slow the horse so they could make the turn onto the Masts' long gravel driveway.

"*Danki* for bringing us home, Paul, and for your kind words."

"I'm glad I could help."

"You're a *gut freind.*"

Paul nodded. He wanted to be so much more than that, but he would accept friendship for now. He would pray that one day—preferably before he was old and gray-haired—Rosanna would regard him as more than a mere *freind.*

He stopped the buggy near the back door of the two-story house and hopped out. "Wait right there," he called over his shoulder. "I'll help you." He raced around the gray buggy and held out his arms for Mollie. He shifted her to one arm to help Rosanna step down. A tiny movement in his arms caused him to look down. Mollie's big blue eyes had opened to gaze right into his face.

"*Ach,* Rosanna! She smiled at me!"

"She doesn't smile yet except for that little quirk of her lips when she sleeps."

"Honest! She smiled. Look! She's doing it again!"

Rosanna stood on tiptoes to get a closer look. "You're right, Paul! She is smiling!"

She stroked Mollie's little cheek. "Aren't you a precious one," she cooed.

"*Danki.*"

Rosanna laughed. "Not you, Paul Hertzler. The *boppli.*"

"I'm not precious?"

"Well, maybe. Mollie certainly thinks you're special. She bestowed her first real smile on you."

"I'm honored." Would Rosanna ever think he was special, too? "I'll carry her inside for you. I know you're tired."

Rosanna climbed the cement steps and opened the back door leading into the mudroom. "*Kumm* into the kitchen. It should be warm in there."

Paul obediently followed, murmuring to Mollie as he walked.

"Would you like more tea or *kaffi* or a glass of milk?" Rosanna crossed the room, lifted the lid on the wood-stove, poked around a bit with the long iron poker to stir up a flame, and added a chunk of wood. She lifted the teakettle and set it back down. "*Jah*, there's plenty of water. Would you like something?"

He'd like very much to prolong his time with her, but he should be getting home for evening chores. Such a quandary!

Rosanna must have sensed his dilemma. She seemed to have a knack for reading his thoughts. Not all of them, he hoped. "Why don't you sit for a minute with Mollie while I hang up my cloak and bonnet? Then I'll fix a quick bottle for Mollie and get you some cookies for the road. Do you have the time?"

"Sure." He'd make time. He pulled a heavy oak chair back from the table and eased himself down onto it. Mollie still gazed at him. If she was hungry, she didn't seem too upset about it. He could get used to Rosanna bustling about the kitchen while he held their *kinner* without any problem at all. Instantly his cheeks burned. He'd better rein in those thoughts fast. He dipped his head to smile at the infant and to give the flush time to fade from his face. "What a *gut* little girl you are," he whispered.

"She certainly is."

Oops! Rosanna caught him talking to the *boppli*. Oh well, maybe that was a positive thing.

Rosanna smiled as she closed the door behind Paul. What a caring fellow he was, and he certainly seemed at ease with Mollie, even though there weren't any little ones at his house.

"Isn't he nice, Mollie?" The infant had managed to get one tiny fist to her mouth and sucked vigorously. Rosanna chuckled. "You sure aren't going to get any nourishment out of that. Let's get you changed and fed."

By the time Rosanna had Mollie tucked into the cradle, she heard footsteps downstairs in the kitchen. Her own bed called to her, but she forced herself to ignore it. She didn't think Mamm would be home yet, but her younger *schweschders* had probably darted into the kitchen for a snack. She needed to recruit them to help with supper. As tired as she felt, she might fall headfirst into the pot of stew she planned to heat up.

"One cookie each." Rosanna entered the kitchen to find a scuffle over the cookie jar.

"Mamm lets us have two," Katie wailed.

"It's close to supper time, and I need your help."

"Where's Mamm?" Sadie bit off a huge chunk of a peanut butter cookie.

"She stayed with Becky and the twins a little longer."

"Twins!" Katie squealed. "I can't wait to see them. Did she have *buwe* or girls?"

"One of each."

"Are they cute?" Sadie asked around her mouthful of cookie.

"All *bopplin* are cute. You need to swallow that wad in your mouth before you speak."

Sadie wrinkled her nose before gulping down her bite of cookie. "There."

Rosanna wagged her head. "You're going to get choked one of these days. Where's James?"

"He came in before us. I heard the cookie jar rattle before he ran out to help with chores. I bet he took more than one cookie, too."

"Don't worry about it, Katie. I don't think you'll starve. Can you get the canister of flour, and Sadie, would you pull out the pan for biscuits?"

Both girls stuffed the remainder of their cookies into their mouths before doing as asked.

"Can we help roll out and cut biscuits?" Sadie always seemed so eager to help and to learn new things. Katie usually preferred to race outside to check on the animals or discover some new facet of nature.

The biscuit making would take longer with the two of them, but Rosanna couldn't refuse their request. With any luck, she'd still have supper on the table before Daed and her *bruders* came inside. Mamm should be home soon, too, and she would be even more tired than Rosanna. "Let me stir the stew, and then we'll start on the biscuits. I'll get down the big measuring cup and the mixing bowl, and you two find the rolling pin and spoons."

A short time later, Rosanna heard four pairs of feet

clomping up the steps and through the back door as she pulled the pan of biscuits from the oven. "Perfect timing," she told the little girls who were hovering around the oven to see the emerging biscuits.

"Some of them look funny," Katie observed.

"*Jah*, they're kind of lopsided." Sadie frowned as she looked at the pan.

"That's okay. They will all taste delicious. Are cookies always perfectly shaped?"

"*Nee*," two voices answered simultaneously.

"Don't they taste yummy anyway?"

Both girls nodded.

"Then these biscuits will all taste great whether they are round or oblong or triangles."

"Triangles?" Katie and Sadie giggled.

"Do you think your *bruders* will even notice the shape of the biscuits?"

"*Nee*. They'll gobble them up like they're starving." Katie knew her *bruders* well.

"Exactly." Rosanna slid the biscuits off the baking pan and into a napkin-lined basket. "Here." She handed the basket to Sadie to set on the table. "Katie, will you please set the apple butter and honey on the table?"

"Mamm's home!" Sadie squealed. "I saw a buggy drive up."

"Everything worked out just right, ain't so? Supper is ready, and everyone is here." Rosanna began ladling stew into ceramic bowls for everyone.

"You'll never guess who I saw today," Tobias said around the bite of biscuit he was chewing.

"Swallow first." Rosanna shook her finger at her

older *bruder*. "I can see why Sadie talks with her mouth full. She learned from you."

Tobias made a face at Rosanna and gulped his tea. "As I was saying before I was interrupted, you'll never guess who I saw today."

"I'm sure you'll tell us." Joseph elbowed his *bruder* before reaching for another biscuit.

"I was on my way back from picking up some supplies for the furniture shop when I passed Henry Zook and Frannie Hostetler. Riding together. In an open buggy. In broad daylight."

"Don't go spreading rumors, Tobias," Mamm admonished.

"It's no tall tale. I saw them with my own two eyes."

Rosanna's last bite of biscuit hit her stomach with a thud. She only hoped it stayed there and she wouldn't have to make a mad dash from the table. Evidently Henry and Frannie didn't care who saw them. A pinprick to her heart let all her hopes and dreams escape. She stared hard at the peas and carrots floating in her stew so her family couldn't see the tears flooding her eyes.

"Maybe they simply had been at the same place at the same time and shared a ride home," Sarah suggested.

"I don't know. They looked pretty cozy to me." Tobias scooped up a spoonful of stew and stuck it in his mouth.

Rosanna blinked and stared harder. Why did Tobias have to bring this up now? When she wanted him to talk to her, wild horses couldn't drag information out of him. Now he prattled on like his tongue was loose at both ends. Did he want to make sure she knew Henry was probably out of her reach? Rosanna stirred her spoon around in the bowl but didn't dare raise a bite to her lips. There wasn't any way it could possibly slide past the boulder nearly clogging her throat. She had thought Henry and Frannie looked pretty cozy, too.

"Do you know anything about that, Rosanna?" Tobias lowered his spoon to the bowl and stared at her.

"Why would I?" Rosanna tucked her napkin under the edge of her bowl and jumped up. "I-I think I need to check on Mollie." She ran from the room but could still hear Tobias' voice.

"What's up with her? I didn't hear the *boppli*."

The pent-up tears overflowed their banks as soon as Rosanna's feet hit the stairs. She raced up with one hand over her mouth to try to contain a sob. If Henry and Frannie didn't care who saw them, they must truly be a couple. Rosanna would have to say goodbye to her dream.

She slowed her pace when she reached the door to her room and tiptoed inside. She had almost made a little bed for Mollie downstairs but at the last minute had decided to tuck her into the cradle next to her own bed. Now she was glad she'd done that. She needed to be alone. A quick peek through the film of tears told her Mollie still slept.

Rosanna threw herself across the bed and buried her face in the pillow to muffle the sound of her sobs. She should have kicked her door completely closed but couldn't drag herself off the bed to do that at this point. She cried for her lost dream. She'd pinned her hopes for marriage on Henry Zook about six months ago and had thought she'd been moving closer to realizing that dream. She talked to Henry after each singing, inquired about his work and his family, extracted his opinion on current happenings, and learned his likes and interests. He had always treated her politely and even smiled and nodded. He never seemed eager to escape, so he must have at least found her presence tolerable. Her last sob ended as a hiccup. But wait . . .

Rosanna pulled her face from the pillow and rolled to a sitting position. She gulped in a quivery breath. Something clicked in her brain, something she hadn't noticed previously. Or maybe she had *chosen* not to notice. Had Henry ever once asked about her likes and opinions? Had he ever asked about her day or how she spent her time? She couldn't remember his ever showing such an interest. Had he even taken the initiative to seek her out, or had she always gravitated toward him?

Her thoughts traveled back to the singings over the past six months. Rosanna had always been the one who had wandered in Henry's direction. He'd never sought her out. She had been the one to offer him a cup of juice or to take him brownies and cookies, particularly if she'd been the person who baked them. Henry had never offered to get her a drink. Had he merely been enduring her presence?

How embarrassing! Rosanna slapped her palms to her burning cheeks. Had she appeared foolish or even desperate to Henry and everyone else? She'd never noticed the other youngies watching them. They all seemed to pursue their own interests. So maybe she'd only looked completely ridiculous to Henry. Should that make her feel better?

A little lip-smacking sound from the cradle captured Rosanna's attention. Her *boppli*. She'd focus on her *boppli*. Henry never asked her about Mollie or seemed interested in her at all. He'd probably make a terrible *daed* anyway! She'd worry about being the best *mudder* she could be and forget about all the fellows she knew.

Rosanna swiped at the remaining tears and slid from the bed to tend to Mollie. She had her little girl and her family. She didn't need one of those *buwe* who wouldn't want to be a *daed* to her *boppli*. But then a little voice way in the back of her brain whispered, *One fellow is different.*

Chapter Ten

Despite the napkin full of cookies he'd gobbled up on the drive home, Paul didn't have any problem polishing off his supper. Mamm's macaroni and cheese had to be the best in the world. His silence at the table appeared to have gone unnoticed—a *gut* thing, for sure. Mamm had chattered so much about Becky's twins that it would have been hard to sneak a word in anyway. He didn't know if anyone loved *bopplin* as much as his *mudder* did, except maybe Rosanna.

Rosanna. Now there was the real reason for his silence. She filled his thoughts so completely that talk of her would surely pour out of his mouth if he attempted to speak. His younger *bruders* would tease him mercilessly. One of them would be bound to utter something to a *freind,* who would tell a *freind,* who would tell a *freind,* until the whole community knew the secrets of his heart. It was definitely to his advantage to keep mum at the supper table. He listened, nodded from time to time to show interest, and ate.

Alone in his room, he could give in to those thoughts. Since he was fortunate enough to have a room to himself, he could even give voice to his thoughts, if he wanted. Sometimes it helped to sort things out if he could say them aloud. Actually, nothing needed to be sorted out. The more time he spent with Rosanna, the more he liked her. Period. End of story. If she experienced the same emotions, his story would be complete.

Paul hadn't missed her absorption with Henry after singings. She'd done nothing wrong, of course. She'd never flirted or batted her eyes like some girls did with a fellow. From where he'd sat on a bale of hay with a few other fellows, munching on treats, he'd stolen peeks at the various couples chatting away. Rosanna usually ended up talking to Henry, though he'd never been certain who sought out whom.

She always looked so pretty in her blue or purple dress. Her dark hair contrasted nicely with her white *kapp*. But it was her big chocolate drop eyes and easy smile that snatched his breath away and sent his heart rate soaring. If Rosanna looked at him the way she looked at Henry, he might melt on the spot. From his observation point, he'd never been sure if Henry's expression mirrored Rosanna's, but he knew they never left together. On the way home after every singing, Paul kicked himself for lacking the courage to approach Rosanna before she had the chance to gravitate toward Henry.

If today had been any indication, though, Henry had not had his heart in any of those conversations with Rosanna. What was wrong with the guy? How could he pass up Rosanna Mast for Frannie Hostetler? He didn't mean that in a bad way. It was simply that there couldn't be any comparison whatsoever between the two girls. Frannie was nice enough, he supposed, but he always thought she could be rather bossy and

maybe a touch nosy. If things went her way, she smiled
and could be right pleasant. If they didn't, well, a surly
look crossed her face. And she really needed to get
those glasses adjusted. She was forever pushing or
tugging on them.

Sure, he knew outward appearance wasn't the most
important quality, but Rosanna possessed an inner
beauty to go with her outer attractiveness. She always
acted sweet and polite. Even if she'd been up all night
with a woman giving birth or with Mollie, her smile
could still thaw an icicle.

Could Henry's loss be his gain? Paul hoped so. How
did he go about winning Rosanna's heart? How did
he get her to consider him as more than a *freind*? *Ach!*
He wished he had someone to talk to about this. He
didn't have any *schweschders*, and his younger *bruders*
wouldn't be any help at all. His older, married *bruder*
was practically a newlywed but probably wouldn't
prove helpful, either, since he and his new *fraa* had
known since the cradle they would eventually marry.
Maybe he could ask Mamm's advice. *Nee*, that would be
too embarrassing.

One thing Paul did know, though, was that he
couldn't be anything other than who he was. He worked
hard at the furniture shop and on the farm. He loved
Gott and his family. He loved *kinner* and animals. Were
those qualities Rosanna held dear? He wanted to
marry and have a family—and he wanted to do that
with Rosanna and Mollie. Paul eased his weary body
onto his bed. He needed sleep. He needed answers.

Rosanna settled Mollie in a little nest in the corner
of the Kurtz's big living room. The huge quilting

frame occupied the center of the room. Enough chairs surrounded it for all the women, young and old, who were expected to attend the quilt frolic. They would be working hard to finish the king-sized quilt in time for the upcoming annual auction. Many items would be auctioned off, not only the quilts the women had stitched during the past year.

The auction always drew a huge crowd and helped them raise money for their community fund. The Amish did not carry any health insurance or home-owner's insurance or any of those things the *Englischers* considered necessary. When some catastrophe occurred or someone suffered a health problem requiring expensive medical care, the community pulled together to help the person or family in need. The funds raised at the auction helped out at such times.

Women began arriving bearing bowls and baskets of food to share at the noon meal and at snack time. Since it was a weekday, many of the *kinner* were at school. Only the youngest ones tagged along with their *mudders*. They would be tended by the girls who had finished school but weren't yet ready to join the experienced quilters. Of course, lots of stories, news, and laughter would be shared during the frolic. Rosanna had been looking forward to a fun day.

A few other young *mudders* found resting places for their infants as Rosanna had done. Maybe she would fit in more with these young women rather than her usual *freinden.* But she didn't have a husband and home to talk about as they did. It was entirely possible that she didn't fit in anywhere. She tried hard not to let that thought take root in her brain and make her sad.

Rosanna's attention shot to a group of girls chattering and giggling in the corner. Of course, Frannie Hostetler stood in the center of the group. Her hands flew about as she spoke. Every few moments, one hand fiddled with her glasses.

"Really?" Rosanna heard someone ask.

"*Jah*. We had such a nice time. We talked ever so much. Henry is a lot of fun to be with." Frannie's voice rose louder than the others.

Rosanna found it hard to imagine Henry talking "ever so much." Pulling conversation from him, other than polite answers to questions, had been like tugging a bone away from a dog.

"But in daylight for all the world to see?" another voice chimed in.

Rosanna saw Frannie shrug. "We didn't care. It isn't like we ran into a lot of people."

"It only takes one person to set the grapevine atwitter."

"It doesn't bother me." Frannie giggled. She turned her head and cut her eyes to Rosanna. A smirk overtook her smile.

She knew I was standing here. She wanted me to hear every word. Rosanna attempted a smile and nodded at Frannie. She wouldn't give the girl the satisfaction of knowing she had been upset by the comments. She jumped when long, slender fingers clamped around her upper arm.

"I'm so glad you came and brought Mollie."

Rosanna looked up into Emma's clear blue eyes. "Hi, Emma." She knew her response lacked enthusiasm.

"Don't pay her any mind," Emma whispered. "She's only trying to get attention. She probably never went anywhere with Henry."

"She did. Tobias saw them together—and so did I.

She really was out riding with Henry. That part is true for sure and for certain. I don't know about the part about Henry being a chatterbox, though."

Emma clapped her other hand over her mouth, but still a tiny giggle escaped. "I don't quite see that happening, either."

"Who knows? Maybe with the right person, he's totally different."

"And maybe Frannie prattled enough for the both of them. She usually only needs someone to listen, not to actually speak."

"*Ach*, Emma! You're terrible!"

"But truthful. Let's sit over on this side, where you can keep an eye on Mollie." Emma tugged on Rosanna's arm and led her to a seat at the quilting frame. "Mollie is really growing, ain't so? You're a natural with her."

"And you're a *gut freind*."

As Rosanna and Emma took their places, other women followed suit. Rosanna breathed a sigh of relief when Frannie and her rapt listeners chose seats at the opposite end of the big quilting frame. Surely Frannie wouldn't speak of her outing with Henry now when all the older women could hear her. Rosanna threaded her needle and plunged it into the fabric, taking small, even stitches. The log cabin wasn't an unusual pattern, but the colors of this quilt were quite unique. It should go for a high price at the auction. Rosanna's tension began to ease when Emma's *grossmammi* began one of her stories from her growing-up years in Southern Maryland. The wizened old woman could always spin a *gut* yarn.

Rosanna left her spot once to tend to Mollie, the same as the other young *mudders* took turns slipping away to care for their infants or youngsters. The morning flew by as first one and then another woman told a story or shared news from relatives in different parts of the country. At noon, they all stretched their fingers and backs as they rose from their positions and scurried off to set out dishes for the meal. Rosanna checked on Mollie again before joining the other young women.

"I thought you were going to say something to her," one girl hissed as she nudged Frannie.

Rosanna pretended not to hear the comment and glanced around for Emma.

"Well?" The girl issued another challenge.

Frannie shuffled over to Rosanna, who couldn't find any means of escape. "I'm sorry if I stole your fellow from you. I guess he wasn't interested in being an instant *daed*."

"You couldn't steal something I didn't possess. Henry and I didn't have any understanding. He was free to choose any girl he wanted."

"But you two talked after singings."

"We only talked. I talked to other people, too, *buwe* and girls."

"You talked mostly to Henry. I noticed. I've had my eye on Henry Zook for years."

"Really? Henry didn't let on . . ." Rosanna's voice trailed off. Henry never offered much in the way of his personal feelings anyway.

"*Jah*. He didn't seem to do much talking to you, but we sure talked a lot."

"I'm glad for you, Frannie." Rosanna turned to head in another direction, any direction, as long as it was away from Frannie.

"You know, your chances for courting may be slim

to none now that you have that *boppli.*" She jerked her head toward the corner where Mollie was sleeping and then shoved her glasses back into place.

"If that's so, I'll accept that. Mollie is my *boppli.* I love her as much as any other *mudder* loves her *kinner.* If a fellow wanted to court me, he'd have to be willing to take Mollie along with me. If not, then he definitely wouldn't be the right fellow for me!"

"Well said, dear."

"*Ach,* Mary! I didn't hear you approach." How much had the older woman overheard?

"You were busy, and I didn't want to interrupt. I wanted to tell you I'd tend to Mollie for you next time she needs something and give you a little break."

Rosanna smiled. "*Danki,* Mary. It's so nice of you to offer."

"It's also selfish." Mary chuckled. "I love *bopplin,* and that one in particular." She squeezed Rosanna's hand. "By the way, Frannie, Rosanna is absolutely right. If a man can't love and accept that sweet little girl, he's definitely not *gut* enough for Rosanna." Mary gave Rosanna's hand another squeeze and hurried toward the kitchen.

Mary's words provided a balm to Rosanna's wounded heart and soul, injuries inflicted by Frannie's words. From the corner of her eye, she caught Frannie staring after Mary with her mouth agape. For once she didn't reach for her silver-framed glasses. Rosanna bit back a smile.

"What was that all about?" Emma looked from one woman to another.

Chapter Eleven

Rosanna watched Frannie snap her mouth shut and shuffle back to her *freinden*. She couldn't hold a grudge against the girl, though. If Henry would rather be with Frannie, then so be it. She mentally shored up her spirits. It was certainly better to know where Henry stood before she invested any more of her time, effort, and heart into a relationship not meant to be.

She whirled around to face the owner of the whisper at her ear. "Where were you?"

"I had to help my *mamm* get some dishes down from the top shelf of the cabinet," Emma said. "I told her to let me climb up and fetch them before everyone arrived today, but she wanted to wait to see if we needed them. Of course we needed them!"

"So you've been scaling cabinets while I've been fending off arrows."

"Arrows shot by whom? *Ach*, wait. Let me guess. It wouldn't be a mud-brown-haired girl with slippery silver glasses, would it?"

Rosanna stifled a giggle. "You always make me feel better."

"I aim to please. It sounds like Mary Hertzler came to your rescue."

"She did, indeed. I don't know how much she heard, but she certainly said some kind words."

"I'm sure she put Frannie in her place. I don't believe I've ever seen Frannie Hostetler speechless. And I don't believe I've ever seen her keep her pudgy hands off her glasses for that long."

"Emma, you're awful!"

"I'm not saying a single thing that isn't true."

"I don't really think Frannie intended to be mean." At Emma's raised eyebrows, Rosanna elaborated. "I think she wanted me to know I should give up any hope of winning Henry's attention."

"She wanted you to know some fellow finally took an interest in *her*."

"Emma!"

Emma shrugged but didn't apologize for her words. "You're so nice, Rosanna. You always look for the *gut* in everything. My glasses aren't so rose-colored. I tend to call things as I see them. And I see Frannie as a manipulator—not vengeful or anything, but manipulative just the same. Poor Henry probably didn't stand a chance."

"Frannie does like to talk."

Emma rolled her big blue eyes. "That's an understatement. You know, I never understood what you saw in Henry anyway."

"He's a nice fellow."

"He's nice enough, I'll grant you that much, but he's not right for you."

"Are you the expert? When did you take up matchmaking?"

Emma burst out laughing. "I'm not any matchmaker. If I was, I wouldn't be unattached myself."

"Tell me why you believe Henry is wrong for me."

"For one thing, if he could be so easily swayed by Frannie, he's not very, um, intelligent."

Rosanna gave her *freind*'s arm a playful punch.

"You need someone big and strong—which Henry definitely isn't. You need someone who isn't afraid to voice his feelings—which Henry doesn't seem capable of doing. You need someone who loves Mollie as much as you do, and I don't even know if Henry likes *kinner*."

"Whew! That's a pretty tall order, Emma. You let me know when you find such a fellow."

"I will. And I hope he has a twin for me. *Kumm* on. Let's get something to eat before we're left with scraps."

The afternoon passed much as the morning had with more talk, laughter, and storytelling. Rosanna mulled over Emma's words as she pushed and pulled her needle through the quilt top, batting, and backing. Was Henry as unsuitable for her as Emma believed? As her *freind* had pointed out, Henry wasn't big. He was barely taller than Rosanna. He could be strong, though. A person didn't have to be a giant to have strength. He'd never really shared his feelings with her. They'd only had polite conversations that skimmed the surface of any serious subjects. Emma could be correct on that point. But then again, maybe she wasn't the girl he wanted to share his feelings with. Maybe Frannie was that person. Rosanna stole a glance to the opposite end of the quilting frame, where Frannie sat with an index finger stuck in her mouth. She must have jabbed the needle into her flesh. Rosanna jerked her eyes back to her own work. She didn't want to share that particular experience.

The final characteristic Emma had detailed was the most important one, and the most troubling one. Henry didn't seem to care a whit about Mollie. In his defense, though, probably most young fellows wouldn't give Mollie a second thought. Their thoughts would be occupied with their jobs and which girl they would ask home from a singing. They definitely would not be thinking about their prospective *fraa*'s infant. Frannie's comment may prove accurate. Rosanna's hopes of courting might be nil.

"Psst! Where are you?" Emma nudged her arm so hard Rosanna nearly stabbed her finger with the needle she held ready to plunge through the quilt. Then she'd be sucking on her finger like Frannie. "What?"

"I only asked you three times if you plan to attend the next singing."

"I'm sorry. My mind has been wandering."

"I think it got lost somewhere. Maybe we should go look for it."

Rosanna laughed and then lowered her voice to a whisper. "I called it back, smarty-pants. I don't know if I'll go to the singing. Maybe everyone feels like Frannie does, you know, that I don't belong anymore." Besides, she didn't think she could stomach the sight of Frannie slipping out with Henry when the songs were finished.

"Don't pay any attention to her. I don't think everyone feels that way at all. And I really think Frannie said that just to puff herself up."

"Emma!"

"Maybe you should thank her. I'm sure she did you a favor."

"You're incorrigible!"

"Well, now you can concentrate on looking for a fellow who will be *gut daed* material."

"I think Mollie will keep me plenty busy. We'll be fine, just the two of us. Right now, I'd better concentrate on this quilt."

"You can't fool me, Rosanna Mast. I know you want a husband and a houseful of *kinner* just as much as I do."

"Sure, but a person doesn't always get what he or she wants. We take whatever the Lord Gott gives us. He gave me Mollie, and if she is the only *boppli* I ever have, I'm happy to have her."

"Hmmm. I'm thinking she won't be your only one. I'm also thinking you won't be raising her alone."

"I haven't any idea what or who you're talking about." Rosanna nudged Emma with an elbow. "Start stitching. Listen, your *grossmammi* is about to launch into another story. She's always so much fun to listen to."

Mollie barely let out half a whimper before Mary jumped up from the table and skittered around the quilting frame. Rosanna started to push herself from her chair but caught Mary's nod and her whispered, "I've got her." Mary had moved faster than either Rosanna or Sarah. Usually the two of them raced to see who would reach Mollie first.

"She sure seems infatuated with your *boppli*." Emma nodded in Mary's direction.

"*Jah*, she seems to really love holding and caring for Mollie."

"I hear her son rather dotes on Mollie, too."

"Where did you ever hear that?"

"A little birdie told me. Maybe Mary's son dotes on Mollie's *mudder*, too."

"If your little birdie told you that, too, it must be a cuckoo."

Emma laughed. "Would that be a bad thing?"

"What? That your birdie is a cuckoo?"

"*Nee*, silly. Would it be so horrible if Paul Hertzler was interested in you?"

Emma's voice had dropped so low, Rosanna practically had to read her lips. She spoke equally as soft. "Paul is a very nice fellow . . ."

"Don't you dare say, 'But he isn't Henry Zook'!"

"Shhh! I wasn't going to say that."

"Then what were you going to say?"

"Before I was interrupted, I was going to say but Paul was just being kind. He's the type of person who would go out of his way to help someone."

"What's wrong with that?"

"Absolutely nothing. It's a *wunderbaar* quality. The point is he's nice to everyone, so it's not like it's anything special if he's nice to me."

"I think there might be a little flaw in your logic."

"How so?"

"You apparently haven't seen him stealing glances at you during church services."

"You haven't, either."

"I have, too. You were too busy peeking at Henry."

"You must have missed every sermon if you've been so busy watching everyone else. And which fellow's eye were you trying to catch?" Rosanna slid a sideways glance at her *freind*. Emma's normally pale face took on a rosy hue.

"Um, not anyone in particular."

"Somehow I'm not convinced that's entirely true."

Emma clapped one hand to her chest and gasped in mock horror. "Are you saying I'm telling a lie?"

"Never! But maybe you are in denial. I'm sure you must have been looking at some certain person."

"We'd better quilt more." Emma dipped her head, but not before Rosanna saw the other girl's scarlet cheeks.

"Uh-huh. *Now* you want to quilt." Rosanna made a few stitches before turning her attention to Mary. The older woman sat in a well-used oak rocking chair near the stove. She shook the bottle to mix the formula as she gently rocked Mollie. After she placed the nipple in the infant's mouth, she looked up at Rosanna and smiled. Rosanna returned the smile. She experienced a twinge of guilt that someone else was caring for her little one's needs, but she knew Mollie was in capable hands. And Mary seemed to enjoy caring for the *boppli* so much. How could Rosanna possibly refuse her help?

Mamm sure had been in a *gut* mood since she got home from the quilting frolic. Paul amended that thought. Mamm was normally pleasant. She always had a smile and a kind word for everyone. It was just that this evening she seemed extra chipper and chatty. At supper, she'd caught them all up on the latest news and had even shared a story or two told by Grossmammi Martha, as everyone called Emma Kurtz's elderly *grossmammi*.

Most of Mamm's chatter, though, centered around a certain fair-haired infant and her dark-haired *mudder*. Paul was reluctant to admit, even to himself, his interest in the same two people. He struggled not to appear too eager to hear Mamm's report, lest his *bruders* commence their teasing the moment they all left the supper table. Paul feigned a casual interest while in reality he soaked up his *mamm*'s comments like the sponge absorbed the milk his youngest *bruder* spilled all over the table when they first sat down to eat.

"And the *boppli* has the cutest little dimples, just like Rosanna," Mary gushed. "You could almost believe Rosanna gave birth to her."

Paul had noticed the dimples, too. Another little tidbit he'd stored away in his treasury of Rosanna's qualities. That observation was filed away with the images of big chocolate eyes, silky, dark hair, and a smile that could light up a room . . . "Hey!" His fork flew from his hand, causing peas to fly off and roll across the table like marbles. He rubbed the arm that Joshua, his twenty-year-old *bruder*, had elbowed none too gently.

"I asked you three times to pass me the biscuits. You've been mooning over something—or someone. I had to get your attention somehow."

"I'm not mooning. I'm thinking. Here." Paul plunked down the basket with only a few biscuits remaining next to Joshua's plate. He chased the escaped peas and dropped them onto his own plate.

"Heavy-duty thinking if you couldn't hear someone sitting right beside you." His *bruder* sliced the biscuit open and spooned a dollop of jam inside before smashing the halves back together. Strawberry jam oozed out around the edges as he took a huge bite. "Who's got your thoughts all befuddled?"

"You've got jam all over your face." Paul avoided the question.

Joshua flicked his tongue around to mop up the mess made by his drippy biscuit. "Who?"

"Not a soul, Josh. Eat your supper."

"Did I hit a nerve, Bruder?"

"Of course not." Paul briefly considered shoving the rest of the biscuit into Joshua's mouth to keep him quiet but thought better of that action. He knew Josh was teasing, but he was not in any mood to be teased at the moment. Besides, he didn't want his family to figure out he had feelings for Rosanna when he didn't know if those feelings would ever be returned. Thankfully, Daed asked a question that drew his *bruder*'s attention. With a slightly shaky hand, Paul scooped up a new forkful of peas and sought to get them into his mouth without spilling any.

Mamm shot him a knowing glance, as if she could read his mind. She probably could. *Mudders* seemed to have a knack for that. At least his did. Paul wondered if Rosanna would be able to do that same thing with Mollie. There he went! Right back to thinking of Rosanna! He would have turned his internal sigh loose if it wouldn't draw more attention to himself. He had to determine what he should do. He lifted a bite of meat loaf—one of his favorite foods—to his mouth and chewed without tasting it. His thoughts could not stay focused on the meal before him.

If Rosanna attended the next singing, could he muster his courage and approach her afterward instead of watching the action from a hay bale and stuffing himself with cookies? She most likely wouldn't seek out Henry, not if Frannie had her way. Frannie and Henry might slip out early anyway. That would give him the opportunity he needed. Would Rosanna ride home with him? Should he even ask, or was it too soon?

Maybe she needed time to get over Henry, if she truly cared about him. But if he hesitated, might some other fellow beat him to Rosanna's side?

What if she didn't attend the singing? Should he show up at her house in the dark of night to shine a light in her window and toss pebbles at the house? What if she didn't respond? Worse yet, what if she refused to *kumm* outside but sent him away instead? He'd be humiliated, for sure, but his heart would be crushed. This courting business was so hard to figure out. Did all fellows feel this way?

Another nudge from Josh brought his thoughts scurrying back to the present. He quirked his eyebrows at his *bruder*. Josh probably didn't have a single problem talking to girls. In fact, Paul had seen him head out of the barn with several different ones after singings.

"If you're just going to play with that meat loaf, I'll eat it." Josh nodded at Paul's thick slice of meat with only two small bites missing. He reached his fork over, ready to spear it.

Paul scooted his plate out of reach. "Keep your hands off my food."

"I hate to see *gut* food go to waste."

"It isn't going to waste. It's going in my stomach."

"It sure seems to be taking a long time to get there."

"Not everyone inhales their food like you do. You probably don't taste a thing."

Paul hadn't tasted a thing either. He cut another piece of meat loaf and popped it into his mouth. A quick glance around the table told him everyone else had nearly finished second helpings of food. He didn't know how many biscuits Josh had consumed while his mind gallivanted. The basket was almost half full when he set it down a while ago. Now one lonely biscuit crouched in the corner. When had Josh eaten all the others? That guy could pack away more food than all the horses in the barn. Paul forced himself to eat a little faster.

"Is there pie for dessert, Mamm?"

"*Nee*, Josh. I was gone all day and didn't get pies made. Someone ate all the pie from yesterday." She wagged a finger at her second-oldest son. "I did bake a chocolate cake this morning, though."

"Chocolate cake will do just fine, Mamm. And I'll take Paul's piece too, since he's never going to finish his supper."

Chapter Twelve

"I really don't want to go, Mamm."

"You need to get out and have some fun. You're only young once."

"I don't want to leave Mollie."

"Don't you think I can take care of her properly?"

"I know you can. It isn't that at all."

"I'm offering my services free of charge—not that I would ever charge to watch my *grossdochder*."

Rosanna smiled. It warmed her heart to hear her *mudder* call Mollie that. She counted her blessings that her family loved and accepted Mollie as their own. "What if you need to attend a birth tonight?"

"None of my women are due this month or next month. You know that as well as I do."

"Right, but someone might need you anyway." Rosanna bounced Mollie in her arms.

"If one of my women goes into labor tonight, she will need lots more help than I can give. She will have to call the rescue squad."

"But . . ."

"What is the real reason you don't want to attend the singing, Rosanna? You always liked to go before."

"Before I wasn't a *mudder* with responsibilities. I was young and carefree."

Sarah burst out laughing. "And now you're old and decrepit and can't have fun?"

"*Nee.*" Rosanna's lips twitched. She tried hard not to laugh along with her *mamm* but gave up the effort and joined her. "Sometimes I feel old," she gasped when her laughter faded.

"Every sleep-deprived new *mudder* feels that way. You could use a little break."

"Other women don't get a little break to run out on their *bopplin* to have fun."

"Other women have slightly different situations."

"Exactly. I don't really fit in with the youngies anymore."

"Ahh! So there's the issue."

"That's only a small part. Mainly, though, I just like being with Mollie."

"I completely understand that. Other new *mudders* sometimes take little breaks and leave their infants with a family member or a *freind* for a while. A break is *gut* for you. It helps keep you energized." Sarah reached out to stroke Mollie's soft pink cheek. "It helps keep you sane. It doesn't mean you don't love your *boppli*. Being a *mamm* is a full-time job, but unlike other jobs, it doesn't end after eight or ten hours. It's a twenty-four-hour-a-day job. That's why it's important to sneak a little break when you get the chance. And you have that chance right now."

"Honest, Mamm. I really don't feel like going."

"You'll be glad once you're there and start having fun."

Rosanna seriously doubted that. She wouldn't exactly be thrilled to watch Henry and Frannie talk and slip out the door together. And despite her protests, Emma had her eye on someone, and would most likely rather spend time talking to that fellow instead of to her. She'd be alone, watching from the sidelines. "I talked to people after church today. I don't need another break."

"You talked to other *mudders* while toting Mollie around. I never saw you talk to your *freinden*."

"I talked to Emma."

"Briefly. And she probably tried to persuade you to attend the singing, too, ain't so?"

"Well . . ."

"See? Your *freinden* want you there."

"Only Emma." Rosanna bent to kiss Mollie's forehead.

"The others do, too."

"They don't seem to know how to act around me anymore."

"All the more reason to go and show them you're still the same girl."

"But I'm not."

Sarah blew out an exasperated sigh. "Inside you are still the same Rosanna. It is true you have taken on responsibilities none of the other youngies have. Your life has changed drastically. But you are still the same thoughtful, kind person you've always been."

"My priorities are different now. Mollie is my main concern. I am definitely not complaining about that. I love her dearly." Rosanna bent to kiss the little forehead again.

"I know you love her. And it is right for a woman to put her infant's needs before her own, but you can't deny yourself the opportunity to court and marry."

Rosanna smiled. "I get it, *Mamm*. You're afraid you'll be stuck with me forever."

Sarah laughed and playfully swatted at her *dochder*. "If it was your desire to never marry and add to your little family, I wouldn't have any qualms about your living here forever. But somehow, I don't think it is your real desire to remain a *maedel*."

"It never was." Rosanna had to admit the truth. "I always figured I'd marry and have a houseful of *kinner*, but if that's not Gott's plan for me, I can be content with only having Mollie."

"Content, maybe. Happy? I'm not so sure. You won't know if it's Gott's plan for you to marry if you don't mingle with the others. Simply because you have a *boppli* doesn't mean you can't court and marry. Widows with more than one little one remarry."

Rosanna didn't mention she had thought Henry was the one for her, but that dream had marched right out of her life. Her heart was still sore, and now confusion settled in her brain. How did a girl know who was the right fellow for her? If she had made such a drastic mistake pinning her hopes on Henry, how could she be sure who to give her heart to? It was all so confusing. Would any of the young fellows she knew want to take on a girl who already had a *boppli,* or would she have to settle for an older, widowed man with *kinner* of his own? Maybe she'd have to look outside her own community. Rosanna suppressed a shiver. She definitely didn't want to have to "settle" for someone. She wanted to be in love with the man she married. She wanted him to love her, not need her to be a *mudder* to his passel of little ones. Was that too much to hope for?

"What is it, dear? You're frowning like you're trying to solve the mysteries of the universe."

"I'm thinking, that's all." Rosanna made an effort to smooth her brow.

"About what?"

"I'm, um, wondering how to ever know who the right fellow is."

"You'll know. Your heart will sing at the very thought of him. And it will thump wildly whenever you see him." Sarah smiled and patted Rosanna's arm.

"Was that how it was with you and Daed?"

"Your *daed* still makes my heart sing, even after all these years." Sarah's smile broadened. Little crinkly lines fanned out around her brown eyes.

"How did you know he was the one? Was it love at first sight?"

"I'm not sure *love* at first sight ever really happens. It was *like* at first sight. He was so kind, thoughtful, and generous. He made me feel special, and he made me laugh. He still has all those qualities. There are fellows out there with remarkable qualities, Rosanna. You'll see."

"I suppose." Rosanna chewed on her tongue for a moment and then released it to utter, "Do you truly think there's someone for me and Mollie?" The image of Henry and Frannie laughing together trotted through her mind.

"I'm sure there is." Sarah squeezed the younger woman's arm again. "The right person isn't always the person we have in our own mind. The Lord Gott's plan might be totally different from ours, but you can be sure He has a plan for you."

"I wish I knew what it was. And I wish I knew how to tell who is right for me."

"Pray about it, dear. Ask for Gott's wisdom and guidance."

"I've been doing that."

"The Bible says to pray without ceasing. Gott's timing is not always the same as ours."

Rosanna nodded and blinked back the sudden tears that pricked the backs of her eyes.

"I know someone who sure seemed to be looking for you after church today."

"Really? Who?" It couldn't have been Henry. From her spot near the window, Rosanna had seen him leave the group of fellows he'd been talking with after the noon meal to follow Frannie around. Of course, she didn't know if Frannie beckoned to him first or not. It had been pretty hard to tell from her hiding place in the kitchen with Mollie and two or three other young *mudders*.

"If you'd socialized a little more after the tables had been cleared, you would have known that Paul Hertzler asked several people where you and Mollie were. He specifically asked after you *and* Mollie."

"How do you know that?"

"I heard him ask Emma, and then he asked me."

"What did you tell him?"

"I told him you were in the house, probably feeding Mollie. Why didn't you leave the kitchen?"

Rosanna shrugged. "I felt more comfortable there."

"The other young folks are your *freinden*. I'm sure you'd fit right back in if you gave yourself the chance." Sarah held out her arms. "Now give me this precious girl. You haven't gone to the last several singings. You need to get out. Mollie will be fine. You know how Katie and Sadie dote on her. She won't lack for attention."

Rosanna looked at her *mamm*'s outstretched arms but still hesitated. Part of her wanted to go, but a bigger part of her wanted to bathe Mollie, cuddle her, and tuck her into bed.

Sarah wiggled her fingers. "You can go and return with Tobias, so you won't be alone."

"He might want to take someone home. He wouldn't want me around."

"He can take someone home. He can simply drop you off before he takes home whichever girl he chooses."

"I don't want to spoil his evening."

"You'll only spoil my evening if you don't hurry and get ready to go," Tobias said from the doorway. How much of the conversation had he heard? Not much, Rosanna hoped. He crossed the room in several long strides. He gently tweaked Mollie's nose and playfully punched Rosanna's arm. "Besides, I might not want to take anyone home this evening."

Rosanna threw him a mock look of disbelief. "What? Are my ears playing tricks on me?"

Before Rosanna realized what he was doing, Tobias had lifted Mollie from her arms and plunked her in Sarah's waiting arms. "Now go get ready!"

"But . . ." Rosanna looked from Sarah to Tobias, feeling totally helpless.

"Go have a *gut* time," Sarah said. "We'll be just fine." She stroked Mollie's cheek.

Rosanna sighed in defeat. She wasn't at all certain she'd be "just fine." Maybe she could sneak back outside and hide in the buggy until Tobias was ready to go home. The weather was a bit cold, though, to stay in a dark, unheated buggy for too long. And it would be nearly impossible to hide in Tobias' open courting buggy. She dragged herself toward the stairway.

"Hurry up!" her *bruder* barked out behind her. "I move faster than that in my sleep."

Rosanna turned and wrinkled up her nose at him. She might have poked out her tongue if Mamm hadn't been watching. That probably wouldn't be a very mature thing to do, though, and she did need to set a *gut* example for Mollie.

Reluctantly she pulled her blue dress from the peg on the wall. She should be excited to go to a singing. Instead she dreaded the entire evening. She changed her dress, smoothed her hair, and straightened her *kapp*. She imagined Tobias was standing at the bottom of the stairs with his arms folded across his chest and the toe of one foot tapping furiously.

"It's about time!" he said when she emerged from her room.

Rosanna had been mostly correct. Tobias was standing at the bottom of the stairs. He already had on his jacket and black felt hat. His toe tapped. Instead of having his arms crossed, though, his fingers drummed on the handrail. "I didn't take that long."

"Right."

"What's your hurry? Are you anxious to see someone special?"

"*Nee.* I just don't like being late for anything."

Rosanna supposed that was true. Tobias generally arrived early for any activity he needed to attend. For all his joking and lightheartedness, he was a very punctual person. "I don't think anyone will care if we're a teensy bit late, but we probably won't be."

"Here." Tobias held out Rosanna's cloak and bonnet.

"You really are anxious. I think there's something you're not telling me, Bruder."

"I think I'm going to pick you up and carry you out the door."

"Let me kiss Mollie."

Tobias sighed and rolled his eyes. His toe tapping increased in intensity and volume.

"I'll be right back."

A few moments later, Rosanna settled herself beside Tobias on the open buggy seat. It would definitely be a chilly ride. She scooted a little closer for extra warmth. "So who is it?"

"Who is who?"

"Who is the girl you're so anxious to see?"

"I didn't say I was anxious to see anyone, if you remember."

"I remember you *said* that, but my gut tells me otherwise."

"Maybe you should have taken some medicine for that gut problem."

Rosanna elbowed his upper arm. "I won't tell anyone, you know."

"There's nothing to tell anyway."

She sighed. "If you say so. Just remember you have to take me home."

"Maybe you'll ride home with someone else."

"Not a chance. I'm sorry, Bruder, but you're stuck with me."

"Could be worse, I guess."

Chapter Thirteen

Rosanna's attempt to sneak into the singing as Tobias' shadow was thwarted when Emma spotted her almost immediately and tugged her to a seat on the girls' side of the Bylers' big barn. She had hoped to sit near the door and plan her escape, but Emma apparently had other ideas. Rosanna couldn't easily refuse to accompany her *freind* without causing a ruckus and drawing unwanted attention. As she had told Tobias, they weren't late, but they arrived barely before the singing began.

By the start of the third song, Rosanna had relaxed. The tension in her shoulders eased, and she felt the wrinkle between her brows smooth out. She loved to sing and soon lost herself in the songs, which were sung a cappella. Her gaze wandered from time to time. When her eyes flicked in Frannie's direction, a pain wrenched her gut with a vengeance, and she nearly choked on her own saliva. Rosanna would have to be blind to miss Frannie's less-than-subtle glances at Henry. "Out-and-out staring" might have been a more apt description. She tried hard to suppress a strangled cough but couldn't quite hold it in.

"Are you all right?" Emma whispered.

"I swallowed wrong." Rosanna coughed so hard tears flooded her eyes. So much for not causing a commotion or drawing attention! She gasped for breath and swiped a hand across her eyes before waving at the song leader to continue. If they started singing the next song, she could cough a little more inconspicuously and try to get herself together. Her cheeks burned hot enough to light a bonfire on a windy, wet day. She stared hard at her feet.

A prickling sensation crawled up Rosanna's spine, raising the little hairs on the back of her neck to stand at full attention. Someone was staring at her as he or she sang. She tried to ignore the ripple that washed over her, but her curiosity won out. She lifted her eyes ever so slowly and scanned the girls' section. They were all focused on their books or stealing glances across the barn at the *buwe*. None seemed even remotely interested in her.

When Rosanna's eyes traveled to the male faces on the opposite side, her heart began to pound. Would Henry be looking at her instead of at Frannie? *Nee*. His eyes roved to where Frannie sat. Rosanna struggled to keep disappointment at bay. The certainty she was being watched persisted. She shifted her eyes slightly to discover Paul Hertzler staring at her. When their eyes locked, the smile he offered was so warm and sincere Rosanna couldn't help but smile back. Why was Paul watching her?

Rosanna's cheeks grew warmer. She snapped her attention back to the singing and threw herself into the rhythm of the next song. She needed to forget about Henry. She didn't want to analyze the smile she had exchanged with Paul. She simply wanted to sing and make an escape as soon as she could.

Hearing only silence from the girl next to her, Rosanna peeked at her *freind*. Emma had stopped singing. Rosanna followed the other girl's gaze to where it landed smack on Tobias' face. Tobias? Emma was interested in Tobias? From her *bruder*'s smile, the interest appeared mutual. Rosanna's nudge startled Emma. She jumped nearly off the bench and immediately joined in the song.

"Tobias?" Rosanna whispered.

Emma jabbed Rosanna with a sharp elbow in answer. She ducked her head, but not before Rosanna glimpsed the other girl's glowing face. Rosanna nearly laughed aloud. How interesting!

Paul's heart warmed and its tempo increased when Rosanna smiled back at him. She had such a lovely smile. It lit her whole face. He'd been troubled by her solemn expression when she entered the Bylers' barn a short time ago. It appeared that Emma practically dragged her inside. Even after the singing had begun, Rosanna seemed skittish, like she was set to take off at any moment. She sang each song with great fervor, but in between songs, that frightened-doe look took over. At least she had made the effort to attend tonight for the first time in a while. Paul prayed the right words would enter his mind to reassure Rosanna, and he prayed he got the chance to utter them before she bolted.

Whatever transpired between her and Emma obviously amused Rosanna. She looked as if she was about to burst into laughter. Her mirth brought a smile to Paul's lips. He'd give anything to be the one to bring Rosanna joy. He had wanted to rush to her side to pat her back or to offer her a drink when she had that earlier coughing fit. He'd forced himself to remain seated. He'd felt her embarrassment as his own. He really wanted to talk to her when the singing concluded. Someday, somehow he had to show Rosanna how much he cared about her and Mollie. So far, suitable words hadn't popped into his head to start even a general conversation, much less a serious one, and they were getting ready to sing the final song of the evening.

As soon as the last note died, Paul made his move. He didn't want to be rude, but he feared he might have to trample over the fellow next to him to reach Rosanna before she slipped out the door. He saw Emma lay a hand on Rosanna's arm, halting her, momentarily at least. *Keep talking, Emma!* Paul scooted past the other fellow but couldn't make it any farther. A thump on his shoulder stopped him in his tracks. Ugh! Of all times for Ammon Byler to want to talk about his *daed*'s new horse! He tried to listen but was too preoccupied to give Ammon his full attention. He hoped he made appropriate responses. Before he could politely make his escape from his *freind*, he glimpsed Rosanna creeping out the door and disappearing into the darkness beyond.

Evidently satisfied with the conversation, Ammon shuffled off toward the refreshment table. Paul considered grabbing a few cookies to take to Rosanna, but figured any further delay in getting outside would give Rosanna time to put distance between herself and the barn, if she had taken off on foot toward home. Maybe she had decided to wait in the buggy for Tobias.

Paul paused for a moment after he stepped away from the doorway to allow his eyes to adjust to the darkness. He strained to hear any crunch of footsteps

on the gravel or dried leaves to give him a hint as to
which direction Rosanna took. All he could hear,
though, was the sound of muffled voices from the
barn. He looked around but couldn't detect any movement. The night must have swallowed her and left no
trace of her whereabouts. Would she even answer if
she heard him call her name?

"Rosanna?" Paul whispered as loud as he dared. He
certainly didn't want to draw the others out of the
barn. Rosanna would be mortified to have an entire
search party trail her.

"Rosanna?"

Not a whisper, a gasp, or a grunt in response. He
hadn't been that far behind her. How fast a runner
was she? He'd check the buggies first to make sure she
wasn't hiding there in the dark. With the nip in the air
tonight, she'd freeze if Tobias lingered very long.

Paul swerved onto the grass so his footsteps didn't
create any noise. Now to discover which buggy belonged to Tobias. Surely if Rosanna was here he'd see
her even in the blackness of the moonless night. His
eyes swept each open buggy as he passed. He stopped
when his gaze fell upon a lump in the last buggy. This
one had to belong to Tobias, since he and Rosanna
had been the last to arrive tonight.

"Rosanna!" He called a little louder since he was
most likely out of earshot of the folks in the barn. She
didn't answer, but he saw her hunkered beneath a
blanket. He climbed into the buggy and laid a tentative
hand on the blanket. "That is you, isn't it, Rosanna?"

"*Jah.*" The reply was soft, muffled by the blanket.

"Why are you out here? You're going to freeze."

"I-I'm okay."

"Then why are your teeth chattering?" The blanket

moved beneath his hand. He assumed she shrugged her shoulders. "Didn't you want something to eat?"

"I-I'm not hungry."

"Didn't you want to talk to your *freinden*?"

"I shouldn't have *kumm* at all."

"Why not? We're your *freinden*. We've missed you. I've missed you." It was a *gut* thing Rosanna was still hiding beneath the blanket and couldn't see him. Surely his cheeks glowed brighter than any full moon ever could.

"You have?"

Paul barely heard her voice. "I have. I was hoping to talk to you."

"I-I figured everyone would pair off or would want to do that. I didn't want Emma to think she had to babysit me if she wanted to talk to someone."

"I don't think Emma would feel like she had to babysit you. And you know very well not everyone pairs off. Some of us just like talking to everybody."

"You're right. I don't know what's wrong with me." The lump shifted. Rosanna poked her head out and gulped in a breath of air.

Paul chuckled softly. "I wondered when you were going to emerge for oxygen."

Rosanna snaked a hand out from under the blanket to straighten her bonnet and to swipe at her face. Paul wasn't sure if she had brushed away stray strands of hair or tears. Without giving his brain a chance to gain control over his hand, he reached over to capture her cold, much smaller one. "Your poor hand is as cold as an icicle." He briskly but gently rubbed it between both of his own hands. He was surprised but encouraged that she didn't immediately pull away. "Do you want to tell me what's wrong? I'm a *gut* listener."

"*Ach*, Paul! I don't fit in anywhere anymore. I'm not sure where I belong. I'm not a carefree youngie now, but I'm not a married woman, either. I'm a single *mudder*, and let's face it, there aren't many of those in this community." Rosanna gave a little laugh, but the sound was not at all joyful.

"We're still your *freinden*, Rosanna. That hasn't changed because you have Mollie. I, for one, think it's *wunderbaar* that you took Mollie in without any hesitation."

"I love Mollie."

"That's obvious." Paul gave her hand a little squeeze. "She's easy to love. She's a very special little girl." He paused a moment before blurting, "And you're a very special *mudder*."

"I want to be a *gut mamm*, but I don't feel like it when I'm here instead of home with her."

"Is this the first time you've left her in the two months you've had her?"

"*Jah*, except for when Becky's twins were born and your *mamm* watched her for a few hours."

"Don't you think you deserve a little break once in a while?"

"Most *mudders* don't . . ." Her voice trailed off.

"Sure they do. *Daeds* or grands or neighbors help out so they can catch their breath a bit."

"That's what Mamm said, too."

"Sarah is watching Mollie tonight, ain't so?"

"*Jah*."

"I'm sure she's happy to do so."

"She is. She loves Mollie, too. All my family dotes on her." A huge sigh escaped. "It's me. I guess I'm the one who's changed, not everyone in there."

Paul could barely see Rosanna's nod toward the

barn. "But you've changed in *gut* ways. *Ach!* That didn't sound right. I didn't mean you needed to change at all. You were perfect as you were, but your nurturing and protective instincts kicked in. It makes me think of Misty, our barn cat. She was a gentle, loving cat, but when her kittens came, she became more loving as she lavished attention on her *bopplin*." Paul chuckled. "I guess that didn't *kumm* out right, either. I didn't mean to compare you to our cat."

Rosanna squeezed his hand this time. "That came out exactly right, Paul. It was an ever so nice thing to say. I'll always remember your kind words. You know, I've always loved cats, so it's rather fun to think of myself as a *mudder* cat."

This time they laughed together. Rosanna's laugh ended with another sigh. "I hope . . ."

"You hope Mollie is okay."

"How did you know that's what I was thinking?"

"Like I said before, you're a *gut mamm*. *Mamms* always worry about their *kinner*. I'm sure Mamm worries about me and my *bruders*, even if we are older. And I'm sure Sarah is taking great care of Mollie."

"I know she is. Mollie is probably sleeping right now."

"Why don't you *kumm* back inside to grab some cookies and warm up a bit?"

"I think I'll just wait here for Tobias. He probably wants time to visit. I'll be fine huddled under the blanket. But you go ahead. You must be hungry and probably want to talk to the others. Maybe you even want to talk to someone special."

Paul could hear the smile in Rosanna's voice. The thought that persisted in his head slipped out before he could catch it. "I'm already talking to someone special."

"*Ach*, Paul! You're such a *gut freind*."

Paul struggled to swallow his disappointment. Would she ever think of him as more than that? He tried to reassure himself. That was a *gut* start, wasn't it? He couldn't expect her to be ready for anything more at the drop of a hat. Patience was a virtue he would apparently need to cultivate more of.

He'd called her perfect and special. Could Mamm have been right? Did Paul think of her as more than a *freind*? Did he have other, deeper feelings for her? She could picture his red cheeks beneath his big, hazel eyes when he'd uttered that remark. He was probably glad the darkness masked his face. He could be inside enjoying himself, but instead he sat out here in the cold keeping her company.

Maybe she should go back inside the barn for his sake. But if they were spotted entering the barn together, everyone would think they had slipped out together, too. Oooh! Everything was so confusing? Besides, that glimpse she caught of Frannie slipping away with Henry and walking so close to him a gnat could barely squeeze between them left her feeling wounded and miserable. "I'll be fine, Paul, if you want to go inside."

"*Nee*, I don't mind waiting with you, unless you're trying to get rid of me."

"Of course not! I don't want to spoil your evening, that's all." She'd actually like to be a fly buzzing around inside the barn to see if Tobias and Emma ended up talking. She most likely wouldn't be able to pry any information out of her *bruder* on the way home. She wasn't sure Emma would confide in her, either, even if they had been best *freinden* since they were ten years old. With her mind flitting about, she nearly missed Paul's comment.

"An evening, or part of one, spent with you can't be considered spoiled."

Rosanna wasn't sure how to respond. Instead, she squeezed the hand that continued to hold hers. She should pull her hand away, but didn't quite know how to do that without hurting Paul's feelings. He truly was such a nice, considerate fellow. When a sudden breeze blew, she shivered despite the heavy blanket wrapped around her like a cocoon.

"I, uh, could take you home, if you want. You don't have to consider it as anything more than a *freind* giving you a ride, if that will make your decision easier. I don't want you to freeze out here."

"I'll be okay." Rosanna forced the words out through teeth that wanted to chatter. "Tobias surely won't be much longer."

"You're talking about Tobias Mast? Your *bruder*?"

Rosanna laughed. "I see your point."

"I could sneak back inside and tell Tobias you want to check on Mollie and since I was leaving anyway, I could drop you off. How does that sound?"

Rosanna wavered. She did want to check on Mollie. And she was growing colder by the minute. If the wind kept up, she'd surely be a block of ice by the time Tobias exited the barn. If Paul could discreetly seek Tobias out and give him that message, she could be home in minutes. "Okay. That sounds like a fine idea. *Danki*, Paul."

Paul dropped her hand and pulled the blanket tighter around her before hopping to the ground. "I'll be right back out to hitch up my buggy."

Rosanna could barely see his silhouette floating toward the barn. Did she make the right decision? She didn't want to give Paul a false impression. She hoped the ride home wouldn't be too awkward.

"She's trying to roll over already," Rosanna said. Paul had been asking her about Mollie, a subject she never grew tired of discussing. Just like any other *mudder.*

"Already?"

"*Jah.* I can't believe it. She's quite strong. I think she'll figure it out any day now. And I think she's working on some teeth the way she gnaws on her hands and practically anything else she can get into her mouth."

"Next thing you know she'll be crawling and then walking."

"Not too soon, I hope. She's so adorable." Rosanna slapped a hand across her mouth and spoke between her fingers. "Oops! I didn't mean to sound braggy or prideful."

Paul laughed. "You didn't. You sounded like a *mamm.* It's obvious you love your *boppli.*"

"I surely do. Sometimes I forget I didn't give birth to her. She's such a part of me."

"I'm sure all adoptive parents feel the same way. At least, I hope they do. All little ones need to feel loved and cherished."

"You really love *kinner,* ain't so?"

"I suppose I do. I've never been asked that before, so I guess I've never thought about it. But I do have a fondness for them."

"You must have inherited that from Mary."

"Mamm sure does like caring for little ones. She smiled the whole time she watched Mollie for you."

The horse clip-clopped along at a moderate pace, but Rosanna didn't seem to feel the cold any longer. Either she was already frozen or Paul's ability to draw her into easy conversation warmed her.

As if reading her mind, he asked, "You aren't too cold, are you?"

"I was just thinking I didn't feel the cold so much now."

"*Gut.* I've enjoyed talking to you, Rosanna."

"It has been fun. I hope I haven't bored you with tales of Mollie's every smile and coo."

"Not at all. I like hearing about her. And I like hearing how happy you are. I do hope you'll continue to attend the singings, though."

"I'm not sure. Tonight didn't go so well."

"You aren't used to being away from Mollie. That's probably the problem."

"Maybe." Rosanna didn't mention that watching Henry and Frannie exchange meaningful glances hadn't exactly made the evening pleasant. She had to let him go. They had never been a couple. She'd never even sat in his buggy with him. Any relationship with him had been purely wishful thinking on her part. It was time to banish all those thoughts. Some little niggling voice whispered that she had already relinquished her silly crush on Henry Zook. She exhaled in a deep sigh, but a contented one rather than a despondent one.

"Are you tired?"

There he goes being considerate again! "I suppose so.

Mollie doesn't sleep through the night yet, so neither do I."

Paul laughed. He had an easy, happy laugh that didn't sound forced or strained at all. Rosanna doubted he had a dishonest or pretentious bone in his body. What he said, he meant. And he was so easy to talk to. She hadn't felt one bit fidgety or nervous during the whole ride. What could that mean?

Chapter Fourteen

Rosanna knew she should ask Paul if he would like a cup of *kaffi* or a piece of pie. After all, she had kept him from indulging in a snack after the singing, and he was kind enough to drive her home. If she asked him inside, though, Mamm and Daed would jump to the wrong conclusion. There was a chance they had already gone to bed—a very slim chance. Mamm was most likely still fussing over Mollie.

Ach! What should she do? She didn't want to be rude, but she didn't want to give her parents or Paul the wrong impression. She wrung her hands beneath the blanket Paul had tucked over her earlier. She had to make a decision. The buggy rolled along the Masts' long dirt driveway and would arrive at the white two-story house before she could inhale two more frosty breaths.

"Here we are." Paul stopped close to the back door. "I'm glad you came tonight, even though you didn't stay."

"*Danki*, Paul." Rosanna chomped on her tongue, indecision warring in her brain. "Would you like a cup of *kaffi* or cocoa to warm up?" There. Her tongue decided for her. She laughed. "I kept you from your snack, so I can at least offer you a bite to eat and a drink to warm you up." She held her breath, hoping he would refuse the offer so she wouldn't have to explain his presence to anyone.

"Sure, I could *kumm* in for a few minutes, if it isn't any trouble."

Rosanna forced enthusiasm into her voice. It wasn't that she didn't enjoy Paul's company, because she did. It was, *ach*, it was confusing, that's what it was! "Of course it isn't. There should be some pie or cookies, and there's always hot water in the kettle."

"May I take a peek at Mollie if I promise not to wake her up?"

"Do you really want to?" Rosanna couldn't believe a young fellow would actually ask to see a *boppli*. She figured they would try to pretend Mollie didn't exist—that is, if they showed any interest in her at all.

"Sure. I'd like to see her, if that's okay."

"Okay. She usually sleeps in a crib in my room, but we moved the cradle to the living room, so that's probably where she is right now." Rosanna scooted to the edge of the seat and prepared to climb from the buggy.

"Wait! I'll help you."

Startled, Rosanna pulled her foot back. She'd been climbing in and out of buggies all her life. She was pretty sure if she jumped she would land on her feet like a cat, but she waited for Paul to dash around to her side. He reached up for her hand and then practically lifted her down. Her heart thudded, either from the exertion or from Paul's nearness or both. She couldn't be sure. "*Danki.*"

Surprised by her reaction, Rosanna hesitated before moving toward the house. Now what was that all about?

She willed her racing heart to slow down. Paul's hand cupping her elbow did nothing to calm her. She didn't have any choice but to follow his lead.

"I'll try to tiptoe so I don't wake Mollie," Paul whispered as they mounted the cement steps leading to the back door.

"You forget that Mollie lives in a house full of rowdy *kinner*. She can sleep through just about anything."

Rosanna hoped it wasn't wrong to pray that everyone had gone to bed and was deep into dreams. Then she wouldn't have to explain why Paul had brought her home instead of Tobias and why he had followed her into the house. Her black athletic shoes didn't make so much as a squeak as she tiptoed across the linoleum floor in the kitchen. As she'd told Paul, Mollie could sleep through any noise, so it wasn't the *boppli* that concerned her. Mamm, on the other hand, could wake up if a gnat sneezed at the opposite end of the house.

Paul crept along behind Rosanna. He'd let go of her arm but still walked close enough that Rosanna could practically feel his breath on the back of her head. A single kerosene lamp glowed in the kitchen. The brighter propane-powered light had been turned off. Rosanna's huge shadow kept pace on the wall beside her as she made her way through the kitchen. Paul's giant shadow overlapped hers.

A soft humming from the living room alerted Rosanna that her prayer had not been answered in the manner she had wanted. Another single lamp glowed from within that room. One peek inside dashed all her hopes. Sarah sat in the old oak rocking chair near the black woodstove with a tightly swaddled Mollie in her arms. She softly sang a tune Rosanna had heard her sing to Sadie, Katie, James, and Joseph when they were small. Undoubtedly Sarah had sung the same song to Rosanna and her older *bruders* as well. The gentle rocking and hushed singing ceased when Rosanna crossed the threshold into the living room. Sarah's eyebrows shot upward when her glance fell on Paul. The question in her eyes didn't cross her lips.

Rosanna lifter her shoulders ever so slightly. "Is she awake?" Rosanna's whisper sounded more like a shout in the quiet room.

Sarah nodded. "I fed her a few minutes ago and couldn't bear to put her right back to bed."

Rosanna smiled. Many times she continued to hold or gaze at Mollie long after she'd returned to her slumber. Rosanna crossed the room with Paul on her heels. She'd better offer some sort of explanation before Sarah's imagination ran away with her. "I-I wanted to check on Mollie," she confessed. "I knew Tobias wouldn't want to leave the singing early, so Paul offered to bring me home." That should satisfy her *mudder*'s curiosity for the time being. Rosanna didn't mention that she'd fled from the barn after the last note of the final song and that she would have waited in the cold for Tobias if Paul hadn't sought her out.

Paul scooted around Rosanna. "Isn't she the sweetest *boppli*?"

Rosanna thought so, of course. There couldn't be any sweeter sight in the world than little Mollie sleeping peacefully or cooing or reaching for a rattle. She figured every new *mudder* believed her little one was the most precious thing in the world.

"*Ach! Gut* evening, Sarah. I didn't mean to ignore you."

Sarah stopped rocking. "Hello, Paul. It was nice of

you to bring Rosanna home. I didn't think it was late enough for everyone to leave. Had the singing even ended before you left?"

"*Jah.* I-I didn't want to stay, but I knew Tobias did, so I-I . . ." Rosanna couldn't say she hid in the cold buggy to avoid talking to anyone and to lick her wounds after watching Frannie and Henry slip out together.

"I knew Rosanna wanted to check on Mollie since she isn't used to being away from her."

Rosanna threw Paul a grateful look. He had jumped right in to save her further stumbling around for justification.

"Well, as you can see, Rosanna, Mollie is fine. We have had a pleasant evening."

Rosanna nodded. "I knew she would be fine with you, Mamm. It was just hard to be away from her." She reached down to lightly pat the tiny body in Sarah's arms.

"She sure is a *gut boppli.*" Paul leaned closer. "She's definitely growing, too."

Rosanna beamed. Mollie was the best *boppli* ever. She didn't dare say the prideful words aloud, but she couldn't help thinking them. "I-I told Paul I'd feed him a snack since we left before he could even grab a handful of cookies."

"And you can see that I'm wasting away, too." Paul patted his solid but flat belly.

Rosanna and Sarah laughed. Sarah resumed her gentle rocking. Rosanna fought the urge to snatch Mollie from her *mamm*'s arms so she could hug her and breathe in her sweet scent. But she needed to be a gracious hostess first. "I promised Paul a cup of cocoa or *kaffi* to warm up for the ride home. It's gotten colder out."

"The water is hot, and there are some little packets if you want cocoa, unless you want to make it from scratch with milk."

"The instant kind is fine," Paul assured her.

Rosanna gave Mollie another little pat before shuffling toward the kitchen with Paul on her heels.

"There is some peach pie left, and cookies, too," Sarah called softly.

Rosanna nodded. She crossed the kitchen to the cabinet where the boxes of cocoa usually sat. "We have some with or without the little marshmallows. Which would you prefer?"

"Without, please. Here, I can help. Where are the mugs?"

"You don't have to help."

"I'm used to helping in the kitchen. I told you once before, my *bruders* and I used to take turns helping Mamm."

"You did say that. The mugs are in there." Rosanna pointed to a different cabinet. When she saw Paul set two mugs on the counter, she pulled out another packet of cocoa for herself. Holding the mug would at least give her hands something to do once she sat at the table with Paul. She couldn't very well just sit and stare at him. That wouldn't be polite at all. And she could take a little sip when she couldn't think of anything to say. "I'll get the kettle."

Paul passed behind her to set the mugs down. A little shiver shot up Rosanna's spine at his nearness. She tore open the packets of cocoa and dumped brown powder into each mug. He stood close. Too close. Her breath caught. Her brain seemed incapable of issuing the command to step back. She caught a whiff of Paul's soap as he held a mug still for her to pour water into it. She prayed she wouldn't slosh it and scorch his hand. She had to move away from him.

"Would you like pie or cookies or both?" Rosanna scooted around Paul to retrieve the big cookie jar. She could get a breath into her lungs now that she'd put a little distance between herself and the big blond man with the most amazing chameleon eyes.

"Either one will be fine. I'm easy to please."

"Which means you'll eat anything, if you're like my *bruders*." Rosanna chuckled. They would eat anything that didn't get away from them or eat them first.

"That about sums it up." Paul laughed along with her.

Rosanna carried the cookie jar to the big oak table and pulled paper napkins from the holder. She returned to the counter to cut a healthy slice of peach pie and slid it onto a dessert plate.

Paul had located the silverware drawer and retrieved spoons to stir the cocoa. He carried both frothy mugs to the table. "Aren't you having any pie?"

"*Nee*, I'll just have cookies." She dropped onto a chair and stirred her cocoa. Why had her stomach turned into a giant ball of nerves? She doubted it would accept a single bite of cookie, even though the chocolate chunk cookies that filled the bear-shaped jar were her absolute favorites. She swirled the cocoa, laid the spoon on a napkin, and raised the mug to her lips.

"You might want to let that cool for a minute. I nearly burned the taste buds off my tongue." Paul smiled before turning his attention to the pie in front of him.

"*Gut* idea." Rosanna peered through the steamy fog at Paul. She lowered the mug but kept her icy hands wrapped around it.

"Great pie! Did you make it?"

"Actually, I did."

"It's very tasty."

Seeing what quick work Paul made of the pie, she slid the cookie jar closer to him.

"You first." Paul held the jar over for her to select a cookie.

She reached into the jar and pulled out a single cookie. She laid it on the napkin beside the spoon but didn't make a move to pinch off a bite.

"Only one?"

"One is fine for now." Even one cookie probably wouldn't make its way down her throat.

"Did you make these, too?" Paul dipped his hand into the jar and extracted three cookies.

"I did."

He bit off a chunk. "Mmm! Delicious! These are my favorites."

"Mine, too." Rosanna broke off a bite and popped it into her mouth. Somehow Paul had a way of putting her at ease. Tension drained from her body, her shoulders relaxed, and she actually tasted the chocolaty, sweet concoction. She might even persuade her stomach to unknot and accept the entire cookie.

"Mollie sure looks great." Paul licked his lips after polishing off his first cookie. "She really is beautiful." He looked down and plucked a chocolate chunk out of a cookie. "Like her *mudder*," he added in a whisper.

Rosanna's heart tripped over itself. Did Paul really say what she thought, or were her ears playing tricks on her? One peek at his tomato red face told her she surely must have heard correctly. Heat rose in her own cheeks. Should she respond, or pretend she hadn't heard the comment? Paul half raised his eyes and caught her looking at him. Now she had to say something. "*Danki*," was all she could manage. She broke off another piece of cookie to give her nervous fingers something to do. How were they going to recover from this?

Paul grabbed his mug and took an audible gulp. He immediately began to cough.

"Are you all right?" Rosanna reached across the table to take the mug from his hands before cocoa rained down on them and the table.

"It went down the wrong way." Paul thumped his chest and coughed a few more times.

"Would you like a glass of water?"

"*Nee,*" he croaked. "I'll try another sip of cocoa."

His fingers brushed hers as he took the mug she still held for safekeeping. A tingle shot up her arm and ran straight to her heart.

"I'm better." Paul took one more sip before setting the mug down. "I hope I didn't wake Mollie."

Rosanna patted his hand that rested on the table. "If she can sleep through Katie's and Sadie's squealing, she can sleep through a little coughing."

"Is she trying to crawl yet?"

Rosanna smiled. "It's a bit too early for that, but she managed to roll over, and she pushes up when she has tummy time on the floor. She looks like a little turtle emerging from its shell."

Paul chuckled. "Tell me more."

Rosanna relaxed again as she regaled Paul with Mollie's feats. He continued asking questions, seeming genuinely interested. Any other fellow would have mumbled a polite question or two and then maneuvered the conversation to another topic. Not Paul. He smiled, nodded, and encouraged Rosanna to keep sharing. When she glanced down, she discovered she'd eaten her entire cookie at some point.

"I'm going to tuck Mollie in and head to bed myself." Sarah spoke from the doorway.

Ach! How late had it gotten? How long had Sarah been close by? Rosanna had completely forgotten her *mamm* had been sitting in the next room. Her eyes flicked to the battery-operated kitchen wall clock. Two hours! She and Paul had been sitting at the kitchen table for two hours! Had Sarah been waiting for Rosanna to relieve her?

"I'm sorry for keeping you up, Mamm. I can take Mollie upstairs."

"You didn't keep me up. I dozed off in the chair. I've never figured out if it's a blessing or a curse to be able to fall asleep anywhere. I guess it's a trait of all midwives." Sarah's smile morphed into a yawn.

"*Danki*, Mamm. Get some sleep."

"It was *gut* to see you, Sarah." Paul pushed off the chair and crossed to the doorway in several long strides. "And you, too, Mollie." He touched one large index finger to the infant's cheek.

"You, too, Paul. Say hello to your *mudder* for me."

Rosanna tiptoed over to stand beside Paul and Sarah. She bent to kiss Mollie's cheek. "I'll be up soon."

"Take your time, Dochder. This little one should sleep a while longer yet. She ate like a little piggy at her last feeding."

Was Mamm encouraging her to stay here with Paul? Did Mamm think there was something going on between them? She'd have to set her straight in the morning. Rosanna watched her *mamm*'s retreat until she and Mollie rounded the corner and were completely out of sight.

"Mollie looked like a little angel sleeping in your *mudder*'s arms."

Paul's voice brought Rosanna out of her reverie. "I think of her as my little angel, but all *kinner* are a gift from the Lord Gott, ain't so?"

"For sure, but there is something extra special about this one." Paul gently squeezed Rosanna's arm.

"I'm blessed He chose me to raise her."

"That you are."

Rosanna smiled up at Paul. "Let's finish our snack."

"If you want to get some sleep while Mollie is sleeping, I can leave now."

"Finish your cocoa first." What was she saying? Paul had given her the perfect opportunity to end this little gathering, and she didn't pounce on it. She didn't have any choice now but to return to the kitchen and her hostess duties. Somehow the idea appealed to her rather than annoyed her. "Would you like more cocoa? That mug has probably grown cold now."

"This will be fine. I even like cold cocoa."

Rosanna slid onto the chair she'd vacated as Paul settled across from her. "Help yourself to more cookies."

"I believe my stomach is finally full. I'll just finish my cocoa."

Rosanna raised her mug and took a sip. "You're right. Cold cocoa isn't bad."

They talked a bit longer until Rosanna struggled to suppress a yawn. She dabbed at her mouth with a napkin to hide it.

Paul laughed. "That didn't work, Rosanna."

"Oops! I'm sorry. I tried to stifle it."

"I know you must be tired."

"It really isn't that late." Her eyes wandered to the clock.

"Maybe not, but your sleep is always interrupted, and I'm keeping you up when you should be stealing a nap before Mollie wakes up again."

"You're very understanding."

"I'm thinking how I'd feel if I had to wake up every few hours. I'm not so sure I'd be as pleasant to be around as you are."

Rosanna laughed. "I can't imagine you as being anything except pleasant."

Paul stood and picked up his mug and empty pie plate.

"I can take care of those."

"Let me help you clean up. Then I'll leave so you can go to bed."

What a nice fellow! How many times had that thought crossed her mind recently? Had she ever had such a thought about Henry Zook? Rosanna gathered up her own mug and the cookie jar. She ran a little water in the sink to wash the few dishes they'd dirtied. Paul dried them and returned them to the cabinets.

"*Danki* for inviting me in for the treats, Rosanna." Paul pulled on his black jacket.

"*Danki* for bringing me home."

"It was fun talking to you and great to see Mollie again."

"It was fun." Surprisingly, Rosanna meant those words. She had enjoyed talking to Paul. The time had flown by, instead of dragging, as she had feared it would.

"Will you attend the next singing?"

"I'm not sure about that."

"I hope you do."

Rosanna followed Paul to the door. "I'll think about it but won't promise I'll go."

"I understand, but I'd sure miss you if you didn't attend. You're a special person, Rosanna. *Gut nacht.*"

Paul touched her cheek and then slipped outside while Rosanna tried to devise a reply. Her cheek tingled and a warm feeling flooded her heart. "*Gut nacht,* Paul." She hoped he heard her. She also hoped he didn't encounter Tobias on the driveway. She'd never live down her *bruder*'s teasing, and she'd never convince Tobias that nothing was going on between her and Paul. It was bad enough she had to set Mamm straight first thing in the morning. She didn't need to add her *bruder* to the list.

She decided to leave a battery-operated lamp burning for Tobias instead of a kerosene one. He certainly was late. Maybe he took Emma for a ride. Wouldn't that be something? Her *bruder* and her best *freind.* She smiled and almost giggled out loud when she thought of ways she could persuade Emma or Tobias to tell her about their evening.

Weariness threatened to overtake Rosanna as she trudged up the stairs. She quickly prepared for bed and peeked into Mollie's crib. She sure hoped Mamm was right and Mollie would sleep awhile longer. She knelt beside her bed to say her prayers and whispered a hasty "amen" when her head thumped down on the bed. A few blessed hours of sleep would be *wunderbaar.* Even her eyelashes were tired, if that was possible. Her entire body throbbed with fatigue. Only her brain remained wide awake. It wanted to rehash the entire evening.

Rosanna punched her pillow and turned onto her side. She squeezed her eyes tight, as if that could block out the images parading through her mind. Amazingly the pain of seeing Henry and Frannie together had subsided. Not even a dull ache remained. Paul's kind words and concern had provided a balm to her heart.

She flopped onto her back and, as in the past, tried the technique she always encouraged with laboring women. She tensed each muscle group and then released them to encourage them to relax. She started with her feet and worked her way up her body. By the time she reached her shoulders, sleep claimed her.

Paul tossed and turned. Tomorrow would be a busy workday at the furniture shop. He needed to get at least a little sleep. His body was certainly willing, but his mind had its own agenda. It wanted to replay every moment with Rosanna. Had he said the right things? Should he not have told her she was special or as beautiful as Mollie? Or should he have said more? It was much too soon to confess his true feelings. Rosanna didn't even consider the evening anything other than two *freinden* sharing a snack. Would she ever think of him as more than a *freind*?

The more he tried to shut his brain down, the more images it wanted to display: Rosanna's shiny, dark hair and big chocolate eyes; Rosanna's smile that lit her entire face; Rosanna's laughter that sounded like the music of angels; little Mollie's long lashes against her soft cheeks. *You've got it bad!* How did he get rid of "it" if Rosanna could never consider a relationship with him? He yanked the pillow out from under him and covered his head. Maybe he could smother the images and get some sleep.

Chapter Fifteen

The rooster's shrill crow pulled Rosanna from the dream she'd fallen into what seemed like mere moments earlier. Usually she awakened before him, but today he won. She rubbed her eyes and threw off her covers. Thankfully, Mollie had only awakened once and had gone right back to sleep after swigging down her bottle. She had been sleeping for longer stretches, which was a blessing indeed.

Rosanna clicked on a small battery-operated lamp and dressed in the semidarkness. She didn't need much light to perform actions she'd done for so many years. She pinned her dress, cape, and apron and nimbly wound her hair into its customary bun. After pinning her *kapp* into place, she tiptoed over to the crib to lay a hand on Mollie. Her hand rose and fell with the *boppli*'s breaths. Rosanna had heard about sudden infant death syndrome and constantly reassured herself Mollie was okay. She smiled. How she loved this little one. She tiptoed from the room so she could start breakfast if Mamm hadn't yet gotten up. She hoped she would have a few minutes alone with her *mudder* this morning to clarify any misconceptions about last night.

That plan was immediately thwarted. The aroma of *kaffi* assailed her before she made it halfway down the stairs, so she knew Mamm was already bustling about the room. Muffled voices alerted her that someone else was awake and would soon troop into the kitchen. Rosanna would have to hold off on her discussion until a time they would not be overheard by nosy siblings.

"Is Mollie still sleeping?" Sarah called over her shoulder as she stirred oatmeal bubbling on the back burner of the stove.

"*Jah*. She ate about an hour or so ago, so I expect she'll sleep for a while. Do you want me to scramble or fry the eggs?"

Sarah tapped the wooden spoon against the side of the pan and laid it in the ceramic spoon rest. She gave Rosanna a quick glance and a little wink. "Scrambled will be easier. You look pretty tired."

"I'm not any more tired than usual. Mollie only got up once. Maybe she'll be sleeping through the night soon." Rosanna opened the door of the propane-powered refrigerator and slid out a carton of eggs.

"Once we start introducing solids, her little tummy will probably stay full longer."

"We can do that in another month or so, ain't so? She'll be six months old then."

"*Jah*. She is growing so fast."

"She sure is." Rosanna cracked eggs into a large mixing bowl and added salt, pepper, and milk. "We aren't frying bacon today?" Usually she scrambled eggs in the bacon grease, but the cast-iron skillet hadn't been pulled from the cabinet.

"I don't think there is enough bacon for everyone, so I didn't bother with it. I'll make some French toast now that the oatmeal is about done. That should fill everyone up. Did you notice if the *kinner* were awake?"

"I heard noises, but I didn't see anyone. I assumed James was outside with Daed and Joseph."

"He should be, but I didn't hear them go outside." Sarah gave her *dochder* a sheepish grin. "I wasn't up very long before you appeared."

"You certainly got *kaffi* and oatmeal going quickly." Rosanna bit back a smile. The old rooster must have beaten Mamm, too.

Sarah patted Rosanna's arm as she passed by. Rosanna heard her shuffle to the stairway to call Sadie and Katie. A moment later, she heard four feet hit the wood floor overhead. She pulled out two pans and dumped the egg mixture in one. She would use the other pan for the French toast. As tired as she was, she hoped she could cook both things at once without ruining either one.

Rosanna breathed a sigh of relief when the flurry of activity in the kitchen had abated and everyone had eaten and been sent on their way. Tobias had thrown odd looks at her across the table but hadn't made any teasing remarks or asked any embarrassing questions. Once or twice he opened his mouth to speak, but Sadie's spilled milk and Katie's incessant chattering kept him from getting any words out. Now, finally, everyone was well on the way to work or school. She and Mamm were alone with a mountain of dirty, syrupy dishes.

Rosanna sighed again as she scooted toward the doorway for a moment to determine if Mollie was making any sounds of stirring from sleep. Satisfied all was well upstairs, she crossed the room to the sink and filled it with hot, soapy water.

"How was your evening?" Sarah dropped silverware into the dishwater before picking up the towel to dry the dishes stacked in the drainer.

Here we go! "Mamm, before you get any wrong ideas or crazy notions, you need to know that Paul and I are not seeing each other." Rosanna scrubbed furiously until Sarah lifted the plate from her hands.

"I'll take that before you destroy it . . ."

"Paul is just a *freind*. He offered to bring me home last night to spare me from sitting in the cold while waiting for Tobias."

"Okay." Sarah picked up another plate. "You did invite him in, ain't so? He didn't force his way inside and steal cookies, *jah*?"

Rosanna cut her eyes to the right in time to see her *mamm*'s mouth twitching. The very idea of Paul forcing his way inside was hilarious. She couldn't hold back a giggle. "Of course he didn't." She used an arm to wipe her eyes. "I had to be polite and offer him food since he left the singing before getting refreshments, didn't I? That seemed to be the right thing to do."

"It was the right thing to do, but it seems he stayed awhile."

"I couldn't hand him a cookie and push him out the door, could I?"

This time Sarah burst out laughing. "I see. You want me to mind my own business, ain't so?"

"Truly, Mamm, there's nothing between Paul and me."

Sarah raised an eyebrow but kept silent.

"I know that look, Mamm. Paul and I talked while eating a snack, mainly about Mollie, not about us."

"If you say so."

"Mamm!" Rosanna stomped her foot on the little rag rug covering the section of the linoleum floor beneath the sink.

"Not many fellows would spend time discussing a *boppli* unless they were interested in the *boppli*'s *mudder*." Sarah elbowed Rosanna, causing her to drop the mug she'd been washing. Soapsuds flew in all directions.

"Please, Mamm, don't go spreading rumors or plan a celery patch or anything else. We won't be needing any creamed celery or any other celery dishes for a wedding supper, not mine, anyway."

"Calm down, Dochder." Sarah flicked soap from her nose. "I'll keep my mouth shut. But let it be known, I wouldn't object one bit if Paul was your beau."

"Mamm!"

"Okay. Okay."

At least Sarah got off the subject of Paul Hertzler for the rest of the time they cleaned up the kitchen. Instead, they talked about Mollie or the work planned for the day. When the kitchen had been restored to order, Sarah headed for the baskets of laundry surrounding the old gas-powered wringer washer.

"I'll be back to help as soon as I tend to Mollie." Rosanna galloped up the stairs two at a time. What a blessing to have a little one who woke up in a pleasant mood. She could hear Mollie cooing and gurgling to herself. Ever since she had become aware of her toes, Mollie talked to them or played with them when she awoke. Rosanna thought it was adorable. She slowed as she neared the top of the stairs so she could sneak to the doorway of her room. Sure enough, Mollie's feet were in the air, and she was babbling to her toes.

Rosanna waited for Mollie to spy her before rushing to the crib and scooping the infant up into her arms. She twirled around and planted kisses on the little cheeks. "Let's get you ready for the day and fed, my angel." Rosanna tickled and talked to Mollie as she changed her diaper and dressed her. "Now we'll go downstairs where it's warmer for your bottle."

Once she had settled into the rocking chair with Mollie happily slurping her bottle, Rosanna's thoughts turned to Sarah's words. If Sarah thought there had been more to last night than two *freinden* chatting and sharing a snack, did Paul get that same mistaken impression? She certainly didn't want to lead him on or hurt him. She knew the pain of rejection and didn't want to inflict that on anyone else.

Paul was a nice fellow, for sure and for certain, and always so interested in Mollie. Rosanna couldn't recall Mamm ever saying she would approve of Henry as a beau. But, then again, Henry had never come to the house—not to see her, anyway—and Rosanna had been careful not to reveal her feelings or hopes. Had she ever been wrong about Henry! How could she have let her feelings run away with themselves? How had she not seen he didn't have any interest in her? Had he always been interested in Frannie and simply bided his time until he received some sort of signal from her? How humiliating! How painful! Well, she wouldn't make that mistake again. No matter how thoughtful Paul might be or how much her *mamm* liked him, they would never be more than *freinden*. She'd just as soon live out her days as a single *mudder* rather than risk her

heart again. Somehow she would have to ensure Pa
got that message.

"It's only you and me, right, Mollie?" Rosanna s
the empty bottle on the floor, lifted the infant to he
shoulder, and patted her back. "Of course, you hav
aentis, *onkles*, a *grossmammi*, and a *grossdaddi* who lov
you, too. We'll be fine." Rosanna pulled the *boppli* bac
to look into her face. "I love you, you adorable girl.
She kissed a soft pink cheek. As much as she'd like t
rock and cuddle Mollie all day, that huge pile of laun
dry awaited.

The sky had become a thick, gray mass of clouds
and the wind had a bite by the time Rosanna made he
way out to the clothesline. Darkness would swallow
them early this evening with so many clouds. If it didn'
snow, it was sure missing a *gut* chance. Rosanna fough
to release the clothespins from the flapping trousers,
shirts, and dresses. The diapers threatened to wrap
around her and encase her like a mummy. She shivered
and wished she had remembered to pull on a pair of
gloves before stepping outside.

The constantly jiggling clothesline and slapping
clothes kept her attention so focused on her task that
she didn't hear the approaching buggy until it had
nearly reached the house. It was almost supper time.
Who would be visiting now? She wrestled the clothes
into the wicker laundry basket before turning to face
the gray buggy.

Chapter Sixteen

"Emma!"

Emma hopped to the ground, tethered her horse, and jogged to the clothesline. "This looks like a losing battle." She swatted at a diaper that smacked her in the face.

Rosanna chuckled. "It sure seems that way, but I'm determined to win." She yanked another one of Sadie's dresses from the line and tossed it into the basket.

"Brrr! I'm surprised the clothes aren't as stiff as boards."

"I think the wind has kept them dancing so they didn't freeze."

"You must be frozen, though. Look how red your hands are."

"I am pretty cold. I remembered my gloves after I got out here."

Emma quickly unclipped diapers and folded them. "You probably won't even feel your fingers by the time you're done. I think winter has moved in for sure."

"I believe you're right—on both counts." Rosanna's fingers had already stiffened. She flexed them twice and pulled the rest of the misbehaving clothes from the line as Emma corralled the remaining diapers. "So what brings you by so late in the day?"

"I would have *kumm* earlier, but my *mamm* took a notion to beat all the rugs and wax the wood floors after we did all the laundry."

"You must be tired."

"I am, but I wanted to get out. Mamm didn't need my help for supper since she threw everything but the kitchen sink into a big pot of soup."

"It's a perfect day for soup. We've got a pot of stew simmering ourselves. So to what do I owe the pleasure of this visit?" Rosanna bent to hoist the overflowing basket to her hip.

"I wanted to make sure you were okay." Emma trotted to the house behind Rosanna.

"As you can see, I'm as healthy as ever." Rosanna tossed the words over her shoulder.

"I didn't mean I thought you were *physically* ill."

"Are you implying I am mentally ill?"

Emma giggled. "*Nee*, silly. You stole away from the singing last night without saying a word. I was afraid you were upset."

Rosanna let Emma pull the door open, since her fingers seemed to have frozen to the basket handles. "You were busy, and I didn't want to interrupt."

"Busy? Me?"

Rosanna slid a sideways glance at her *freind*. "It appeared you were making eyes at my *bruder* and vice versa."

"*Ach!* Rosanna Mast! How can you say such a thing?"

"My vision is perfect, and I speak only the truth."

"I think not."

"I think so. Your words may protest, but your face is beet red."

"It is cold and windy out here, you know."

"Uh-huh." Rosanna plopped the basket on the floor as soon as she entered the kitchen. She hurried to the big black woodstove and held her hands out to warm them. "I think my fingers are too stiff to untie my bonnet or take off my cloak."

"Here, I'll help you." Emma helped Rosanna out of her outerwear and hung everything on a peg near the door.

"*Danki.*"

"Sure. What are *freinden* for?"

Rosanna flexed and extended her fingers several times. "I believe they will work again soon. Aren't you frozen, too?"

"Not quite. I wasn't out there as long as you were."

"It's a *gut* thing. Now, tell me who you talked to after the singing?"

"Is Mollie taking a nap?"

"She is, but don't change the subject."

"I wasn't aware we were discussing anything in particular."

"Oh, but we were. Just before we came inside."

"Funny, I don't seem to remember."

"Selective memory. Isn't that what they call it?"

"I don't have an idea what you're talking about." Emma shrugged out of her own cloak and hung it on a peg beside Rosanna's.

"Let me refresh your memory. Could it possibly be my own dear *bruder* Tobias who you chatted with? Did he take you home?" Rosanna nudged the taller girl with an elbow.

"That's for me to know."

"And me to find out! If your face glows any brighter, I'm afraid it will burst into flame."

"You're so funny, Rosanna."

"Maybe I should put my still-icy fingers on your cheeks to cool them off."

"And maybe you should tell me why Paul Hertzler disappeared from the barn right after you did."

Rosanna shrugged her shoulders. "How should I know what went on after I left?"

"I'm guessing you didn't walk home. And you didn't wait for Tobias."

"Aha! You wouldn't know if I waited for him or not if you didn't leave with him."

"Not necessarily."

"Explain it, then."

"I don't owe you an explanation."

"True, but we're *freinden*. Best *freinden*."

"So?"

"So spill."

"You first."

"I have nothing to tell." Rosanna turned toward the cupboard and reached to open the door. "Would you like some tea or cocoa?"

"Now look who's changing the subject." Emma's blue eyes twinkled. She hopped onto a kitchen chair. "I'll have tea, by the way."

"Okay, me, too." Rosanna dragged down two mugs and plopped a tea bag into each. She felt Emma's eyes on her as she turned her back to pour hot water into the mugs. She knew for sure a smirk would be plastered on Emma's face.

"*Danki*," Emma said when Rosanna set the mug in front of her. She reached for the sugar bowl in the center of the table and dumped three heaping teaspoons of sugar into her tea.

"Did you want a little more tea to go with all that sugar?"

"This is fine."

"I don't know how you stay so skinny. You have the biggest sweet tooth in all of St. Mary's County."

"I'm just lucky, I guess."

"Maybe."

"I'm waiting."

Rosanna sat in the chair across from Emma. She took her time stirring a single spoonful of sugar into her tea. She purposely ignored Emma's stare, though she had to work hard to keep from squirming. She raised the mug to her lips to take a tentative sip. Steam swirled around her face.

"You might want to wait a minute on that."

"Oooh! I think you're right. It is a tad hot." Rosanna set her mug on the table but kept her hands wrapped around it. Knowing her *mamm* was probably sitting in the living room mending, she lowered her voice. "I'll tell you what happened, like I told Mamm this morning, so you won't jump to the wrong conclusion."

"I'm all ears." Emma wiggled in her chair as if getting ready to receive some juicy snippet of gossip.

"Wipe that silly grin off your face. This is not going to be some happily-ever-after love story."

"Really?" Emma poked out her bottom lip in a pretty little pout.

"*Nee*. I'll let you provide that." Rosanna attempted another sip of tea but again set the mug down without doing so. "This stuff might be drinkable by next week."

"You're stalling. Go on with your story."

"As you know, I didn't feel totally comfortable at the singing. I enjoyed the actual singing and seeing everybody, but by the time we finished the last song, I wanted to leave. I wanted to check on Mollie."

"Your *mamm* was watching her, ain't so?"

"True, but I've rarely been away from her."

"Okay. I can understand that. Even though I'm not a *mudder*, I imagine it would be hard to leave your *boppli*, at least the first few times."

"Right. I was missing Mollie and thinking I should be home taking care of her."

"Everyone needs a break, though, and you're still young and single."

Rosanna nodded. This time when she raised her mug, she did take a gulp of tea. "Ahh! It's just right now."

"Would Henry's slipping out with Frannie have had anything to do with your desire to leave?"

"*Nee. Jah.* Maybe. Others were slipping out or pairing up, even you."

"Me?"

"*Jah*, but I expect you to tell your story in a minute. Anyway, I had told Tobias he was stuck bringing me home, but I didn't want to rush him or spoil his evening. I figured I would wait for him in the buggy."

"But it was cold outside."

"It certainly was. I thought about walking home while I was huddled under a blanket. I guess Paul was leaving early. He saw me shivering in the cold and offered to take me home. End of story."

"I don't think so."

Rosanna raised her eyebrows and ventured another sip of tea.

Emma sipped, too. "Yum. Nice and sweet." She

lowered her mug. "I don't think Paul just happened to leave. From what I observed, he shot out of the barn practically on your heels. I'm thinking he *deliberately* left when he did in search of you."

Rosanna lifted and dropped her shoulders. "I wouldn't know about that."

"All right. He drove you home. Did he *kumm* inside?"

"As I told Mamm, I couldn't be rude and not offer him a snack since he was kind enough to give me a ride and it was my fault he didn't get any refreshments at the singing."

"Of course not."

Emma's look of expectancy almost made Rosanna ball up a paper napkin and throw it at her. "It wasn't anything romantic at all."

"Didn't you talk while you ate?"

"We did. Mamm was still up rocking Mollie when we tiptoed into the house. Paul wanted to see Mollie before Mamm took her upstairs. While we ate our snack, we talked about Mollie."

"That's a *gut* thing, ain't so? After all, most fellows wouldn't be too concerned about a *boppli*."

Rosanna shrugged again. "I don't know. But I do know that Paul and I aren't interested in each other in any way except as *freinden*."

"Are you sure about that?"

"I've learned my lesson."

"I'm sorry things didn't work out with Henry. I know you talked to him a lot at singings."

"That's just it. I talked to him. I sought him out. I guess he was never interested in me, though."

"Unless Mollie's arrival scared him off."

"That's silly. Mollie is the sweetest little thing ever."

"You know that, and I know that. Maybe Henry didn't want any extra responsibility."

"It's best I know that now." Rosanna sighed. "I'm okay with being Mollie's *mudder*. I don't have to be someone's *fraa*."

"You will be." Emma reached across the table to squeeze Rosanna's hand. "With the right person. And I think I know who that person might be."

Rosanna looked up and gave her head a shake.

"Don't dismiss Paul like that." Emma snapped her fingers for emphasis. "He's a very nice fellow, and he's obviously crazy about you."

"You're crazy!"

"*Nee.* I've seen him watching you. He is definitely more than a little interested."

"I told you, Emma, we're only *freinden*."

"Give it time. Just don't write him off until you've given him a fair chance."

Rosanna rolled her eyes. "It's your turn. Did you talk to Tobias after the singing?"

Emma squirmed, bumping the table so hard their tea nearly sloshed onto the table. "I talked to a lot of people."

"Uh-huh. Did you talk to my *bruder* more than the others?"

This time Emma shrugged and stared into her mug.

"I've seen you two sneaking peeks at each other."

Emma clapped her hands to her cheeks.

Rosanna giggled. "Your strawberry red cheeks are so pretty." She yanked one of Emma's hands down. "Did you and Tobias go for a ride?"

"We did not. We only talked."

"Would you like me to put a bug in his ear, you know, put in a *gut* word for you?"

"Don't you dare!"

Rosanna laughed harder. "I could help you out."

"And I could talk to Paul for you. I could offer him some encouragement."

"I don't think so."

"Then we'll both have to wait and see what happens, ain't so?"

"As far as you're concerned, anyway. I already know for me. I've resigned myself to being single all my days."

"Such a martyr!" Emma chuckled. "You mark my words, my *freind*. You'll be getting married before the rest of us."

"Such crazy talk, Emma Kurtz. That is not in my plans at all, not anymore."

"Don't let one bad apple spoil the whole bunch."

"*Jah*, but I've made my plans." Rosanna crossed her arms over her chest and stared at the pretty blonde girl. "And they don't include apples, bad or *gut*."

"Sometimes the Lord Gott's plans might be different from ours, ain't so? He probably created the perfect shiny red apple for you." Emma smiled sweetly before raising her mug to her lips.

Chapter Seventeen

Rosanna sighed in relief when Mollie finally dozed off in her arms. Poor angel had been teething and suffering so much discomfort with a tooth that stubbornly refused to break through the red, swollen gums. Rosanna wanted to cry along with her miserable *boppli*. She had been so worried that Mollie was sick, since she had seemed too young to be teething, but Mamm assured her little ones teethed at all different ages. Mollie apparently was an earlier teether.

She would have gladly taken on her little girl's pain if she could have. She carried her downstairs to the living room to keep her from waking the rest of the family. Elongated shadows cast by the single flickering oil lamp danced on the walls of the dimly lit room. Only the occasional squeak of the rocking chair or the crackling of wood in the stove broke the tomb-like silence of the room. Rosanna leaned her head back against the thick, blue cushion lining the back of the chair. Her body had passed beyond tired, but her brain whirred.

"The Lord Gott's plans might be different from ours." Those were Emma's earlier words. Did His plan for her include a special person who would be her husband and Mollie's *daed*? If so, who was this mystery man? It obviously wasn't Henry Zook. She'd given him enough opportunities to move any relationship forward. The reticence she had mistaken for shyness could only have been disinterest. She was okay with that now. She was over him. Even her embarrassment had faded once she realized most of the other young people at the singings had been too absorbed in their own conversations.

Rosanna squeezed her eyes shut. She couldn't crawl into the past to change it. She could only do her best in the present. Right now, she'd love to sleep for a few minutes while the house was peaceful. Her eyes popped open when her ears detected a shuffling sound. She squinted into the darkness until a lumbering shape came into view. "Tobias?" Her whisper was little more than an exhalation, for fear of waking Mollie.

"Rosanna? What . . . ?"

"Shhh!"

Tobias stumbled into the living room. He groaned when he stubbed a toe, but he didn't cry out. "What are you doing up?"

"I might ask you the very same thing."

"Is Mollie all right?" Tobias scooted closer to the rocking chair.

"She's teething and was fussy. I brought her downstairs so she wouldn't disturb anyone."

"Little chance of that. You know we all sleep like dead men's bones. Is she asleep?" He leaned over to peer into the little cocoon of blankets.

"Finally. What's wrong with you?"

"Aside from the toe I just broke, you mean?"

"*Jah*." Rosanna stifled a giggle.

"My stomach rumbled so loud I thought a freight train crashed in my room."

"It must have been some rumble if it woke you up. There was some peach pie left from supper unless someone else crept in and finished it off."

"I'll check. Do you want a piece?"

"*Nee.* I'm fine."

"You don't seem so fine."

"Go get your pie!" Rosanna loved her *bruder* but hoped he'd stay in the kitchen to eat his pie. Maybe she should ease herself out of the rocking chair and carry Mollie upstairs before Tobias had a chance to return. Her *bruder* could read her too well. He already suspected something wasn't quite right. She'd managed to slide to the edge of the chair before Tobias shuffled into the living room with the metal pie plate in one hand and a fork in the other.

"Tobias!"

"What?"

"You've got the whole plate!"

"Hey! There was only one piece left."

"One big piece."

"I've got a ferociously big hunger." He patted his belly. "I'll share with you, if you want."

"You go right ahead. I certainly wouldn't want you to starve or even go to bed the teensiest bit hungry."

"I appreciate your concern. You're such a kind, thoughtful person."

"Why, *danki.*" Rosanna tried not to show her disappointment when Tobias plunked down onto the chair nearest the rocking chair. She peeked over the rim of the pie plate. "Tobias Mast, that's a third of the pie!"

"What can I say? I'm a growing fellow."

"You'll be growing sideways."

"Not a chance. I work too hard."

"You work your jaws more than your muscles."

"Ha ha! I'm glad to see you haven't lost your wit, even if you are so down in the mouth."

"I'm not down in the mouth." The lamplight cast shadows across Tobias' face, but Rosanna could still see the quirk of his eyebrow before he forked an enormous bite of pie into his mouth. "I'm merely pensive."

"Did you learn a new word today?"

"Now look who's being funny. Don't you know the meaning of 'pensive'?"

"Of course I do. You must be having some mighty sobering thoughts."

"I'm tired and have been trying to comfort a fussy *boppli*."

"I don't think that's all there is to it."

"I don't know why you say that." Rosanna prepared to hoist herself and Mollie from the chair. "I'll leave you to your *smidgen* of pie."

Tobias reached out and grasped Rosanna's wrist. "Wait. Please."

"My, such manners."

"Talk to me, Rosanna."

"About what? Would you like me to tell you a bedtime story?"

Tobias' fork halted halfway to his mouth. "Tell me the story of why you didn't want to stay at the singing and why Paul Hertzler took you home."

Rosanna gulped. She knew this would happen. She should have escaped earlier. How many times was she going to have to repeat her explanation? She tried to pull her arm free, but Tobias' grip tightened. "I'm tired, and there's nothing to tell."

"Tell me anyway."

"You already know. Paul went back into the barn to tell you. Very simply put, I wanted to go home and check on Mollie. I was waiting in the cold for you. Paul discovered me and offered to drop me off at home. That's it in a nutshell."

"Do they all live happily ever after?"

"What?"

"Don't bedtime stories end with everyone living happily ever after?"

"I don't know. My story ended happily. I arrived home safely to take care of Mollie. Did your own story end happily ever after?" Rosanna needed to get the focus off herself before Tobias tried to dig deeper.

"What story?"

"The story of Tobias and Emma. Does it have a happy ending?"

"I don't know that story."

"I think you do. I saw the two of you stealing glances at each other. It looked to me like you were drifting toward each other as I slipped out the door."

"Emma and I talked. But I talked to a lot of people." He shoveled another bite of pie into his mouth.

"Did you talk to a lot of other *girls*?"

Tobias shrugged and chewed. "You know me. I talk to everybody."

"Swallow before you talk."

He gulped. "You asked me a question, so I answered."

Rosanna sighed. "Are you interested in Emma?"

"Are you interested in Paul?"

"Paul is a *freind*."

"Emma is a *freind*."

"I saw you staring at her, Tobias. And I saw her staring back. You can't fool me."

"I saw Paul looking at you, too."

"You couldn't have. Your gaze was totally focused in a different direction."

Tobias wiped his mouth with the back of his hand.

"We do have napkins, you know."

"True, but they're in the kitchen. I'm in here."

Rosanna rolled her eyes. "I just want to tell you I think it would be *wunderbaar* if you and Emma, uh, get together."

"Don't go planning a wedding or anything."

"It might be kind of fun."

"Then plan your own."

"I don't have any intentions of getting married."

"Why not? You're pretty nice and decent enough to look at."

Rosanna nearly choked. "You certainly have a way with words, Bruder. I hope you didn't say anything like that to Emma."

"I didn't say anything bad."

"Decent-looking? What girl wants to hear she's decent-looking?"

"Should I have said I am blinded by your beauty, and you are the most magnificent creature ever put on earth?"

"That's better. Emma wouldn't object to that."

"We'll never know about that, will we, since I don't have any intention of saying those words to her or anyone else."

"Don't you want to get married?"

"When you do."

"You're older than I am."

"Oooh! By a whole two years." Tobias licked a finger, pressed it to the plate to pick up pie crumbs, and popped it into his mouth.

Rosanna reached over to slap his hand away from

his face. "Seriously, Tobias, you do plan to get married, don't you?"

"Sure, but not tomorrow."

"I didn't think you were planning to get married tomorrow. I do think Emma would be perfect for you, though."

"It's such a relief to have your approval." He slapped a hand across his chest and heaved an exaggerated sigh of relief.

"I'm trying to be serious."

"Then seriously think of yourself. Paul is a great guy. He'd be just right for you. From what I hear, he sure seems taken with Mollie. You ought to give him a chance."

"What do you hear?" Rosanna's heart skipped a beat. Had people been talking about her and Paul? Why?

"It's a known fact that he brought you home after Becky's twins were born. He was at the right place at the right time after the singing. And Mamm said he always asks about Mollie and seems interested in her—and probably you, too."

"Mamm? Have you been talking to her about me?"

"I asked her if you got home okay and if she knew what happened. She told me Paul wanted to see Mollie and then you two had a snack in the kitchen. She said you seemed to get along well."

"Why wouldn't we? As you said, I'm pretty nice. Paul and I are only *freinden*. Remember that. I told Mamm the same thing. I'm grateful he showed up at the right place and time after the singing. I could have turned into a lump of ice waiting for you."

"You could have stayed inside. If you were waiting for me and figured I'd be a while, you could have visited with some of the others instead of running out to

hide in the buggy—an open buggy, mind you, on a
cold night."

"I wasn't hiding." Rosanna lowered her voice even
more. "Not exactly."

"If you say so. Why did you run out, Rosanna?"

"*Ach*, Tobias! I didn't seem to fit in. Nobody else
there was a parent, so I felt like I didn't belong. But
I'm single, so I don't really belong with the young married women, either." She was too embarrassed to tell
her *bruder* how the sight of Frannie and Henry leaving
together had pierced her heart and brought tears to
her eyes.

Tobias scooted to the edge of his chair and set the
empty pie pan on the floor. He gently patted Mollie
before squeezing Rosanna's arm. "You fit in everywhere. We're all different and have different things to
offer people. Sure, the other girls at the singing don't
have *kinner*, but they are still your *freinden*. They still
care about you. They probably look up to you for taking
on the responsibility of raising an infant. They'd probably like hearing about her. The other young *mudders*
could probably be a help and support for you. They
know what you're going through with the sleepless
nights and teething. Give people a chance."

Rosanna stared at her *bruder*. She'd never heard
such a serious speech from him before. "Maybe," she
whispered.

"The point is, dear Schweschder, you are the same
Rosanna inside whether you have one *boppli* or ten or
none. You are still you. You don't have to believe you
are a misfit and hide from people. We care about
you and Mollie."

Rosanna remained silent for a moment as the words
sank in. "You make a lot of sense for a *bu*."

"I'll take that as a compliment."

"It was meant as one."

"And as for Henry and Frannie . . ."

"Never mind about them."

"If you say so. He wasn't the right fellow for you anyway. But that doesn't mean the right one isn't out there. Maybe someone you haven't considered before. Maybe someone right under your nose. Maybe Paul Hertzler."

"I get your point, but I'm not anxious to make another mistake or make a fool of myself again."

"You did neither. This is the time we're supposed to get to know people and figure out what's right for us before we make a commitment that will last our whole lives."

"When did you get so smart? Emma would be very fortunate to have you."

"Hey!"

"Hey, yourself. Help me out of this chair so we can go to bed."

"That sounds like the best idea I've heard in a while. My stomach is happy now, so I can probably sleep. We do need our energy. We never know what tomorrow will bring, ain't so?"

"Life is full of surprises, for sure and for certain."

Chapter Eighteen

Just before Christmas and Mollie's six-month birthday, two stubborn teeth finally erupted through her gums, returning her to her sweet-natured disposition.

"I sure hope her other teeth aren't as difficult." Rosanna carried a smiling Mollie into the kitchen, where Sarah had already begun breakfast preparations. "Just look at these two beautiful teeth." She tickled the little girl until she broke into a wide smile.

Sarah pushed the skillet of bubbling eggs off the heat to focus her attention on the *boppli*. "Well, lookee there! She does have two teeth. The first ones are usually the toughest."

"You'd think you two never saw teeth before." Tobias stomped into the kitchen from the mudroom.

"Mollie has never had teeth before. Just look, Tobias. Aren't they the prettiest teeth ever?" Rosanna held the infant out for her *bruder*'s inspection.

"Teeth are teeth. When is breakfast going to be ready?"

"*Ach*, Tobias, you always think with your stomach. Here, Mollie, your *onkle* will hold you while I help get breakfast on the table." Rosanna thrust the little girl into Tobias' arms. "We certainly don't want this poor fellow to waste away to nothing."

"Not a chance of that happening," Sarah mumbled. "Either he or Joseph slipped into the kitchen for a midnight snack last night and ate all the applesauce cake that was left."

"How do you know it was one of us? It could just as easily been Daed or one of the others."

"James, Katie, and Sadie don't venture downstairs at night." Sarah shook a finger at Tobias.

"And I didn't do it, whatever it was." Samuel entered the kitchen drying his hands on a towel before lifting Mollie from Tobias' arms.

Rosanna laughed. "Daed doesn't know what 'it' is, but he knows he didn't do it."

"Joseph, call your *bruder* and *schweschders* before you plunk down at the table, please." Sarah waved her hand to shoo him toward the stairway.

Moments later, the three younger *kinner* bounded into the kitchen chattering about the upcoming Christmas program at school. The entire community attended, not just the scholars' families, so they were very excited.

"You won't have much longer to wait now. Christmas will be here before you know it." Sarah used the edge of her apron to pull a pan of biscuits from the oven. "Set the table, girls, so we can eat." She handed Sadie a wad of silverware and Katie jars of homemade apple butter and strawberry jam.

Rosanna dropped little plastic bags filled with oatmeal raisin cookies on top of ham sandwiches and apples in the lunch pails lined up on the kitchen counter. She cast a quick glance out the window over the kitchen sink. "I don't see any pink and purple streaks of sunrise this morning."

"It's cloudy," Daed remarked. "It wouldn't surprise me if we saw snowflakes today."

Katie, James, and Sadie cheered while Rosanna shivered. Snow could be pretty and lots of fun for the *kinner* to play in, but Rosanna hoped it held off until Christmas.

"Maybe we'll get out of school early to go sledding." Sadie's eyes sparkled in anticipation.

"You might want to hold that thought, Sadie." Joseph poked her with his elbow and nodded toward the window. "There isn't a single flake falling from the sky."

"You never know what could happen." Sadie wrinkled her nose at her older *bruder*.

"Life is full of surprises. Here, Daed, I'll take my little surprise so you can eat." Rosanna extracted Mollie from Samuel's arms and planted a kiss on top of her little honey-haired head.

Sadie's wish for snow came true on the evening of the Christmas program. The clouds spit out big, fluffy flakes, and the bitter wind chomped at their noses as the Masts hurried to the buggies. Rosanna, Mollie, and Joseph climbed into Tobias' waiting buggy, while the younger *kinner* hustled into the back of their parents' buggy.

"I'm not sure if Sadie is more excited about the program or the snow." Rosanna hugged Mollie close and pulled the buggy blanket tighter around both of them. "It's a *gut* thing the ride isn't too long." She tried hard to keep from shivering, but lost the battle. She scooted closer to Tobias so Joseph could sit in front, too. Maybe squished between the two she could absorb some of their body heat.

"They're bound to have the stove cranking out heat at the schoolhouse, so you'll get warm quick." Tobias clucked to the horse to get them rolling.

"*Jah*, and with all the people crammed in there, we'll probably be sweating in a matter of minutes," Joseph added.

"I doubt I'll be sweating." Rosanna's teeth chattered. "I hope Mollie is warm enough."

"You've got her so bundled up she can barely take a breath." Tobias reached a hand out to touch the lump in Rosanna's arms. "*Gut*. I feel her moving. She's still alive."

Rosanna slapped at his arm with a gloved hand. "You're silly. She's only a *boppli*, you know. I don't want her to get chilled or to get sick."

"Overprotective!" Joseph muttered.

Rosanna nudged him with her elbow. "That might be true, but it's probably not any more than Mamm."

"You're right about that. Mamm keeps us on a short leash. I can't wait until I can have a little more freedom." Joseph sighed.

"One more year and you'll be able to attend singings and activities, Bruder. I hope you aren't planning to go wild."

"*Nee*. I only want to do more things, not wrong things, just different things."

"That's a relief. Don't be like your big *bruder* here." Rosanna giggled.

"Hey! I behave myself."

"I know, Tobias. I'm teasing. If Joseph turns out like you and Roman and Adam, that will be a blessing.

Then Mamm and Daed will only have the three little ones to worry about."

"And Mollie," Tobias reminded her.

"True, but she'll mainly be my worry."

The two Mast buggies followed a long line of gray buggies up the lane to the Amish schoolhouse. A crowd of people, young and old, were already hurrying toward the door. The scholars' program provided a highlight of the season for the entire community.

"What did I tell you, Rosanna? You'll get warm in record time." Joseph pointed at all the folks who weren't wasting time milling about outside on such a raw evening.

"I can let you and Mollie out close to the door," Tobias offered. "Joseph and I can park and see to the horses."

"That would be great."

"Say, you aren't planning to slip out and wait in the cold buggy again tonight, are you?"

"*Nee*, Tobias. I only did that once, and not with Mollie."

"You haven't been back to any more singings, either."

"I've been, uh, busy. Besides, there have only been a couple since that time. Maybe I'll go to the next one."

Tobias stopped the buggy. He tossed the reins to Joseph and hopped out to help Rosanna and Mollie down.

"*Danki*, Tobias. See you later. Hurry so you don't miss anything."

"It's too cold to dawdle. We'll be there before the program starts."

* * *

Tobias had been right. Once everyone gathered in the school, the temperature in the room soared. Wedged in between two other young women with infants, Rosanna gradually thawed. She pulled some of the blankets off Mollie so she wouldn't become overheated. The women exchanged information and brief tales about their little ones' latest accomplishments. A welcome peacefulness settled over Rosanna as she talked with the other *mudders*. They accepted her. They shared with her. Hope surged. Maybe she did fit in after all.

A hush fell over the room when the teacher walked to the front. She explained what the scholars had been working on over the last few weeks and pointed out various papers and pictures pinned to the walls and invited guests to examine them later. The program proceeded with songs, recitations, and the enactment of the Christmas story.

Rosanna thought Katie looked nervous, but she gave a flawless recitation. Sadie almost giggled when her turn came, but she sobered and did a fine job. James had narrated part of the Christmas story and only stumbled over one or two words. The whole program went off without a hitch and brought smiles to the faces of all who watched.

Mollie cooed a couple of times but had otherwise been silent. She happily played with the few soft toys Rosanna had brought or else watched the other *bopplin* in fascination. Before long she would want to play with the others and wouldn't be content to simply stay in Rosanna's arms. Rosanna vowed to enjoy every single day of these precious times with her little girl. One day she'd be watching Mollie stand before the community to recite her part in the Christmas program.

The program concluded with a few words by the bishop followed by a silent prayer. Then everyone could partake of the refreshments or peruse the scholars' work on display. The school program never failed to put Rosanna in the holiday spirit. This year would be extra special since it was Mollie's first Christmas.

"There's that beautiful *boppli*." Mary Hertzler didn't waste any time seeking them out.

Rosanna smiled. "Hello, Mary. The scholars put on a nice program, ain't so?"

"For sure. I remember when my *buwe* participated in programs. It doesn't seem so long ago, but of course, it's been quite a while. They grow up so fast."

The wistful look that crossed Mary's face almost made Rosanna sad, but Mollie's tug on her *kapp* string brought a smile instead. "I had just been thinking that Mollie will be up there reciting before I know it, even though I'd like to keep her safe in my arms."

"*Ach*, Rosanna, they do have to grow up. But we can certainly enjoy the growing-up years." Mary reached out to tickle Mollie's chin and was instantly rewarded with a giggle. "Would you like me to take this one off your hands for a few minutes so you can mill about and get something to eat?"

Rosanna didn't really want to relinquish her *boppli*, but she didn't want to disappoint Mary, who clearly itched to hold her. "Sure. I'll grab a couple of cookies and look at Sadie's Katie's, and James' work. I'll only be a few minutes."

"Take your time." Mary immediately began clucking and cooing to Mollie.

Rosanna hesitated for a moment but knew Mollie

would be well cared for. Mary would make a terrific *grossmammi* one day. She wandered around checking out the colorful artwork and neat penmanship displayed on the walls. She made a mental note to tell the teacher what a fine job the scholars had done with the program.

"Are you looking for anything in particular?"

Rosanna jumped. Her hand flew to her chest to pat her thumping heart. "*Ach*, Paul. You startled me."

"I'm sorry. I guess you didn't hear me call your name."

"I didn't. It's a bit noisy in here, and I was lost in thought."

"Sadie's work?" Paul nodded to the paper hanging in front of them.

"*Jah*. Her handwriting is improving. I tried working with her at home, but she got easily distracted. At school, I'm sure she has to sit still until she completes her assignments."

"That can be hard for little ones."

"Are you speaking from experience?"

"I'm afraid I was one of those scholars who had a thousand other things to do rather than sit and practice writing legibly."

"I believe you've learned patience over the years."

"I'd like to think so. Where is Mollie this evening?"

"I'll give you three guesses."

"I'm sure I'll only need one. My *mamm* has her, ain't so?"

"Exactly right."

"That wasn't too hard to figure out. Did you get some refreshments yet?"

"Not yet."

"Would you like something to eat or drink?"

"Maybe I'll get a cookie."

Paul took her arm and steered her through the throng of people. His manners and concern always made her feel so special. From the corner of her eye, she glimpsed Frannie threading her way through the crowd to reach Henry. Surprisingly, that once-familiar pain did not pierce her heart. Had she let go of that dream? If the wound healed so quickly, would it have been love, or anything akin to it, in the first place?

Rosanna shrugged off thoughts of Henry. She'd made a mistake, pure and simple. Who hadn't made a mistake? She would be extra careful from here on out.

"Would you like a drink?" Paul passed Rosanna a paper napkin and reached for a Styrofoam cup.

"*Nee*, I'll grab a couple of chocolate chip cookies." She selected two plump ones and wrapped them in her napkin. While Paul made his selection, she turned to scan the room to make sure Mollie was still fine. Mary caught her eye, smiled, and nodded. Rosanna relaxed, until she caught a glimpse of Emma's ashen face. What could be wrong?

Chapter Nineteen

Rosanna's heart thundered when she realized Emma was headed directly toward her. Had something happened to Mamm or Daed or one of the little ones? Emma's grim expression sent bolts of fear and dread shooting through her entire body. "Something is wrong."

"Huh? What did you say, Rosanna?"

"Look at Emma. Something is very wrong." Emma pushed past a group of giggling girls and strode straight to Rosanna. "What's happened?" Rosanna could hardly get words past the lump blocking her throat.

"Th-there's a girl outside."

Emma grabbed Rosanna's free hand and squeezed so hard Rosanna feared her bones would snap. "A girl?" Why would that be so troubling?

"An *Englisch* girl." Emma panted as if she'd just run around the school building three times. "She's looking for a *boppli*."

"A *boppli*?" Rosanna clenched her other hand into a tight fist, crushing the cookies in the paper napkin.

"You had better *kumm* see." Emma let go of Rosanna's hand and tugged her arm.

"Why me?" Her voice emerged as a croak, but she couldn't clear her throat to change that.

"She's *Englisch*," Emma repeated. "I doubt she's looking for an Amish baby. She must be looking for Mollie."

"Mollie *is* an Amish baby."

"You know what I mean. You'd better *kumm* now." Emma tugged harder on Rosanna's arm.

"Do you want me to go out there with you?" Paul leaned down to speak directly into Rosanna's ear.

Rosanna couldn't form a coherent thought, much less a coherent sentence. Mollie was her *boppli*. The adoption would be final soon. She stumbled over her own feet and would have fallen flat on her face if Paul hadn't caught her.

"It will be okay." Paul kept his grip on her arm.

Rosanna plodded toward the door on lead feet. Her brain screamed at her to snatch Mollie from Mary's arms and hide. But she had to see what this stranger wanted. Maybe Emma had misunderstood and the girl didn't have any business here at all. She reached a shaky hand out and yanked the door open.

The girl jerked around to face Rosanna. From the light behind her, Rosanna could see the girl's hair was blonde, instead of brown like Jane's. But even in the dim light cast by the lamps, Rosanna could tell the blonde color came from a bottle and couldn't possibly have been a natural hue. Her blue eyes, though, matched Jane's—and Mollie's.

"Hi." The girl, who now appeared older than Rosanna had originally thought, cracked her chewing gum before maneuvering it to the back of her mouth. She thrust out one hand with long, pointy, red fingernails. "I'm Kandis Kottyn. They call me Kandi Kottyn, get it?"

Rosanna stared, openmouthed.

"You know, cotton candy. You've heard of that?"

"*Jah*. I know what cotton candy is."

"Okay. You might have heard of me. I'm an actress and a dancer. I've performed, mainly dancing, in lots of clubs in DC and an off-off-really-off Broadway show."

"I've never heard of you."

"I guess not. Anyway, I'm on my way to the big time, you know, superstardom. I heard my little sister lived here for a while."

"Your *schweschder*?"

"Jane."

"J-Jane?"

"Yeah. And I understand she had a baby."

"Wh-why would you *kumm* here?" Paul's grip on Rosanna's arm tightened. She had the overwhelming urge to fling herself into his arms and bury her head in his chest.

"I believe Jane came here. I don't mean here to this particular place. I mean this area." She gestured to their surroundings. "I'm sorry to interrupt your party, by the way."

"It isn't a party. Tonight was the school program."

"Whatever." She apparently freed her gum to snap it once more before storing it again on a back tooth. "In a letter Jane wrote me—come to think of it, I think it was the only letter she ever wrote me—she said she found some people she admired. She said she was finally going to do the right thing."

"Wh-where is Jane?"

"She passed away."

Rosanna sucked in a sharp breath and swayed. If Paul hadn't gripped her arm even tighter, she might have dropped to the ground. "What happened?"

"Janie had always been a sickly little girl, but I thought she'd gotten better. We sort of lost touch there for a while. I'm a bit older, you know. Anyway, I guess that childhood cancer returned."

Tears pricked Rosanna's eyes. Poor Jane. To die so young. She'd said she was sick, but she certainly gave birth like a champ and climbed from a window to escape. She must have relied on determination and willpower. "I'm so sorry for your loss."

"Yeah. It's a shame she had to die so young. The autopsy report said she'd given birth recently. The post-mark on her letter was this little Podunk town, I mean, Maryland. I've been exploring the area and figured Jane must have been talking about you people when she said she found people she admired."

"What do you want with us?" Rosanna's heart roared in her ears. Surely Paul and Cotton Candy or Candy Cotton could hear it.

"Was my sister here?"

Rosanna hesitated. She had to be truthful. "A girl named Jane came here, but Jane is a pretty common name."

"Here." Kandi rummaged through the oversized handbag she pulled off her shoulder. "This picture is a couple years old, but you should be able to tell if it's the same girl." She thrust the mangled photograph under Rosanna's nose.

Rosanna wanted to lie and say she had never seen such a person, but she couldn't. That didn't mean she had to give this gum-smacking dancer her *boppli*! She raised her chin to look the taller girl in the eye.

"It's hard to be sure in this dim light, but this does look like the same girl who was here."

"Did she have a baby?"

"*Jah.*"

"Where is the baby?"

"I have her. I-I'm adopting her. That's what Jane wanted. She had legal papers."

"A little girl. Janie had a little girl." Kandi sniffed. "Can I see her?"

Silent until now, Paul finally spoke up. "Maybe you could meet tomorrow so we don't interrupt the celebration tonight. Would that be all right?" He looked from one young woman to the other.

"You won't run off with the baby?"

"Of course not. This is our home. I can give you directions to my house and you could drop by tomorrow."

"I guess that will have to do. What's your name?"

"Rosanna Mast. And this is Paul Hertzler."

"What's the baby's name?"

"Mollie."

"Mollie. I like that. Does she look like Jane?"

"She has honey-gold hair and big blue eyes."

"Not quite like Jane, huh? Tell me how to find you."

Rosanna gave directions and held her breath. Would this woman say she planned to take Mollie?

Kandi backed away. "Okay. I'll see you tomorrow, say, ten-ish?"

"That will be fine." As fine as anything could be in her world that had suddenly flipped upside down.

"Here's my card. This is a picture of me from the play I was in. Great costume, don't you think?" She didn't wait for a reply but pointed to her name with one red fingernail. "See Kandi Kottyn. Spelled with Ks to make it fancier. There's a little bit about me on there, too."

Rosanna squinted to make out the picture and barely withheld a gasp at the skimpy outfit. She quickly turned the card over.

"Thanks for taking care of the kid." With that, the woman disappeared down the gravel lane to a car parked at the end.

Kid? Mollie was a precious *boppli*. Her *boppli*. Whatever would she do? She wouldn't have to give Mollie up, would she? Maybe she should find a way to contact that lawyer first thing in the morning. Or should she just wait to hear whatever this Kandi Kottyn said? Surely the woman wouldn't want an infant around if she traveled around dancing and acting. What kind of life would that be for her sweet Mollie?

"Are you all right, Rosanna?"

"*Jah. Nee.* I . . ." She burst into tears and scarcely noticed Paul had pulled her into his arms.

Paul patted Rosanna's back as she sobbed against his chest. How *wunderbaar* it felt to hold her in his arms. He wished the circumstances were different. He wished he knew how to comfort her. "It will be okay, Rosanna."

"Wh-what if she t-takes my *boppli*?"

"I don't think she can do that."

"Sh-she's a relative."

"But Jane wanted you to have Mollie. I don't know much about the *Englisch* laws, but you do have those official papers."

Rosanna sniffed and pulled back to look up into his eyes. "Do you think that will be *gut* enough?"

"I hope so."

"I love Mollie so much."

"I know you do. I'll do whatever I can to help you. I promise." He would make the sun shine at night if he could if that would please her.

"*Danki*, Paul." Rosanna swiped at her eyes with the back of one hand. As if she suddenly realized she stood within the circle of his arms, she took a giant step backward. "I-I'm sorry."

"That's all right." Actually it was more than "all right." It was great. Did she notice how his heart raced? Did any electric current surge through her body as it had his?

"I-I'd better go back and check on Mollie."

"Mamm will take excellent care of her."

"I know, but I need to hold her."

"I understand." Paul had a need to hold and protect Rosanna. A desire to protect and care for Mollie, as well, stirred from somewhere in the depths of his soul. "I'm here for you, Rosanna, and will help you. Mollie belongs with you. The Lord Gott gave her to you."

"You're a great *freind*, Paul." She reached out to pat his arm.

Was it remotely possible that he could ever be more to her and to Mollie? Could he ever mean half as much to her as she meant to him?

Chapter Twenty

"Give me that spoon, Rosanna. You're going to stir a hole clear through the pot." Sarah wrestled the long-handled wooden spoon from Rosanna's hand. She banged it on the side of the pot to shake off the oatmeal clinging to it. "I believe this is done, unless you're planning to use it for wallpaper paste."

"I'm sorry, Mamm. My mind is off and running."

"I'd say it's run completely away."

Rosanna's sigh carried the weight of the world. "What if this Kandi girl wants to take Mollie? What will I do, Mamm? What if I lose Mollie forever? What if . . . ?"

Sarah enfolded her *dochder* in a hug. "Don't play the 'what if' game, dear. Trust in the Lord. Everything is in His hands."

"Paul said the Lord gave Mollie to me. What do you think?"

"I think Paul Hertzler is one smart, caring fellow."

The thundering footsteps of six people hungry for breakfast interrupted their conversation. "We'll take it one moment at a time, Dochder. Let's not borrow sorrow."

* * *

Her *mamm*'s words played in her head as Rosanna paced the living room floor. Periodically she'd pause to glance out the window. "Let's not borrow sorrow," Mamm had said. Rosanna didn't have to borrow sorrow from anyone else. Enough of it had landed on her doorstep all on its own. If wishing could make it so, Kandi Kottyn would never show up at the Mast house today. She'd forget all about seeing Mollie and skedaddle out of Southern Maryland.

That probably wasn't fair or nice. The woman did have a right to see her *schweschder*'s infant, didn't she? *Please, Lord Gott, don't let her want to take Mollie away. I couldn't bear that pain.*

The woman said she would arrive at ten-ish. Ten-ish had *kumm* and gone. Did Rosanna dare hope she'd changed her mind? Mollie had already gone back down for her morning nap. Rosanna had kept her up for as long as possible, but the poor little girl couldn't hold out any longer.

Rosanna paused in her lap around the room to peer out the window again. Her heart jumped into her throat at the sight of a rather beat-up-looking lime green car slowly making its way up the driveway. She jerked away from the window and ran her clammy hands down the sides of her dress. "Mamm! Mamm! I think she's here!"

Sarah scurried into the living room, pushing a strand of brown hair beneath her *kapp*. She grabbed Rosanna's hand and squeezed it. "Take a deep breath, dear one. We'll get through this with the Lord's help."

"You'll stay in here with me?" Rosanna knew she sounded like a panic-stricken girl instead of a mature woman, but she couldn't calm her fears or the violent trembling of her hands.

"I will stay, if that's what you want."

"Please."

Sarah squeezed Rosanna's hand again as a knock sounded at the front door. "Have faith."

"I'm trying."

In the light of day, Rosanna could definitely tell this woman's blonde hair came by artificial means. Not that there was anything wrong with that. Rosanna had seen many *Englisch* women studying boxes and bottles of hair dye on the shelf at the drugstore. She'd even seen some young, and not-so-young, girls with pink, purple, and blue hair. Fine lines fanning out from the corners of Kandi's eyes hinted that she must have been born quite a bit earlier than Jane, or else she'd led an exceptionally hard life.

Sarah nudged Rosanna into remembering her manners. "*Kumm* in." She held the door wide to allow the *Englisch* woman to enter. She introduced Sarah, and then her mind went totally blank.

"Let's have a seat in the living room." Sarah led the way.

Rosanna waited for Kandi to pass and trailed along behind like a lost puppy. *It's a gut thing Mamm is here or we'd still be standing in the doorway gawking at each other.* She perched on the edge of the sofa next to Sarah. Kandi sat in the rocking chair opposite them and looked as uncomfortable as Rosanna felt. Rosanna expected to hear the woman chomp on a piece of gum any second.

Kandi wiggled in the chair and tugged at her tight, short skirt, which had risen halfway up her thighs when she plunked onto the chair. One red-nailed hand reached to swipe a stiff strand of platinum hair off her face. With the toes of her high-heeled black boots she set the chair in motion.

Rosanna clasped her hands in her lap to keep from picking at her nails. It took every ounce of her will-power to sit still. What she really wanted to do was race up the stairs, snatch Mollie from the crib, sneak out the back door, and disappear from sight. But she sat still. Waiting. Wondering. The silence grated on her raw nerves.

Kandi cleared her throat. "Where is she?"

"Mollie is taking a nap," Sarah answered when Rosanna didn't.

Rosanna tried to coax her voice out, but that proved quite a chore, since simply breathing had become nearly impossible. "I-I tried to keep her up, but she got too sleepy."

"Yeah. I guess I was a little late. I overslept."

The three women stared at one another for another moment. Rosanna's heart thudded so hard she feared it would fly right out of her body.

"How is she?" Kandi reached into her huge fuchsia handbag and pulled out a pack of gum. She held it out toward Sarah and Rosanna, who both shook their heads, before unwrapping a piece and popping it into her mouth. She chomped for a few minutes, keeping time with the rocking chair.

"Mollie is fine." Rosanna finally got words past the knot in her throat.

Sarah jumped up from the sofa. "Let me get us all something to drink. Miss Kottyn, would you like water, *kaffi*, or tea?"

"I've had a gallon of coffee already. The motel had free stuff. A glass of water would be nice."

"Rosanna?"

"Just water, Mamm. I'll help you."

"I can handle it. You sit."

Rosanna feared her legs wouldn't support her right

now anyway, so sitting was probably the best option. She glanced at Kandi, waiting for and dreading her next statement. She shifted her gaze to the window. She'd give anything to be outside in the cold instead of in this room opposite the woman who presented such a threat. The popping gum dragged her attention back to the rocking chair.

"Can I see her?"

"Of course. She should be awake soon."

Kandi rocked, chomped, and shook her head. "I don't get it. Why would Jane want total strangers to have her baby instead of her own sister?"

"Maybe she thought a *boppli* would hinder your career. You'd have to tend to her all hours of the day and night or find a babysitter. Jane probably thought it would be hard for you to be a working *mudder*."

"Hmmm. Maybe. But there are zillions of single working mothers in the world."

"But your work requires you to travel and work different hours, ain't so?"

"You're definitely right about that. Just last week, I had a gig that went on until almost four in the morning. I would have needed to have a babysitter all night."

Exactly. And what kind of life is that for a little girl? To be dragged around from one place to another or left with sitters for hours and hours. Rosanna bit her tongue to keep from giving voice to her thoughts.

"Here we are." Sarah bustled into the room carrying a tray with three glasses of water and a plate of cookies.

Rosanna breathed a sigh of relief to have her *mamm* back in the room, even if she did look like she was serving *freinden* at an afternoon frolic.

Sarah set the tray on an end table and passed

glasses of water around. "Help yourself to cookies, Miss Kottyn."

"Thank you. And you can call me Kandi." She reached for a plump oatmeal raisin cookie.

Rosanna wondered what the woman would do with the gum while she ate cookies. She didn't have to wonder long, though. She could see that Kandi used her tongue to push the gum to the back of her mouth before she bit into a cookie. How did she manage not to get the two mixed together? Rosanna's own stomach churned so much that it surely wouldn't accept so much as a crumb of a cookie. She'd better stick to plain water.

"Rosanna said you were an actress." Sarah returned to her spot on the sofa.

Thank goodness her *mamm* could engage in polite small talk. Rosanna's own mind resembled one of those little slates she'd seen in the dollar store. Any thought she had immediately got erased, like lifting a corner of the filmy cover on one of those slates.

Kandi gulped down her bite of cookie and sipped her water. Rosanna wondered how she kept from swallowing the gum along with the cookie. "I am an actress, or I want to be. I've done more dancing than acting. I hope to get my big break soon."

Did Mamm understand what that meant? Rosanna sure didn't have a clue.

"You must stay very busy." Sarah sipped her water.

"Usually I do. I get regular gigs. Sometimes I do a little singing, too." Kandi popped the rest of her cookie into her mouth.

"My, you have many talents."

"I hope the folks I audition for think so, too." Kandi

reached for another cookie. "I really shouldn't eat all these calories, but the cookies are so delicious."

"You probably work hard enough that you don't need to worry about the calories in a few cookies." Sarah smiled and slid the cookie plate a little closer to their guest.

"I do rehearse a lot." Kandi nibbled the edges of her cookie, apparently saving the plump raisins for last.

It reminded Rosanna of what she used to do as a little girl when Mamm let her purchase an ice cream bar from the truck that came around in summer. She always tried to bite off the hard outer chocolate coating first and save the vanilla ice cream for last.

"Had you known Jane long? We hadn't been in touch much." Kandi's tongue snaked out to capture a few crumbs.

"I actually only met her when Mollie was born," Sarah admitted.

"Really?" Kandi turned her gaze on Rosanna.

"I met her that day, too."

"What? My sister gave her baby to people she'd never seen before?"

"Not exactly," Rosanna whispered.

"You just said you hadn't met her before."

"True, but Jane told me she had been watching me. She knew about me, my habits, even my name. I guess she lived nearby and followed me whenever she could."

Kandi shivered. "That's kind of creepy."

"Not if you didn't know it was happening. Jane seemed to really care that her *boppli* have a *gut* home."

"I could have given her a good home." Kandi brought the gum out of reserve and chomped it again as she rocked harder. "Did you go to the hospital and get the baby or did Jane leave her here in a basket on the doorstep with a note, or what?"

Sarah chuckled. "Nothing like that. Jane gave birth here."

"Here? In this house?"

"*Jah.* Mamm is a midwife, and I often attend births with her." Rosanna read horror mixed with surprise on Kandi's face.

"Jane didn't even have medical care?"

"Birth is a natural experience, not a sickness," Rosanna replied.

"What if something went wrong?"

Sarah leaned forward a bit. "I have attended many births. I do not hesitate to send a woman to the hospital if necessary. In fact, I encouraged Jane to give birth at the hospital since I had not seen her prenatally and did not know her history. I did not know she was sick when she arrived. Her labor progressed so quickly there was not much time to do anything but deliver the infant."

"Wow! She wouldn't even consider going to the hospital?"

"She wouldn't hear of it."

"I suppose that sounds like Jane. She always was feisty, even stubborn. Did she have any problems?"

"Everything went well with the birth." Sarah sat back and took another sip of water.

Kandi popped her gum. "I don't get it. Did Jane stay here a few days and then decide to leave her baby?"

"She snuck away before she had two full days to recover following the birth." Sarah set her glass on the end table and clasped her hands in her lap.

"So you're telling me my sister gave birth one day,

jumped out of bed less than forty-eight hours later, and hightailed it out of here?"

Rosanna cut her eyes over to her *mamm*. She had the insane urge to giggle. What would Kandi say if she knew Jane had somehow found the strength to climb out a second-story window to flee? She had better let Mamm handle that question.

"Actually, that's exactly what she did. She never even wanted to hold her *boppli*."

Kandi raised her over-plucked eyebrows. Her red-tinted mouth opened, but not a single sound came out.

"I-I think she didn't want to form any attachments." Rosanna recalled Jane's absolute refusal to hold or even look at her newborn, but tried to soften the blow for Kandi. "You know, it probably would have been ever so much harder to let the *boppli* go if she'd cuddled her."

"I guess." Kandi chewed harder and harder. Rosanna expected to see her spit out bits of her tongue any second.

"I'm sorry to ask, but couldn't Jane have gotten help for her medical problem?" Instantly Rosanna regretted her question. She didn't want to add to the other woman's pain. "Forgive me. You don't have to answer."

"That's quite all right. I'm surprised Jane didn't tell you herself."

"We didn't talk much except for getting through the birth."

"Jane had a rare childhood cancer. I don't understand all the medical stuff. They said it could return when she was older, which it did. It showed up in her liver, and there was nothing they could do about it. At least that's what the coroner's report said."

"Jane never talked to you about it?" Rosanna didn't want to appear nosy, but she couldn't imagine a family that didn't communicate about such things.

"We weren't that close. She wrote me that letter to tell me goodbye, I guess."

"I'm sorry." Rosanna struggled to resist the urge to cry. What a sad story. Did poor Jane die alone? She wouldn't ask that.

"What about your parents?" Sarah asked.

"Our parents passed away a long time ago, and there were just two of us kids. What about the baby's father?"

"She never mentioned him that I heard," Sarah replied. "Did she say anything to you, Rosanna?"

"*Nee.* She didn't even tell me how sick she was." Rosanna found it so hard to believe that a girl so desperately ill could give birth without any medication and then steal away like a wounded animal that wandered off to die alone. Rosanna barely suppressed a sob.

Kandi pressed down with the toes of her boots to stop the chair from rocking. "Do you suppose I can see the baby now? We've really got to get moving. I've got to dance tonight at a club in DC."

Rosanna started to rise, but Sarah stretched out a hand to stop her. "I'll get Mollie."

We. Kandi said *we.* Did she plan to take the *boppli* right now? Mollie belonged to her! She had all the legal papers to prove it. "What are your plans?" Rosanna feared the answer but had to ask the question anyway.

"Well, I'm the only family the baby has."

"We're her family." *Please, Gott, don't let her take my* boppli *away.*

"She just woke up." Sarah entered the room with a

wide-awake infant in her arms. She crossed to the rocking chair, where Kandi sat stock-still, not even chomping on her gum. "This is your *aenti*, Mollie."

Kandi clapped her hands to her face. "She's beautiful."

"Would you like to hold her?"

"I, uh, I guess, uh, but I don't know how."

"I'll put her in your arms." Sarah lowered the little girl into Kandi's stiff arms. "You won't break her. She's pretty strong."

"Hi." Fear shone in Kandi's eyes. "I-I'm your aunt."

Mollie apparently picked up on Kandi's discomfort. How could she not, with those wooden arms around her? Her little forehead wrinkled, and her lower lip trembled.

"Hey, don't cry, kiddo." Kandi looked up with a helpless expression on her face. "I don't think she likes me."

"She's not used to you, that's all," Sarah assured her.

Rosanna pretended glue held her to the sofa. Otherwise she would have darted over to the rocking chair and snatched Mollie from Kandi's arms. The other woman might be a blood relative, but Rosanna was Mollie's *mudder*. How could Kandi possibly think she could raise the *boppli* when she was afraid to even hold her? How would she feed her or change her diaper?

"She doesn't look a lot like Jane, does she? I mean, Jane had brown hair. The baby's hair is blonde."

"A lot of *bopplin* are born with blonde hair, and it darkens when they get older, ain't so, Mamm?" Rosanna's arms ached to hold her little girl, but they didn't hurt nearly as badly as her heart did.

Mollie's wail startled all three women. She cranked her little head around as if searching for a familiar face.

"Take her!" Kandi held the infant away from her.

Rosanna shot off the sofa and gathered Mollie close to her. "You're okay, sweetheart."

"She's probably hungry. I'll get her bottle." Sarah rushed from the room.

Mollie immediately calmed in Rosanna's arms. Rosanna bent to kiss the *boppli*'s little forehead and caught Kandi's look of dejection. Suddenly filled with compassion, she attempted to smooth things over. She would be crushed if a niece or nephew rejected her. "You're new to her, Kandi, and she's probably hungry, too."

"You're good with her. You calmed her right down."

"I've had practice."

"Here we go." Sarah shook the bottle of formula as she walked into the room. She held the bottle out toward Kandi. "Would you like to feed her?"

"Uh, no, I think I'd better watch. I don't want to upset her again."

"All *bopplin* cry for all sorts of reasons." Sarah passed the bottle to Rosanna. "It doesn't mean they don't like someone or that anything is necessarily wrong. Crying is their way of communicating with us."

Rosanna took the bottle and lowered herself to the sofa. She was glad Kandi refused to feed Mollie. Maybe she wouldn't want to take the infant, since she was obviously so uncomfortable with her. Rosanna positioned Mollie in a semi-upright position and touched her lips with the nipple. Mollie smiled at her before swigging down her formula.

"Look at that! She smiled at you."

Because I'm her mamm. "She's used to me."

Kandi pulled up a sleeve to check the chunky silver watch strapped to her wrist. "Oh my gosh! I've got to drive all the way to DC and get ready for tonight. I don't have a car seat, so . . ."

Rosanna gasped. "You weren't thinking of taking Mollie, were you? You know she is legally in my care. The adoption will be final soon."

"Not if I contest it."

But you don't have the first idea how to care for an infant. You wouldn't even feed her. Rosanna opened her mouth to protest, but Sarah jumped in first.

"I can understand how you feel obligated to care for your niece, but raising a *boppli* is a full-time job and a huge responsibility."

"You think I don't know that?"

"You seem to really enjoy your work."

"You bet I do. My work has been the most important thing to me. I'm so close to reaching my goal, so close to being a star."

Sarah's voice took on that soothing tone she used with laboring women. "If you continued your work, you'd have to pay someone to watch Mollie. And, of course, you'd have all the other expenses, like diapers, formula, clothes, and so on."

"Yeah, so?"

Rosanna wondered how a job could be more important than a person but didn't say anything. Apparently *Englischers*, or this one at least, had different priorities. She'd keep quiet and let Mamm finish this conversation lest she say something she regretted.

"I'm only saying you need to think things through carefully, weigh all the pros and cons."

"And think of what Jane wanted, too," Rosanna whispered.

"I-I've gotta go. I guess I can't call you, can I?"

"We don't have a phone in the house. Wait and I'll give you a number where you can leave a message." Sarah scurried from the room and then right back. She handed Kandi a slip of paper.

"Okay." Kandi stuffed the paper into her pocket. "I guess this will have to do."

Maybe she'll lose it, Rosanna thought, *but then she'd probably show up unannounced. It would definitely be better to have a little advance warning of her visit.*

Kandi rushed to the door without so much as a wave in Mollie's direction. "Thanks for letting me visit." She didn't even turn back to look at them. Before the door closed behind her, Rosanna heard Kandi mumble, "I wonder how much a lawyer costs."

Rosanna set the empty bottle on the end table and lifted Mollie to her shoulder to pat her back. She kissed the top of the honey-haired head. When Sarah turned from the door to look at her, Rosanna burst into tears. "What are we going to do, Mamm? We can't let her take Mollie. She's mine!"

Sarah crossed the room and dropped to the sofa beside Rosanna. "I don't think she really wants the *boppli*."

"She mumbled something about a lawyer when she left."

"True, but I'm wondering if she only feels obligated to take her niece. You heard her. She wants to be a famous actress. It would be pretty hard for her to concentrate on that goal while caring for a little one all alone."

"She could hire a nanny or a babysitter."

"I gathered money was not in abundant supply."

"Maybe, but I'm worried just the same. Should I contact the lawyer who checked over all my paperwork, or maybe Social Services?"

"It might be a *gut* idea, but you'll probably have to wait until after the Christmas holiday."

"*Ach*, Mamm, I couldn't bear it if Mollie was taken away from me."

Sarah opened her arms into a hug that encompassed Rosanna and Mollie. "Let's not borrow trouble, *jah*?"

Rosanna sniffed. "I'll try not to." She sniffed harder. "You don't think the court or whoever makes decisions will give Mollie to Kandi just because she's a relative, do you? Mollie has a *gut* home here, a loving, stable home with lots of family who care about her. They'll take that into consideration, won't they?"

"I would certainly hope so. We will do everything we can to keep this little one." Sarah leaned over to plant a kiss on Mollie's head.

"I feel like running off somewhere with her and hiding."

"You can't do that. They would surely take her away if you did that."

"I know. I wouldn't do anything so foolish, Mamm. I love her so much. She *is* my *boppli*."

"I'm well aware of how much you love her, dear. We all love her. She's one of the family. We will pray the Lord Gott will see fit to leave her with us."

Chapter Twenty-One

A skim of snow covered the grass and frosted the tree limbs early on Christmas morning. Fat, fluffy flakes continued to drift earthward as Rosanna gazed out the kitchen window after adding wood to the stove. She stood staring for a few moments, enjoying the peace and solitude. Once her younger siblings awoke, there wouldn't be any more silence for the rest of the day, except at prayer times.

How fitting that it should snow for Mollie's first Christmas. Just because the calendar said December did not mean there would be snow. Rosanna remembered many Christmases where the temperature in Southern Maryland rose upward of sixty degrees. She welcomed this cold, snowy Christmas. She couldn't wait to show Mollie the scene that looked like the little plastic snow globe she had shaken in the dollar store a few weeks ago. She hoped to make Mollie's day extra special, even though the *boppli* would not remember it. She prayed this wouldn't be Mollie's only Christmas with them.

Enough! This was the Lord Jesus' birthday. She would be joyful. Easier said than done, but she would give it her best effort. Rosanna lifted the heavy black skillet to the stove and removed a slab of bacon from the propane-powered refrigerator. *Kaffi* already perked in the silver pot on the back stove burner. Daed, Tobias, and Joseph were already outside caring for the animals and performing only necessary chores. Surely the smell of bacon frying would draw everyone else out from beneath their warm blankets.

Ordinarily Mamm would be working right along beside her, but a nervous new *daed* had fetched her late the previous evening. It had been a false alarm, but Mamm had stayed with the frightened young couple until the wee hours of the morning. Rosanna had just finished checking on Mollie when she heard her *mamm* trudge up the steps. Even if Mollie slept through the night, Rosanna didn't. She kept getting up to check on her, lightly touching her little chest to make sure it rose and fell with her breaths. Mamm told her most other *mudders* did the very same thing, so Rosanna didn't feel so peculiar.

"*Ach*, Rosanna! I didn't mean to oversleep." Sarah bustled into the kitchen, weariness still written on her face.

"It's okay, Mamm. You could have slept longer. You got home so late."

"Or early, depending on how you look at it."

Rosanna laughed. "I guess you're right. I can fix breakfast. Why don't you pour a cup of *kaffi* and relax for a few minutes."

"Have you ever known me to do that?"

"Well, *nee,* I can't think of a single instance."

"Then I won't start doing that now." Sarah reached for the large ceramic mixing bowl. "Pancakes to go with the bacon?"

"That sounds *gut*. We could have banana bread and muffins—or would you prefer oatmeal?"

"The bread and muffins are fine. We have plenty to use up."

"I'm sure they won't go to waste around here."

"Pancakes, yum! Can I help?" Sadie shuffled into the kitchen rubbing her eyes.

"Sure, but wash your hands first," Sarah replied.

"I washed my hands."

"Last night doesn't count, Sadie." Rosanna wagged a finger at her youngest sibling.

"How do you know I didn't wash them this morning, smarty?"

"Because I know you!"

Sarah pointed to the doorway. "Wash—with soap. Then you can help."

Rosanna laughed. She loved all her siblings, but Sadie was so loving, sweet, and funny. Adam and Roman, Rosanna's two oldest *bruders,* and their *fraas* would be arriving later for dinner. Both women recently announced they were expecting their first *bopplin,* so next Christmas there would be three little ones. Today would be a nice family day. They would exchange presents later and enjoy one another's company. Tomorrow, Second Christmas, they would go visiting or receive visitors. The day after that, Rosanna would make sure Mollie was legally hers and that she stayed that way.

The dinner table had been nearly overflowing with large platters of sliced ham and turkey, heaping bowls of creamy mashed potatoes, green beans from last summer's garden, creamed corn, a variety of pickles and relishes, and baskets of golden-brown biscuits. They had squeezed four more chairs around the long oak table and enjoyed feast and fellowship.

The adults visited and played board games while the younger *kinner* enjoyed their new toys. Mollie had been passed around from person to person, each one cooing to her and playing with her. Rosanna tucked the exhausted infant into her crib shortly after evening fell. Not much later, Rosanna succumbed to her weariness and dropped into bed herself. The next day would be another busy one, but maybe there wouldn't be such a mountain of dishes to wash.

A little more snow fell on Christmas night, so that when Rosanna awoke on Second Christmas, a couple of inches of new fluffiness covered the ground. Katie awoke with a sore throat and sniffles, so Rosanna volunteered to stay home with her while the rest of the family visited *freinden* and neighbors. Secretly, Rosanna was relieved that she and Mollie would have a quieter day at home.

The family hadn't been gone long when Christmas bells jingled in the driveway. Katie had been coloring in her new coloring book when she wasn't sipping hot tea with honey or napping on the couch. She was the first to hear the bells. "Someone came to visit," she called to Rosanna, who had just crept up the stairs to check on Mollie.

Satisfied the infant still napped peacefully, Rosanna bounded down the stairs to peek out the window. "I wonder who is visiting us."

Katie had dragged a chair over to the kitchen window, climbed onto it, and leaned over the sink to peer outside. "It looks like Paul Hertzler."

"I wonder what . . . Katie Mast, get down off that chair before you fall and break your neck!"

"Aw, Rosanna, I climb on stuff all the time."

"That doesn't make it okay. How would I ever explain to Mamm and Daed that you broke your neck while you were supposed to be resting?"

Katie giggled. "You're silly. I'm not going to fall. I've never fallen out of any of the trees I climbed."

Rosanna clucked her tongue. Just then, Katie leaned a little too far, causing the chair to slide. Rosanna raced across the room to grab Katie before she hit the floor. "Whew! That was close." She set the little girl on her feet. "What were you saying about never falling?"

"I *almost* never fall. Why don't you let Paul inside?"

"And why don't you go back to coloring or some other safe activity?" Rosanna hurried to the back door to let Paul in, since she figured, being a single fellow visiting alone, he might feel uneasy simply walking inside as most Amish *freinden* and neighbors did. She pulled open the heavy outer door just as Paul mounted the cement steps. "Merry Christmas, Paul."

"Merry Christmas. I hope it's okay for me to stop by."

"Of course it is. *Kumm* in out of the cold."

"*Jah*, it has turned much colder."

"Is your family well? Did you have a nice Christmas?"

"*Jah* to both questions. The family has headed to my oldest *bruder*'s house. John's family spent yesterday with his *fraa*'s family, so we'll visit with them today. I'm on my way there but wanted to stop by here first."

Rosanna assumed it was okay to invite Paul into the kitchen since Katie could serve as a chaperone of sorts. "Would you like *kaffi*, tea, or cocoa?"

"I don't want to put you to any trouble."

"The water is already warm. I've been plying Katie with hot tea and honey all day."

"Is she sick?"

"She has a sore throat and a bit of a cough. I volunteered to stay home with her so the rest of the family could make their visits as planned."

"That was nice of you."

"I kind of wanted to keep Mollie in out of the cold anyway."

"She isn't sick, too, is she?"

"*Nee,* but she had a busy day yesterday, and I thought it best to keep her calm and warm today."

"I'm glad she's okay. Maybe I can see her in a little while."

"Sure. Now, what would you like to drink?" Rosanna led the way into the kitchen.

"I'll take some cocoa, if that's okay."

"That's fine."

"Can I have cocoa, too?" Katie laid down her crayon to turn a pleading look in Rosanna's direction. "With marshmallows?"

Rosanna laughed. "There certainly isn't anything wrong with your appetite."

"Mamm always says I have a healthy one."

"That's a polite way of saying you eat a lot. You can sure pack away a lot of food for a thin little girl. You must burn off your food with all your climbing, ain't so?"

Katie shrugged. "Can I have cocoa?"

"You *may* have cocoa."

"You sound like my teacher."

"Hey, I like your picture." Paul moved to stand behind Katie's chair at the big kitchen table.

"*Danki.* I like to color."

Rosanna prepared three mugs of cocoa and added

a little cold water to Katie's mug. Knowing her little *schweschder*, she'd probably try to gulp the whole mug down and end up scalding her throat. Rosanna plopped a small handful of miniature marshmallows into Katie's mug and set it on the table.

"I could have put in my own marshmallows, you know."

"Uh-huh. You would have dumped in half the bag."

Katie wrinkled up her nose at Rosanna before trying to sink her marshmallows with a spoon.

Rosanna shook her head. "Would you like to add your own marshmallows, Paul?"

"Hey, you asked him but not me," Katie whined.

"Because he's an adult."

"I trust you to give me the right amount." Paul winked at Rosanna.

She turned back to her task, hoping to hide her burning cheeks. Why did that little wink affect her so? She stirred the cocoa, added marshmallows, and carried the mugs to the table. She set her mug beside Katie's and set Paul's directly across the table. She returned to the counter to retrieve the big ceramic cookie jar.

"Yum. Cookies." Katie looked up from dunking marshmallows.

"I thought your throat hurt." Rosanna set the jar out of Katie's reach.

"The cocoa will make it feel better, so the cookies will go down fine."

Rosanna rolled her eyes.

"I like your thinking, Katie." Paul sipped his cocoa before shrugging out of his jacket.

"I think she's a little manipulator." Rosanna passed

the cookie jar to Paul. "You'd better help yourself to cookies first before this little piggy gets hold of the jar."

Paul reached into the jar and withdrew cookies. "Ah! Chocolate chip. My very favorite."

"Mine, too." Katie leaned as far as possible to slide the jar toward herself.

"I thought peanut butter cookies were your favorite." Rosanna passed paper napkins to the other two.

"They're my favorite, too, but chocolate chip are my most favorite."

Rosanna laughed. "Like I said, she's a piggy." She pulled the cookie jar from Katie's grasp and handed her two small cookies.

"I could have gotten my own."

"I don't know where your hands have been."

"I only get two?" Katie glanced at Paul's cookies and then at her own. "Two teensy-weensy ones?"

"We don't want to tax your poor sore throat too much."

Katie made a face, drawing more laughter from Rosanna and Paul. She devoured her cookies and slurped her cocoa while the adults talked. When she started playing with the crumbs and her spoon, Rosanna sent her to the living room to rest. "Put your mug in the sink on your way."

"All right. I guess I am kind of tired."

When Katie left the room, Paul reached down and lifted a paper bag to the table. "I have a little Christmas present for Mollie."

"You do?"

"With it being her first Christmas, I wanted to do something for her."

"That's so nice of you, Paul."

"It isn't much." He pushed the bag across the table.

Rosanna gasped when she pulled a wooden puzzle out of the bag. The base was shaped like a barn and had duck, horse, cow, pig, sheep, and chicken puzzle pieces. "This is *wunderbaar!*"

"I know she's not old enough for this yet, by my younger *bruders* and I all liked puzzles, so I thought . . ."

"It's perfect. We all loved puzzles, too. Did you make this?"

"I did."

"I never knew you were so talented and so artistic. These animals look so real." Rosanna glanced up into Paul's hazel eyes. The flush in his cheeks warmed her heart.

He shrugged. "I don't know how artistic I am, but I like making things."

"You could certainly sell these to *Englisch* and Amish customers. Mollie will love playing with the puzzle. I just know it!"

Rosanna removed the animal pieces from their slots in the puzzle base. Paul had even painted the inside to look like a real barn.

"I have something for you, too."

"For me?"

"It's your first Christmas as a *mudder*, and, well, I had the wood, so I made this." He set a smaller bag on the table.

Rosanna's heart skipped a beat. Her *bruders* had been the only fellows who had ever given her gifts. She was touched by Paul's thoughtfulness. How many young men would buy a *boppli* and her *mamm* gifts, much less make them? She willed her fingers not to tremble as she reached into the bag.

"*Ach*, Paul, it's beautiful!" Rosanna drew out a polished wooden box with a hinged lid. The word

"Recipes" had been carved on top. Her name was etched in one lower corner, and a flower in the opposite one. Rosanna ran her hands over the smooth wood. She lifted the lid and inhaled the scent of the wood. He had even thought to include the perfect size of index cards. "I've been collecting recipes for when I . . . for later. I will cherish this gift always. *Danki*, Paul. You are so thoughtful." She stretched her hand across the table to squeeze his. Now her face probably glowed as bright as his.

Rosanna withdrew her hand and glanced down at the recipe box. Did Paul have any ulterior motive for giving her this box? Did he misconstrue her impromptu gesture just now? What should she say now to defuse the charged atmosphere that swirled around them?

Chapter Twenty-Two

"Rosanna! I think Mollie is awake. Do you want me to get her?" Katie hollered like her throat had never hurt at all.

"*Nee*, I don't need you breathing your germs all over her. I'll get her." Rosanna scooted her chair back and set the recipe box down on the table. Mollie awoke at precisely the right moment.

"Great, I will get to see her after all." Paul started to push back from the table.

"Please feel free to have more cookies. I'll run up and get Mollie and be right back." Rosanna scooted the cookie jar closer to Paul before dashing from the room.

She tickled the cooing, smiling *boppli* before changing her. "You're always such a happy girl. You have a visitor downstairs who brought you a special gift." She lifted Mollie from the crib and carried her downstairs.

"Hi, Mollie," Katie called from her makeshift bed on the couch. "I wouldn't have sneezed on her or anything."

Rosanna smiled. "I know you wouldn't, but you need to rest so you'll feel better to go back to school."

"Ugh!"

"You know you like school."

"Sometimes."

Rosanna laughed. She knew it must be hard for Katie to sit still all day in school when her body wanted to jump around and keep moving. She understood. She liked to keep busy herself. Upon entering the kitchen, she turned Mollie around so she faced the table. "Look who has *kumm* to see you."

"Hey, Mollie." Paul stood and crossed the room in two giant steps. "Don't you look all bright-eyed after your nap." He tickled her under her chin and smiled when she smiled at him.

"You sure are at ease with little ones for having none in your house."

"I guess I inherited that from Mamm."

"Would you like to hold her while I prepare her bottle?"

"Sure." He expertly lifted Mollie from Rosanna's arms as if he'd been handling infants regularly.

Rosanna scooped powdered formula into a bottle, added water and a nipple, and shook the bottle to mix the ingredients. Paul sure would make a great *daed* one day. How many times had that thought run through her head? When she turned back around, she found Paul had dropped onto a chair and was cuddling Mollie in his arms.

"Can I feed her? Do you think she'll take the bottle from me?"

"I don't see why she wouldn't. She certainly seems to like you." Rosanna gave the bottle a final shake before handing it to Paul.

"Let's see if I can maneuver this."

"Here." Rosanna bent down to help re-situate Mollie in Paul's arms. A little tingle shot up her own arm and raced straight to her heart when he looked up at her with eyes full of concern and . . . what? She inhaled his scent of soap, slightly spicy shaving cream, and wood smoke. The combination provided a pleasing aroma that she wouldn't mind smelling daily. Whoa! She'd better back up right now. "All you have to do is put the bottle to her lips, and she'll take it from there." Rosanna gave a nervous little laugh and backed up a bit farther.

When Mollie opened her mouth and started sucking the bottle, Rosanna plunked down on a nearby chair. The scene in front of her looked so natural that it nearly stole her breath away. Would Mollie ever know a *daed*'s love? Goodness knows, she loved the little girl enough for a hundred people, and she knew her whole family adored Mollie. Would that make up for not having a *daed*? Would *she* even have Mollie much longer?

"What's the matter, Rosanna?"

Although his voice was whisper soft, it pulled her mind from the dark path it wandered down. "What?"

"You looked so sad for a moment. Am I doing something wrong?" He looked down at Mollie, who was happily swallowing the formula, and back up at Rosanna.

"You're doing everything exactly right." Too right.

"Then why the sad expression?"

Rosanna didn't intend to air her concerns, but they slipped out on their own. "I'm so afraid of losing Mollie."

"Why would that happen?"

"Her *aenti* did show up for a visit."

"What?" Mollie startled, stopped sucking, and puckered up her little face. "It's okay, little one. I didn't mean to frighten you. Do you want to finish?" He wiggled the bottle against her mouth until she latched onto it again. "What did the woman want?"

Before Rosanna could stop herself, she poured out the whole story. "If Kandi gets a lawyer and tries to take Mollie, I don't know what I'll do."

"Mollie's *mudder* chose you to take Mollie. She must have known her *schweschder* wouldn't be the right person for the job. You have legal papers."

"I do, and the adoption should be final soon."

"Then you shouldn't have anything to worry about."

"But Kandi is family. That might make a difference."

"Do you have someone you can talk to who understands all the legal matters?"

"Mamm and I are going to try to see the lawyer tomorrow."

"If you need me to tell them what a great *mamm* you are and how content Mollie is with you, I'd be more than happy to do that."

"I appreciate that, Paul. Please pray I don't lose my *boppli*." Rosanna's voice wobbled. She chewed her bottom lip and blinked hard to fight back tears.

"I will definitely pray." Paul reached a hand over to give Rosanna's arm a quick pat. "Everything will be all right. I know it. Mollie is yours. The Lord Gott gave her to you."

Rosanna sniffed and nodded. She didn't trust her voice at the moment.

"We can pray right now, if you like."

Rosanna nodded again.

Paul set the now-empty bottle on the table and

again laid a hand on Rosanna's arm. His other arm still firmly held Mollie. "Dear Lord Gott, we ask for Your help here. Little Mollie is such a special gift You gave to Rosanna. Please work everything out so she can stay here in this loving family. We trust You to guide Rosanna and to give her peace. Amen."

"Amen." Rosanna instantly felt better. She didn't know how things would end up, but she believed the Lord Gott had a plan that would work out for *gut*. "*Danki*, Paul."

Paul sat Mollie up a bit to gently pat her back. "Is this right?"

A burp made him and Rosanna laugh.

"Mollie says it was just right." Rosanna's fingers absently played with the puzzle on the table. She plucked out the sheep piece and studied it. The detail was exquisite. Little wavy lines gave the appearance of curly wool. The eyes were, well, sheeplike. They looked real enough to blink. Rosanna expected the little wooden piece to baa at her any second.

She glanced up to find Mollie watching her move the sheep around. "I think she likes it, Paul. She's watching it so intently." Rosanna held the sheep closer and smiled when Mollie reached for it.

"Maybe sheep will be her favorite farm animal," Paul said.

"We might have to get a few for her." Rosanna held up the other puzzle pieces one by one. Mollie looked at each one, but her gaze kept returning to the sheep.

"She's a rather amazing *boppli*, ain't so?" Paul's smile lit his entire face.

"I certainly think so. She definitely likes these *wunderbaar* wooden animals. What *kinner* wouldn't? I might have to hide the puzzle from Katie and Sadie."

"I think they are a little old for such simple puzzles."

"But they like animals and play with stuffed ones. Don't underestimate your talent."

"It's nothing, really."

Rosanna didn't want to embarrass Paul, but she didn't want him to belittle his ability. "Maybe this is one of your Gott-given gifts. You are able to create useful yet beautiful things from wood."

"I hadn't thought of it that way. I only know I like working with wood and paint."

"You could make a whole bunch of puzzles, toys, recipe boxes, and anything else and sell every single one of them next Christmas."

"That's something to think about."

"Just don't make another recipe box quite like mine. It's special." Rosanna's cheeks heated.

"This is a one-of-a-kind box for a one-of-a-kind girl."

The fire in Rosanna's cheeks blazed hotter. Paul's cheeks flushed a tomato red, too. They talked awhile longer, until Katie shuffled into the kitchen.

"I'm bored." She heaved an exaggerated sigh.

"Poor dear. I'm sure you'll be glad to get back to school tomorrow." Rosanna struggled to conceal a smile.

"Maybe I'm not that bored. Hey, what's this?" Katie picked up the wooden pig and cow and fit them into the appropriate slots on the puzzle board.

"It's a puzzle Paul made for Mollie."

"It's great. Can you make me one, Paul?"

"Don't you think you're a little old for a puzzle like this?" Rosanna handed Katie another puzzle piece to put into place.

Katie shrugged. "Maybe. But it's really nice. I like the animals. Maybe Paul could just make some little wooden animals."

"There's another idea for you, Paul," Rosanna said. "By next Christmas you could have a whole line of products to sell. You could have your own shop."

Paul rubbed a hand across his jaw. "I don't know about a shop, but Eli might let me have a corner of his furniture store to display things. As long as I keep up with the furniture assignments he has for me, he'd probably go for it."

"Why not? It would definitely bring more business into his shop."

"Rosanna, you've given me some great ideas to think about."

"What about me?" Katie stomped one foot in indignation.

"You, too, for sure, Katie."

Paul and Rosanna smiled at each other over Katie's head. Rosanna's heart felt lighter. Her worries had been lifted, at least temporarily. Paul's visit had been exactly what she needed.

"I'd better catch up with my family before they send out someone to search for me. I've enjoyed visiting with all of you." Although he said "all," he looked straight into Rosanna's eyes.

"*Jah*, it has been a nice visit." Rosanna lifted Mollie from Paul's arms. "And we surely thank you for the gifts." Suddenly she wished she had a gift for him as well. Maybe another time. *Ach!* What was she thinking?

Chapter Twenty-Three

Rosanna breathed slightly easier walking down the steps outside the lawyer's office than she had walking up them ninety minutes earlier. She held Mollie tightly in her arms. "You do think I'll get to keep her, don't you, Mamm?"

"The lawyer said all your paperwork was in order."

"But if Kandi tries to fight the adoption . . ."

"She can try, but I think Jane's wishes count for a lot."

"And if it *kumms* down to choosing, they'll have to check which home would be more stable, ain't so?"

"I believe that's what the lawyer said, if I understood correctly."

"We have a stable home. Even though I'm a single *mudder*, I have lots of family around for support. That should count for a lot, *jah*? I mean, our home has to be better than Kandi's. She works nights and would have to get babysitters. She doesn't have family around." Rosanna paused to gulp in a breath. "I don't mean to say anything bad about her, but . . ."

"Calm yourself, Dochder. We've done all we can."

"Have we? There must be something else." Rosanna

paced back and forth on the sidewalk as they waited for Amy, their *Englisch* driver, to pick them up.

"I can't think of anything else. You need to trust the Lord Gott."

"I-I'm trying." Rosanna laid her head on top of the bundled-up infant.

"Don't you think He is big enough or strong enough to handle all your worries and fears?"

"I know He is. It's just that I'm so scared."

Sarah caught Rosanna in mid-stride and wrapped an arm around her and Mollie. "I know, dear. The Lord knows, too. And He knows what is best. Trust him."

Rosanna swallowed hard but couldn't dislodge the massive lump in her throat. She nodded instead and shivered even though the sun was shining and the wind was practically nonexistent. She had to get a handle on her fears. She had to trust, like Mamm said.

"There's Amy making the turn. Just in time before we freeze to death."

"I'm not really that cold, Mamm."

"The shivers must be from nerves, then."

"I guess."

"Everything works out for *gut*. That's what the Bible says."

"I know."

Rosanna reached inside the van to secure Mollie in the car seat before climbing in to sit beside her. Sarah entered the opposite side of the van and fastened her own seat belt. Once the doors slid closed, Rosanna could welcome the heat blasting from the side vents.

"You all let me know if you get too warm and I'll cut the heat down. I thought you might have gotten chilled standing outside." Amy looked at each of them in the rearview mirror.

"It feels fine." Rosanna's shivering had lessened considerably.

"How did everything go?" Amy peered at them again before pulling out into traffic.

"About like you said yesterday when I stopped by your house," Sarah replied. "Our paperwork is in order. We'll have to wait and see if anything else happens."

Wait! The hardest thing on earth to do. Rosanna patted Mollie with one hand as Sarah squeezed her other one.

"Say, are you okay with stopping at the dollar store for a few minutes? I won't be long. I only need to pick up a few things."

Sarah looked at Rosanna, who shrugged. "Sure, Amy. I can pick up some batteries and see if they have that cereal Samuel likes. It should be cheaper here than at the grocery store."

Amy swung into the parking lot and parked near the front door. "Good," she said. "It doesn't look too busy."

Rosanna considered waiting in the van but feared Mollie might get too cold without the heat blowing. Knowing Mamm and Amy, they'd get distracted looking around and a few minutes would turn into an hour. She opened the van's sliding door and jumped out. She reached back inside to unbuckle Mollie from the rear-facing infant seat. "Let's go look around, sweetie." She threw the pink and white blanket she had crocheted over the little girl for extra warmth before trailing behind the other two women.

Since Rosanna didn't need to purchase anything, she wandered around the store aimlessly as Mamm and Amy shopped. She stopped a moment to look at Valentine trinkets and picked up a little stuffed red bear. Its eyes could probably be easily plucked out by little fingers, so it wouldn't be a safe toy for Mollie. She set it back on the shelf and backed up right onto the toes of someone she hadn't heard approach. "Oh, excuse me." She turned around to make sure the other person was all right. "I'm so sorry—Henry!"

"Hello, Rosanna."

"I didn't hear anyone walk up. I hope I didn't crush your toes." She shifted Mollie in her arms.

"I'm fine." His face turned pickled beet red when Rosanna's eyes traveled to the oversized Valentine card in his hand. He cleared his throat. "You still have the *boppli*, I see."

"Of course. She's my *boppli*." Rosanna turned to scan the store. Maybe she'd see Mamm and Amy heading to the checkout area.

"You know, I might have been looking at a card for you if you didn't have it."

Rosanna whirled around in time to see Henry nod at Mollie. "*It* is a *she*. And you never gave any indication you were truly interested in me."

"We talked after singings."

"Mainly I talked. And if you cared about me, you'd care about my *boppli*, too."

"Who wants a *boppli* around when they're courting?"

"Don't you like *kinner*, Henry?"

"They're okay if they belong to someone else. I guess having my own someday would be all right."

"But not an adopted one? That's a pretty selfish attitude, Henry. I guess it's a *gut* thing you decided to take up with Frannie, ain't so?" Rosanna spun on her heel and raced away as fast as she could with a drowsy infant in her arms.

"She'll do for now."

Rosanna stopped in her tracks and looked over her shoulder. "Henry Zook, that's an awful thing to say! I hope Frannie knows how you feel." With that, she zoomed around the corner of the aisle. And to think she'd spent all that time talking to Henry and hoping he'd ask to take her home from a singing. Was she ever wrong!

She concentrated on not causing a scene. She would not stomp her feet or mutter aloud even if she did feel like doing both. How could Henry not feel *kinner* were a blessing regardless of the circumstances of their birth? Mollie was an extra special blessing, a gift. Rosanna hadn't asked for a *boppli* or even thought about having one anytime soon, but when Mollie had appeared, she loved her from the start. In fact, she couldn't love her more if she'd given birth to her.

Rosanna traveled up and down aisles of the store without seeing a single item on the shelves. Even the displays on the endcaps did not reach out and pull her from her thoughts. She would not give in to the tears that had collected in her eyes. She couldn't be sure if they were tears of anger or disappointment or sadness. Whatever their origin, Rosanna refused to let them slide down her face.

She blew out a sigh and glanced down at Mollie, who stared at her with wide-open blue eyes. Rosanna's speed walking must have roused her from her dozing state. Instantly Rosanna's brow smoothed, and her lips curved into a smile. Mollie could always put her in a *gut* mood. She thanked the Lord Gott every day for blessing her with her precious little girl.

She wished she could forget Henry's hateful words. Strange that she never picked up on his true character before. Maybe their conversations had been too superficial, or maybe he was extra *gut* at deception. Ready to take her home! Huh! And then what? Would he ever have revealed his hidden feelings? *Thank You, Lord Gott, for sparing me the disappointment and heartache that surely would have occurred if I'd spent more time with Henry Zook.*

Poor Frannie. Did she know the real Henry Zook? Perhaps she shared his sentiments about *kinner*. They had surely talked a lot more than she and Henry had. It would be interesting to see how that relationship played out.

Rosanna rounded another corner. The store wasn't that huge. Where in the world were Mamm and Amy? Maybe she could ask Amy for the keys to the van so she and Mollie could wait there. Then she wouldn't have to worry about confronting Henry again.

Ah! There! Mamm was rolling a half-filled shopping cart toward the checkout area. So much for batteries and cereal. Rosanna headed in the same direction and was especially glad to see Amy bent over to extract items from underneath her full cart. Maybe, just maybe, they would be able to exit the store before Henry reappeared.

Rosanna slunk down in the seat after fastening Mollie into the infant seat, hoping the high headrests would hide her from view. As the van got rolling, the motion and the hum of the tires lulled Mollie to sleep. The conversation between Mamm and Amy passed right over her head. Her brain kept replaying the run-in with Henry. Should she try to warn Frannie?

Henry made it sound like he would stick with her until someone better came along. What an attitude to have! But if she said anything to the girl, she would think Rosanna was meddling or, worse yet, jealous.

"What's wrong?" Sarah leaned around the infant seat to look Rosanna in the eye.

"Nothing."

"Really?"

"Really. Why?"

"You're drumming so hard on that door I doubt Amy can hear the music blaring from the speaker right beside her."

"I'm not drumming." Rosanna looked down at her fingers in midair, poised to strike again. "Oh, I guess I have a few things on my mind." She dropped her hands to her lap.

Sarah cocked an eyebrow.

"It's nothing important." Not anymore, anyway.

"Okay, if you say so. I'm here if you need to talk."

"I know, Mamm, *danki*."

Rosanna flew around the house sweeping, dusting, and polishing when she wasn't playing with or tending to Mollie. After tucking the infant in for an afternoon nap, she dragged out cookie sheets and mixing bowls. She removed canisters of flour, sugar, and oats. She opened the gas-powered refrigerator to rummage around for eggs and butter.

"Do you want to tell me what's troubling you?"

Rosanna backed away from the refrigerator and threw a quick glance at Sarah in the kitchen doorway before turning back to her task. "What makes you think there's anything wrong?"

Sarah chuckled. "I know you too well, my dear. When you race through the house like a speeding freight train, I know you have something on your mind."

Rosanna shrugged. She couldn't decide whether to tell her *mamm* about her encounter with Henry or not. She wished she could forget about it. She scooped flour into a glass measuring cup and then dumped it in the sifter. She cranked the handle and watched the fine, powdery substance filter into the mixing bowl. If only she could sift the concerns from her mind as easily as she sifted lumps from the flour.

"Are you still thinking about Kandi's possible plan?" Sarah scooted across the room to lay a hand on Rosanna's shoulder.

"I suppose that will always be in the back of my mind as long as the chance she might take Mollie exists."

"I can understand that." Sarah patted the shoulder.

"I only hope everyone sees that we are what is best for Mollie." Rosanna dropped a stick of butter into an aluminum pan and set it on the stove to soften before measuring sugar and oats.

"Didn't you just bake cookies?"

"Those were chocolate chip. Besides, nothing lasts for long in this house."

"Nothing sweet, anyway." Sarah chuckled.

Rosanna was lifting the last batch of cookies from the baking sheets to the waiting cooling racks when she heard Mollie cooing in the cradle in the living room. How blessed she was to have a little one who always awoke in a pleasant mood. She remembered Sadie had not always done that. If she'd slept an extra-long time, she awoke quite cranky until her little tummy got full.

Rosanna set her pan in the sink, wiped her hands on a dish towel, and hurried into the living room to coo back at Mollie. Soon her *boppli* would be too big for the cradle. She was growing so fast. *Please, Lord, let me be the one to watch her crawl and walk and to hear her first words.*

She reached down to tickle the little girl before lifting her from the cradle. She hugged her close and kissed her. "I love you, Mollie. Let's get you changed so you are comfortable enough to eat." Rosanna talked to Mollie as she climbed the stairs and changed her. If she didn't know better, she would say the infant understood every single word. She certainly listened intently and studied each of Rosanna's facial expressions. Such a smart one!

Near the bottom of the stairs, Rosanna's ears picked up the sound of voices in the kitchen. Unless Mamm was talking to and answering herself, a visitor had arrived. Rosanna's chatter to Mollie had completely blocked out any other sound. Who could be visiting so near supper time? Rosanna hurried to the kitchen. She could sit Mollie in her infant swing and start supper so Mamm could visit with her guest. She hadn't quite reached the kitchen doorway when Mamm called out to her.

"Rosanna, look who has *kumm* to visit you."

Me? Someone came to see me? Maybe Emma had dropped by hoping to see Tobias and used Rosanna as an excuse. She smiled. She was all set to tease Emma but stopped short right inside the kitchen.

"Hi, Rosanna. And hi to you, too, Mollie."

"Hi, Paul." Rosanna threw a questioning glance at Sarah, who shrugged her shoulders but offered a sly smile.

"I'm sorry to stop by so close to supper time, but I was on my way home and wanted to find out how things went today." Paul closed the gap between himself and Rosanna and reached out to tickle Mollie's chin. He was instantly rewarded with a smile.

"Why don't you have a seat in the living room, Rosanna? I can get supper just fine."

"Okay." Rosanna headed from the room with Paul right behind her.

"May I hold Mollie? I think I brushed all the sawdust from the furniture shop off of me before I came in the house."

Rosanna stopped abruptly, causing Paul to nearly crash into her. She could feel his warm breath on the back of her neck. He grasped her shoulder to steady them both, sending a surprising electric jolt through her body. "I'm sure you're fine." She turned to hand Mollie to Paul and immediately missed the warmth of his hands when he reached out for the *boppli*.

"My, you're growing, little one."

Rosanna opened the woodstove in the living room to throw in a chunk of wood. She needed to do something with her hands to keep from picking at her nails. Why did she suddenly feel jittery? It must be her frayed nerves from the morning's activities.

"It's nice and warm in here, ain't so, Mollie?" Paul jostled the infant a bit. "Be glad you aren't outside. I think the temperature has dropped ten degrees or more since this afternoon."

"Really? It was cold this morning, but not bad when we went to town. *Kumm* sit near the stove." Rosanna sat in the old rocking chair, leaving the comfortable armchair for Paul and Mollie.

Paul sat and rearranged Mollie on his lap. He

chuckled. "I might get so comfortable I won't want to go back outside. Were you able to see the lawyer today and get some answers?"

"*Jah*. He said my papers are all in order and we'll have to wait and see if Kandi files any petitions. If she does, they might have to determine which would be the best home for Mollie. I'm not really sure how it all works. I only know I can't lose my little girl." Tears sprang into Rosanna's eyes.

"Surely they will take Jane's wishes into consideration."

"The lawyer said they would. I'm trying not to worry."

"But you still do. That's natural, Rosanna. I don't know Kandi, but what I've heard makes me absolutely sure your home would be a far better place for Mollie. You're here with her all the time. You have your family to lend their support. They would have to decide in your favor."

"I sure hope so, but Kandi is a blood relative and that may carry some weight."

Paul stretched to pat Rosanna's arm. "Think positive thoughts and keep praying."

"I've been praying. That's for sure and for certain."

"And the positive thoughts?"

"I'm working on that one."

Mollie's gurgle drew their attention from such a serious subject. They both laughed at the little bubbles she blew and her obvious pleasure at her accomplishment.

"She's a charmer, ain't so?" Paul tickled her again to elicit another giggle.

"She certainly is." Rosanna marveled at Paul's ease with and genuine interest in Mollie.

"Paul, would you like to stay for supper?" Sarah

stood in the doorway drying her hands on a blue-checked dish towel. Her lips twitched as if she wanted to laugh or had some juicy secret.

"*Ach!* I didn't know it had gotten so late. I'd better be getting home, but I appreciate the offer."

Rosanna jumped up from her chair, threw her *mudder* a stern look, and reached down to lift Mollie from Paul's arms. "It was nice of you to stop by, Paul."

"I wanted to make sure everything went all right today." He glanced quickly toward the doorway, now empty, and back to Rosanna. "I care, you know."

His voice had dropped so low, Rosanna had to strain to hear his words. The scarlet tint on his handsome face told her she had heard him correctly. Heat inched its way up her own neck and face. Thank goodness Mamm had disappeared from the doorway. Rosanna hoped she had moved far enough away that she didn't hear Paul's comment. If she had heard it, the questions and comments would fly, and Rosanna had no desire to face that at the moment.

A gentle touch on her arm brought her gaze up and up to meet Paul's lovely hazel eyes.

"I'll be praying for you, Rosanna."

"I appreciate that, Paul."

"Will you attend the next singing? It would do you *gut* to get out."

"I-I'm not sure. You know, I-I don't want to appear a bad *mudder* who leaves her *boppli* with others so she can have fun."

"You could never be a bad *mudder*. I understand, though, if you decide not to attend." His momentary dejected look was replaced with hope. "Maybe I could visit you, then?"

"Sure." Rosanna tried to look away, but Paul's eyes

held her captive. "Uh, would you like some cookies for the ride home? I just baked oatmeal ones."

Paul's face split into a wide smile. "That would be great. Oatmeal cookies are my favorite."

"I thought chocolate chip cookies were your favorite."

"True, but oatmeal cookies are my next favorite."

Rosanna burst out laughing and led the way to the kitchen.

The smile refused to slide from his face as Paul ambled to his gray buggy swinging a small paper bag full of oatmeal raisin cookies. Rosanna's laughter rang in his ears like his favorite hymn from the *Ausbund*. She had answered favorably, sort of, his question about visiting. She'd said, "Sure," so he'd take that as a positive response.

He'd carefully worded his request as a casual visit so he didn't scare her off. If he'd asked about a late-night appearance outside her window, she would have backed so far away from him she'd be standing in the next county. Wouldn't she?

Paul hopped into his buggy and shook the reins to get his horse clip-clopping toward home. Chores were waiting, and some were overdue. He hadn't planned to stay so long at the Masts' house. He'd simply lost all track of time. He always tended to do that in Rosanna's presence. And Mollie's, too. Paul hadn't paid a lot of attention to little ones before, but Mollie captivated him. Sure, he played with various *kinner* at gatherings and after Sunday church services, but Mollie was totally different. Totally special.

Paul had told Rosanna he would pray for her. And he would. He had been. He prayed Rosanna would not have to relinquish Mollie to the care of a woman who might not even be a fit parent. He asked the Lord Gott to keep Rosanna and Mollie safe and healthy. He asked the Lord Gott to remove Rosanna's worry and to give her peace. And maybe it was selfish, but he prayed Rosanna's heart would turn to him.

As the buggy bumped along the dirt driveway toward his family's big two-story home, a sudden inspiration struck him like a bolt of lightning zigzagging earthward from a black storm cloud. What if he and Rosanna were married? They'd have a stable home, complete with a *mamm* and *daed*. Rosanna wouldn't be a single *mudder*. The officials would have to look favorably on that, wouldn't they? Convincing Rosanna to cooperate with this half-baked plan might be a problem, though.

Paul knew beyond the shadow of a doubt Rosanna would do anything for Mollie—maybe even agree to marriage. But he wanted Rosanna to marry him because she wanted to spend her life with him, not merely to present a perfect family image. He wanted her to love him as he loved her.

Whew! Paul smacked his own forehead. That thought crept up on him out of nowhere. But, *jah*, he did love Rosanna Mast, and he desired, more than anything, to make her his *fraa* and Mollie his *dochder*.

The horse had stopped beside the barn and was waiting for Paul to unhitch him. Paul hadn't even noticed. He sat gasping and unable to force his legs to propel him from the buggy. That realization had rendered him breathless and motionless. *Dear Gott, is it too much to ask that Rosanna see me as more than a freind?*

Chapter Twenty-Four

"Anybody home?"

Rosanna heard the voice from where she sat in the rocking chair next to the living room stove with Mamm's mending basket at her feet. Mollie had drifted off into her afternoon nap in the nearby cradle. Rosanna dropped the pair of James' pants she'd been repairing and hurried toward the back door.

"Emma! It's *gut* to see you."

"Brrr! I'll be glad when spring gets here."

"I'm afraid you'll have a bit of a wait." Rosanna wrapped her hand around Emma's arm and tugged her *freind* closer to the big black woodstove. "Tobias is still at work, you know." Rosanna couldn't prevent a sly smile from curving her lips.

"Ha! Ha! You're so funny. For your information, I came to see you and that adorable little girl."

"Only Mollie is adorable? Not me?"

"At the moment, *nee*. You're mischievous."

Rosanna slapped a hand across her chest and gasped. "You wound me."

Emma giggled. "You're certainly silly today. By the way, where is that adorable little girl?"

"She's taking a nap in the living room."

"Oops! I should be quieter, then." Emma dropped her voice to a whisper.

Rosanna chuckled. "It is very rarely quiet around here. Mollie is used to sleeping with all sorts of things going on in the background."

"If you say so."

"If you've warmed up, take off your cloak and sit a spell. Would you like some tea?"

"A cup of hot tea would be great." Emma untied her black bonnet.

"Regular or herb tea?" Rosanna picked up the kettle and shook it to make sure it still contained enough water.

"What kind of herb tea do you have?"

Rosanna sorted through the boxes on a shelf. "Raspberry, mint, or orange. Unless you want chamomile so you can take a nap with Mollie."

"Raspberry will be fine."

Rosanna plopped a raspberry tea bag in one mug and a regular tea bag in another. "There are oatmeal cookies in the cookie jar, too. Help yourself."

"Did you make them?"

"*Jah.*"

"You always make the best cookies—a little soft, yet a little crispy. I don't know how you do that."

Rosanna shrugged. "I don't do anything special." She poured steaming water into the mugs. "We can sit in here or in the living room."

"I'm not interrupting anything, am I?" Emma grabbed a handful of cookies before plunking down at the kitchen table.

"Nothing that can't wait. Mamm has gone to check on Becky and the twins, so I decided to start on the mending. I was just beginning to let out the hems on

James' pants. That *bu* is growing faster than a weed in the summer vegetable garden."

"I don't want to keep you from your work." Emma spoke around the huge bite of cookie in her mouth.

"Trust me, I'd rather sit and talk to you." Rosanna stirred a spoonful of sugar into her mug. "Do I owe this visit to anything special?"

"Can't I visit my best *freind* without a special reason?"

"Of course you can. I only wondered if you had anything in particular you wanted to discuss while we had some time to ourselves."

Emma swallowed another bite of cookie and raised her mug to her lips. She quickly lowered it. "Oooh, that's hot!"

"Maybe that's why it's called hot tea."

Emma wrinkled up her nose. "I didn't drop by to discuss anything in particular. I simply wanted to visit a bit."

"Okay. I'm glad you're here."

"To save you from hemming James' pants?"

Rosanna laughed. "Well, that, too."

While the girls talked and laughed and munched cookies, Rosanna's worries faded into the background. She couldn't help but think how much fun it would be if Tobias and Emma ended up together. There wasn't anyone else she'd like better for a *schweschder*-in-law. She couldn't resist a little probing. "So, Emma, are you and Tobias, uh, interested in each other?"

"Don't be ridiculous!" The rosy spots that danced on Emma's cheeks belied her words. "What about you and Paul Hertzler?"

Now Rosanna squirmed. "Paul has been a great *freind*."

"Really? I think there's more to it than that. I hear he's even fond of Mollie."

"Where do you get such information?"

"A little birdie told me."

"Well, don't believe every little tweet you hear."

"I think Paul would be a perfect match for you."

"And I think Tobias would be a perfect match for you."

"Let's call a truce." Emma reached for the last cookie on her napkin. "I'll finish my cookie, and then I'd better get home to help Mamm with supper."

"You'll be too full of cookies to have any supper."

"I did eat quite a few of them, didn't I?" Emma pushed a wisp of baby-fine, pale blonde hair off her cheek. "This hair of mine won't stay where it belongs. I have a notion to cut off this misbehaving strand."

Rosanna laughed. "Then it would look all lopsided when you took it down."

"I'm the only one who would see it."

"For now. One day your husband will see your hair."

"It will have grown another foot by then." Emma poked the last bite of cookie in her mouth before glancing up. "I'd better go. It's too bad Mollie didn't wake up. I would have liked to hold her." Emma scooted her chair back from the table and stood. "Are you expecting company?"

"*Nee.* Why?"

Emma nodded toward the window directly across from her. "A car is driving up your driveway."

"A car?" Rosanna's heart pounded like a jackhammer inside her chest. "A green car?"

"*Jah.* An odd shade of green." Emma turned away from the window to look at her *freind.* "Rosanna, what's wrong? Your face is as white as freshly fallen snow."

"Kandi. It must be Mollie's *aenti.*"

"Maybe I should slip out the back door and cut through the woods."

"Stay. Please stay, Emma."

"Are you afraid of her?"

"Not of *her*, but I am afraid to hear what she might say." Rosanna jumped to her feet and glanced out the window. She didn't need another look to be sure. "It's her all right."

"I'll stay, if you want." Emma scooted next to Rosanna and squeezed her hand. "*Ach!* Your hand is like a block of ice. Didn't the tea warm you up?"

"It did, but my nerves just shot ice throughout my whole body."

"Everything will be all right."

"I hope so. That's what everyone keeps telling me. I pray they are right. I wonder why she's back again so soon." If Rosanna's heart beat any faster, she wouldn't be able to catch her breath. She willed herself to calm down.

"I guess we'll find out what she wants in a minute." Emma cast another glance toward the window. "She's getting out of the car." She looked back at Rosanna. "Breathe!"

"I'm trying." Rosanna lunged forward, dragging Emma with her.

"What are you doing?" Emma stumbled behind Rosanna.

"I want to catch her before she knocks on the front door. I'd rather she came in back here instead of where Mollie is napping."

"Okay. What kind of name is Kandi Kottyn?"

"It's probably her performing name or whatever they call it."

"Oh." Emma raised up on tiptoe to peer out the window over Rosanna's head. "Her hair kind of looks like cotton candy, ain't so? It's bushy and an unusual color."

Rosanna stifled a giggle. "I don't think it's her natural color. Hush, now. I'm going to let her in."

"This should be interesting."

"Shhh!" Rosanna yanked open the back door and stuck her head out. "Kandi?"

The woman stopped in mid-stride and whipped her head around. Long silver earrings swung on either side of her head. "Oh, Rosanna, you startled me."

"I'm sorry. Would you *kumm* in this way, please?"

"Sure. If that's what you want."

Rosanna wondered how Kandi walked in the pointy-toed, high-heeled boots without wobbling or twisting an ankle. What use would such things be in the ice or snow? She supposed they must be designed for style rather than function. "I-I wasn't expecting you today." Did that sound too rude?

"I couldn't exactly pick up a phone and call you to arrange a visit."

"I suppose not, but Mamm did give you a number where you could leave a message."

The other woman merely shrugged.

"It's awfully cold today. *Kumm* get warm by the stove." Rosanna figured Kandi must be extra cold in her way-too-short skirt and thin leopard print jacket that barely came to her waist. A poke to her back made her remember her manners. "Kandi, this is my *freind* Emma. We were just having tea and cookies. Won't you join us?" She didn't mention that they'd nearly finished their tea and Emma had scarfed down all the cookies on the plate. She could always pour more tea and retrieve cookies from the jar.

Kandi picked her way up the steps and sashayed

into the mudroom. Rosanna scarcely kept from choking on the nearly overpowering floral scent that filled the room like fog. Emma actually did cough and gulped when Rosanna elbowed her.

"It certainly is a frosty day." Kandi gave an exaggerated shiver.

"Well, you don't have on a very heavy coat." Emma's mumble earned her another jab from Rosanna.

"There's hot water in the kettle. I can pour you tea or *kaffi* to help you warm up." Rosanna gave Emma a stern look before pointing Kandi toward the kitchen. She really couldn't be upset with Emma, though. Her *freind* merely voiced Rosanna's own thoughts.

"I came to see Mollie, and I don't have a lot of time."

"Of course. Mollie should be waking up from her nap any second."

"She's always sleeping when I get here."

"*Bopplin* tend to sleep a *gut* bit," Emma muttered.

Rosanna frowned in Emma's direction but wanted to smile. "Would you like something to drink while you wait?"

Kandi huffed out a sigh. "I guess, if you won't wake her up."

"She'll be in a more receptive mood if she wakes up on her own."

Kandi shoved up a sleeve to expose the watch surrounded by four clinking bangle bracelets circling her wrist. "I can wait a little while, but not too long. I'll take a cup of tea. As usual, I've had enough coffee to float a battleship."

"Sure. Have a seat at the table. I'll only be a minute. Would you like some cookies?" Rosanna set another mug on the counter. "Is regular tea okay, or do you prefer herbal?"

"Regular. That herbal stuff is nasty."

Rosanna poured hot water over the tea bag and set the mug in front of her guest. She slid sugar and honey across the table and added cookies to the empty plate in case Kandi decided she wanted a snack. With nothing else to do, she dropped onto the chair next to Emma and sat on her hands to keep from fidgeting.

"Oops!" Kandi's vigorous stirring caused tea to slosh over the side of the mug.

"Don't worry about it." Rosanna passed a couple of paper napkins across the table.

Kandi dabbed at the spill and stirred some more before finally removing the spoon from the mug. She sat back in the chair and ran a hand through her platinum hair.

On closer inspection, Rosanna thought the hair resembled a bristly dish-scrubbing pad rather than cotton candy. She rummaged through her brain to find a neutral topic of conversation. Did the other two women feel the oppressive tension in the room, or was it just her? "Do you have to work tonight, Kandi?"

"Yeah. I have a rehearsal for a play that I'm in, and then I have to dance at one of the bigger clubs downtown." She chomped and popped her gum.

"You certainly have a busy schedule."

"I don't always have two things in one night, so I wouldn't always be away from Mollie most of the evening."

Icy fingers squeezed Rosanna's heart. Kandi still planned to take the *boppli* to the city, where she'd be left with strangers for hours on end and possibly all night? Rosanna's gut wrenched, and she half expected the oatmeal cookies she had eaten to reappear at any moment. "Y-you s-still . . . ?" Rosanna couldn't even get the words out.

Kandi made an especially loud popping noise with her gum before gulping the steaming tea. Rosanna winced. That tea had to be nearly boiling hot. How did Kandi swallow it without yelping in pain? Her own throat would have been on fire. She knew a horrified expression must have crossed her face.

Kandi burst out laughing, almost spraying tea everywhere. "You should see your face!" She slapped the table with one palm. "Your expression is priceless. I should record it for that funniest video show." She ran an index finger under each eye, smudging the black eye makeup and giving herself a raccoon face. "Trust me. I'm used to drinking super-hot beverages. With my crazy hours, I down a lot of hot coffee to get myself going when I have to be up early."

"Oh." That's all Rosanna could utter. So who would get up early to change and feed Mollie?

"And to answer what I think you were about to ask me earlier, I haven't gotten any legal papers drawn up yet."

Rosanna let out the breath that had stalled somewhere between her lungs and nose. Hope surged, only to be dashed by Kandi's next words.

"That doesn't mean I'm not planning to. I just haven't been up in time, uh, had the time to see a lawyer yet."

"Do you have someone to watch Mollie at night while you work? I imagine a nighttime babysitter would be harder to find." Emma asked the question Rosanna couldn't get out.

"Not specifically, but I can probably get whichever of the girls I know who doesn't have a gig that particular night to babysit. We all help each other out."

Mollie wouldn't even have the security of a consistent babysitter. The poor little girl wouldn't have any stability in her life at all.

"Do some of the other girls have *kinner*, I mean, children?" Emma must have been reading her mind. Rosanna wondered the same thing. She couldn't decide if having other little ones around would be a plus or a minus.

"A few of them do."

"So you've helped them care for their children while they worked?" At least that would have given her a little experience.

Kandi threw up her hands. "Oh no! Not me! Changing diapers and cleaning up messes." Kandi paused and wrinkled up her nose. "Well, that's just not my thing."

Did she think Mollie could change her own diapers and clean up after herself? Emma poked Rosanna's leg beneath the table, almost causing her to flinch. "Well, Mollie . . ."

"I know. Mollie wears diapers, and I'd have to clean her up when I'm home, but that's different. Mollie is family."

When she's home? Who would be raising Mollie while Kandi pursued her dream of fame and fortune? Tears burned in Rosanna's eyes. She looked down and blinked hard. Surely Kandi would change her mind and wouldn't want a *boppli* to interfere with her plans. "L-little ones tend to do better with a routine."

"Aw, kids are resilient. They can adapt to anything." Kandi resumed the gum smacking. She made a big show of looking at her watch. "Do you think the little rug rat is about ready to get up?"

Rug rat? Her sweet little angel was not a rug rat. "I'll go check on her." Rosanna focused on walking normally and not stomping off in frustration and anger. The sight of Mollie stretching and smiling instantly calmed her. "How's my precious girl? Did you have a nice nap?"

"Oh good, she's up."

Rosanna hadn't been aware that Kandi had trailed along behind her. "It looks like she just woke up. Would you like to change her?" Rosanna swallowed a chuckle when Kandi jumped back a foot.

"No, that's quite all right."

"It's really not that hard. I'll show you."

"You go right ahead. I'll take a rain check on that lesson."

Rosanna babbled to Mollie as she quickly changed the diaper. "Are you hungry, little one?" Rosanna lifted the infant from the cradle. "Let's go get your bottle." She brushed past Kandi on her return to the kitchen. Emma stood right inside the door with a hand clamped over her mouth. Rosanna could see that her *freind* would burst out laughing with any slight provocation. She had to avert her gaze to keep from laughing herself. If Emma made the tiniest snort, she'd dissolve into a gale of giggles.

Rosanna elbowed Emma as she passed by on her way to prepare a bottle. She shifted Mollie to her left arm but then decided to see if Kandi wanted to hold a clean, dry infant. After all, she drove all the way from Washington, DC, or whatever suburb she lived in. Surely she didn't make the trip to look at Mollie from a distance. How could she hope to raise the little girl if she didn't want to hold her or change her or feed her? "Would you like to hold her while I make her bottle, or would you rather do the bottle? I'll tell you what to do."

"I-I guess I can hold her. Let me sit down first." Kandi plopped onto the chair she'd recently vacated. She tugged at the short skirt. Apprehension wrinkled her brow.

"You have held her before, ain't so?" Emma spoke from the doorway, where she watched in obvious amusement.

Rosanna frowned at her, but she knew Emma would not likely pay a bit of attention to her. "Kandi held Mollie the last time she visited."

"For a few minutes, and she cried like I had pinched her or something."

Rosanna saw Emma's gaze fly to Kandi's long, red-painted fingernails. She quirked an eyebrow. Rosanna had to say something fast before Emma threw out her next barb. "It's just that you were unfamiliar to her. Are you ready?" Rosanna shuffled closer to the table.

"Shouldn't you feed her first so she doesn't start wailing?"

"I need to fix her bottle. Then you can feed her."

"What if she pukes on my clothes? Eww! Then I'd have to drive home like that, and I probably won't have time to change before my rehearsal."

"I can put a cloth over your clothes."

"Why don't you go ahead and feed her?"

"Okay, but you can hold her while I get the bottle ready." Before Kandi could protest further, Rosanna placed Mollie in the other woman's arms. She made sure Kandi got a *gut* grip on the infant before she turned away. Honestly, a grown woman was afraid of a *boppli*? Rosanna couldn't fathom such a notion. She heard Kandi mumbling but couldn't decipher the words.

"Are you about ready? She's squirmy." Kandi's voice rose a notch or two in volume and pitch.

Rosanna shook the bottle on her way back to the table and held it out to Kandi.

The woman jerked back so hard she shook the chair and startled Mollie, who let out a shriek. Kandi held a whimpering Mollie out toward Rosanna. "See, I told you she cries with me. Maybe if you'd fed her first she wouldn't have hollered."

"Maybe if you hadn't jerked so hard you wouldn't have scared her," Emma offered.

Kandi ignored Emma. "Here. Take her. I need to go anyway." She held the infant even farther away from her. Mollie's whimpering turned into sobbing.

Rosanna set the bottle on the table and gathered the *boppli* close. "It's okay, my precious one." She gently swayed to and fro until Mollie calmed.

As soon as her arms were free, Kandi jumped to her feet. "I've got to go." She pulled at her skirt and jacket to straighten them. "Traffic is a nightmare, you know, and I can't be late for my rehearsal." Her high-heeled boots clacked across the linoleum floor. "I'll let myself out. Bye, Mollie." She brushed past Emma and headed toward the mudroom.

"Bye," Rosanna called to the air. She lowered herself onto a chair and offered Mollie the bottle. She stared openmouthed at Emma.

When the back door slammed, Emma broke the silence. "She probably could have gotten away even faster if she hadn't been balancing on those stilts."

Rosanna burst out laughing, releasing the nervous tension that had risen to an almost intolerable level. Mollie stopped sucking and smiled around the nipple in her mouth. "Emma is awful, isn't she, Mollie?"

"*Nee*, Emma is truthful. How does that woman think she can care for an infant if she doesn't even want to hold her or change her? Did you see her expression when you handed Mollie to her? She looked like you handed her a copperhead." Emma imitated Kandi's expression, sending both young women into peals of laughter.

Rosanna gulped in air as she raised Mollie to her shoulder and patted her back. "Emma Kurtz, you should be ashamed of yourself."

"For telling the truth? Rosanna, I truly don't think that Cotton Candy girl will pursue custody, even if she does feel a pang of conscience since Mollie is her niece."

"I don't know, Emma. People sometimes do strange things."

Chapter Twenty-Five

Rosanna greeted each day with a shiver of fear. Would this be the day she received notification that Kandi had filed for custody of Mollie? Sundays were the only days she awoke with peace in her heart. As far as she knew, *Englisch* lawyers did not work on Sundays, and there would not be any mail delivery. Rosanna could completely enjoy the day and every moment with Mollie, her family, and her community.

She had begun to feel more comfortable with the other young *mudders*, and many of her single *freinden* made a point to speak to her and Mollie. Some, like Emma, encouraged her to take part in their activities. Right now, though, Rosanna felt she had to exhibit exemplary behavior. She had to act mature at all times and be a perfect *mamm*. She couldn't risk anyone official showing up unexpectedly to catch her romping around with the other young people.

"We need you to even out the volleyball teams." Emma jogged over to Rosanna after the common meal on Sunday.

"It's cold outside. I think I'll take Mollie in the house." The three-hour church service and meal afterward had been held in a neighbor's big barn. Once folks had finished eating and drifted off in clumps to talk, the temperature in the barn had plummeted. Most *mudders* headed to the warm house with their little ones.

"You'll get warm when you start playing. Your *mamm* will watch Mollie for a little while, ain't so?"

"I'm sure she would, but I don't want to ask her to do that. Mollie is my responsibility."

"I understand, but you can still do something fun. I don't think anyone here will report that you abandoned your *boppli* or anything like that."

"I know, but I still worry."

"Women still have lives even after they have *kinner*."

"I know that, too, but their priorities change. You'll find out."

"Okay, Rosanna. I won't press you. Do what you're comfortable with." Emma squeezed Rosanna's arm. "How about if I join you and Mollie inside?"

Rosanna smiled. Emma was such a dear *freind*. "That's nice of you, Emma, but you go ahead and play. You love volleyball. When your game is over or you get too cold, then you can visit with me."

"I don't know. I don't want you to be alone."

"I won't be. Please, go on and play."

"Are you sure?"

"Absolutely. See you later." Rosanna turned and headed for the house. She didn't want Emma to sacrifice her fun with the other young folks. If she stayed there talking, Emma would miss the game altogether, and Mollie might get too cold.

Most of the older women had gathered in the kitchen to chat. The younger women sat in the living room with their young *kinner*, who played quietly on the floor. Some had already been put down for naps in a bedroom.

"Ah! It feels so nice in here." Rosanna hurried into the warmth of the living room.

"*Kumm* sit by the stove." Katie Yoder eased herself and her sleeping infant from the rocking chair closest to the big woodstove.

"You don't have to get up, Katie." Rosanna held out a hand to stop the pretty young woman, who was probably only a year or two older than she was.

"I've been sitting here for a while. Joanna and I are sufficiently toasted. Here." She patted the chair.

"*Danki.*" Katie's thoughtful gesture warmed Rosanna's heart. Katie had always been kind to the younger girls when they were all scholars. Maybe Joanna and Mollie would be *freinden* one day—that is, if Mollie wasn't snatched from her. Rosanna returned Katie's smile. She would not think worrisome thoughts today.

It had been a pleasant day. Darkness crept in early, like a shade slowly pulled down over a window. Tobias had left for the singing a short time ago. Rosanna knew he was probably glad to go without her so he could do as he pleased and not be responsible for bringing her home. Maybe he and Emma would slip out for a ride afterward. Rosanna smiled.

She sank wearily onto the cushioned rocking chair with her knitting bag in her lap. She had fed Mollie and tucked her into her crib for the night. What a blessing that she had been sleeping through the night for several weeks now. Rosanna still awoke several times to check on her but figured one day she would sleep through the night herself.

She sighed and set the chair rocking. If she wasn't careful, she might rock herself to sleep. She'd try to knit a few more rows on the afghan she'd been stitching for ages before seeking out her own bed.

"Tired, Dochder?" Samuel peered at her over the top of the *Budget*, the Plain newspaper he'd buried himself in. Sarah sat beside him on the couch with her own knitting needles clacking out a soft rhythm.

"I am. I'll probably go to bed soon."

"You could have gone to the singing. We'd have been more than happy to watch Mollie." Sarah paused to glance up at Rosanna.

"I know, Mamm. I'm content to stay home tonight." She pulled her needles out of the ball of yarn and began knitting. With fatigue blurring her vision, she hoped she wouldn't make a mess that she'd have to yank out the next time she attempted to knit. She'd been trying to cast her cares upon the Lord, but she still often awoke in a panic and lay praying that Mollie wouldn't be taken from her. She settled into a rocking and knitting rhythm until a knock at the front door made her drop a stitch.

"Who could that be?" Samuel laid his paper aside. "Do you have any women who might need you?" He looked over at Sarah.

"None of my patients are due right now."

The knock sounded again. Samuel grunted as he rose from the couch. "I guess I'd better let our visitor inside."

Rosanna's heart jumped when she heard the voice greeting her *daed*. She'd forgotten Paul had said he'd drop by. She had assumed he'd spoken out of politeness and wouldn't actually miss the singing.

"Look who I found out in the cold!" Samuel's lips twitched above his full beard.

"Hello, Paul. *Kumm* have a seat near the stove."

"*Danki*, Sarah. The temperature sure drops fast when the sun slides from the sky." Paul rubbed his hands together as he crossed the room. "Hi, Rosanna."

"Hi, Paul. I thought you'd be at the singing by now."

"Not tonight." He perched on the edge of the chair nearest Rosanna.

She glanced up in time to catch Samuel nod at Sarah, who promptly scrambled off the couch with her knitting bag. The two of them stole from the room, leaving Rosanna alone with Paul.

"I hope I'm not interrupting anything."

"Not at all. I'm trying to work on this afghan without making a mess of it."

"It's pretty."

"*Danki*. I don't get a lot of time to work on it these days." She quickly finished the row and plunged the needles back into the ball of yarn for safekeeping.

"I don't want to keep you from your knitting. You can go ahead."

"That's okay. My eyes get bleary by evening anyway."

"I don't want to keep you up. If you're tired and want to get some sleep, I'll understand."

Sarah poked her head into the room. "There is applesauce cake if you want a snack. Or lemon pie, if you prefer. Samuel and I are going upstairs."

"Okay, Mamm. *Gut nacht.*" Why did her parents believe they had to make themselves scarce? Surely they knew she and Paul weren't courting. Now she fought nervousness again. "Would you like pie or cake?"

"Maybe later."

Rosanna nodded. "Didn't you want to attend the singing tonight?"

"Not really." Paul looked at the floor and mumbled, "You weren't going to be there."

Rosanna gulped. What should she say to that? "I-I thought it would be better to stay home tonight."

"I understand. Have you heard anything?"

"Kandi visited again. Her visits are awfully disturbing."

"How so?"

"She says she plans to take Mollie, or to try to take her, in one breath but talks about her crazy work hours in the next one. She won't change Mollie or feed her. She'll barely even hold her. I don't know if she's afraid or if she thinks Mollie will get her dirty or what. When I put the *boppli* in her arms, you'd have thought I handed her a snake." Rosanna shook her head and absently picked at her nails. "What kind of life would that be for Mollie? She'd feel so unloved." Rosanna sniffed and picked harder at her nails.

"Surely the authorities would investigate how Mollie would be cared for if Kandi filed for custody, wouldn't they?"

Rosanna shrugged and continued picking her nails. "Mollie doesn't have a *daed*, but then Kandi is single, too. At least here Mollie has lots of other family members to care for her."

"Do you think it would make a difference?"

"What do you mean?"

"If Mollie had a *daed*."

"They'd probably see that as a stable family unit, but there are lots of single parents. At least that's what Amy Rogers said."

Paul's voice dropped to whisper level. "We can remedy that problem."

"What problem?" And "we" who?

"The issue of Mollie not having a *daed*."

"How?"

Paul reached to still Rosanna's fidgeting fingers. He left his hand on hers. "We could get married. Then Mollie would have two parents."

Rosanna's breath caught. Her heart skipped a beat. Surely she hadn't heard Paul correctly. He was speaking too softly. That was it. "What did you say?" Rosanna sat forward, thinking that would help her hear better.

"We could get married." Paul repeated the words slightly louder. "You know how fond I am of Mollie."

"Marriage is forever, Paul, not something to be undertaken simply to solve a problem."

"I'm well aware of that."

"That means once the issue of Mollie's custody is settled, we'd still be . . ."

"I'm okay with that."

Just okay? Shouldn't there be some sort of declaration of caring, if not love? Did Paul only care about Mollie or did he care about her as well? His proposition sounded like a business deal or a bargain at the market, not like any marriage proposal she had ever heard of or hoped for. She opened her mouth, but not even a squeak came out.

"I know I took you by surprise, Rosanna."

"That's for sure and for certain."

"And I probably said everything all wrong."

"I guess I don't understand. Why would you offer to make such a serious, permanent commitment? Why would you sacrifice your own happiness?"

"Who says I wouldn't be happy? We get along well. We both love Mollie."

"Shouldn't there be more than 'getting along well'?"

Rosanna thought of her parents. They obviously loved each other very much. She'd seen glances of love pass between her *bruders* and their *fraas*, too. Was love too much to hope for?

"I think there would be." Paul took one of her hands between his much larger ones. "You know I care about you, don't you, Rosanna?"

People cared about their horses and dogs, too. "I know you have been a *wunderbaar freind*."

"Lots of couples start out as *freinden* first."

His words might be true, but those couples usually fell in love before they considered getting married. She didn't want to enter marriage hoping her husband would love her one day. "You'd do this for Mollie?"

"For all of us. You are the best *mamm* for Mollie. I want to do everything possible to make sure she stays with you."

Rosanna didn't know what to think, much less what to say.

"I know this came as a surprise."

"Shock" might be a better word. Rosanna merely nodded.

"Will you at least think about it? I really believe we could provide a *gut* home for Mollie and be happy together. Please say you'll consider my offer."

Rosanna nodded again.

"I'll let you get some sleep. I'll talk to you soon." With that, Paul slipped from the room and from the house.

Rosanna rocked. Her knitting slipped from her lap and landed in a heap at her feet. *I didn't offer him any cake or pie.* For goodness' sake, after everything that had transpired, she was fretting over not offering a snack? Her sigh sounded like a gale force wind whistling through the silent room. A loud pop from the stove startled her.

Of all the things she and Paul could have discussed, a marriage of convenience would never have cropped up in her wildest imaginings. And that's what it would be. If there wasn't any love, the marriage would be only a handy solution to a problem. Could she live with that—even if it might help her keep her *boppli*?

Chapter Twenty-Six

Could he have possibly done a worse job than that? Paul didn't even notice the cold or the frost that had already formed to make the winter-weary grass crunch under his feet. Nor did he see the vast array of stars twinkling overhead in the ebony sky. He'd sounded like he was trying to make a deal at a horse auction, not like he was asking the girl of his dreams to marry him. Had he once mentioned he cared about Rosanna, or had he merely offered a proposition for helping her keep Mollie? He couldn't remember exactly what he had said. He had barely been able to hear his own words with his heart thumping like a hundred hammers pounding in his ears. Arggh! How could he have made such a mess of things? It was a wonder Rosanna didn't toss him out the front door and stomp upstairs in a huff.

She wouldn't do that, though. Rosanna was the kindest, sweetest, most considerate person he knew. And her dark hair and chocolate drop eyes made many an appearance in his dreams. Had he told her any of that? *Nee!* What was wrong with him? He climbed into his buggy and clucked to the horse. Thankfully the horse knew his way home, because Paul wasn't paying a bit of attention to where he was or where he was going.

He tried to calm himself and to justify his behavior. Even though he was twenty-four, he hadn't had a whole lot of experience with girls. He'd certainly never asked one to marry him. He'd thought about asking to take Rosanna home after a singing, but he'd thought too long and ended up watching her talk to Henry Zook instead. At least that relationship had gone nowhere fast, especially after Mollie arrived.

Mollie. What a sweet *boppli*. Was he ready to take on the challenge of parenthood? He thought so. *Nee*, he knew so. For some reason, he'd been captivated by Mollie ever since her birth. If that wasn't the Lord Gott's will, he didn't know what was. Would he ever be able to convince Rosanna of that? He'd better figure out a way to gain her trust and maybe, just maybe, her love. That is, if he could make up for tonight's blunder.

Rosanna listened to the fire crackling in the stove beside her. She hadn't moved from the rocking chair or even reached down to retrieve her knitting. Maybe she had dozed off and simply dreamed Paul Hertzler visited this evening. She had certainly been tired when she first sat down with her parents, so that was a possibility, albeit a slim one. She was definitely wide awake now. The faint scent of spicy aftershave assured her that Paul had really been here.

The marriage proposal, if it could even be called that, was nothing like what she'd dreamed of. In her perfect dream world, her handsome suitor would declare his undying love for her and beg her to spend her life with him. She'd be totally swept off her feet and eager to accept the proposal. Paul's words had sounded like a business transaction.

Yet, he did gaze at her tenderly with those chameleon eyes, which had looked green tonight, matching his green shirt. His voice held a sincerity that couldn't be denied. Rosanna didn't have any doubt Paul would live up to his word. He would be the best husband and *daed* he could be. His fondness for Mollie was obvious. He did say he cared about both of them. But people generally cared about their *freinden*. That didn't mean they loved them the way marriage partners should love each other.

Rosanna smiled, remembering Paul's nervousness but determination to speak his mind. His desire to go to such an extreme measure as forming a permanent, irrevocable bond astounded her. What other young man would willingly abandon his own dreams to help a *freind*? Unless Paul really loved her. Could love have been the emotion that had flashed across his face and blazed in his eyes? Love for her? Love for Mollie, for sure. But for her?

She sighed and continued rocking. She closed her eyes to think. Paul was a nice fellow. Extremely nice. He was polite, helpful, and considerate. Those were all great qualities, for sure. And he was definitely pleasing to look at. Would marrying Paul be the best thing for Mollie? Would it help ensure Mollie's permanent placement with her?

Ach, Rosanna! You can't marry someone for the wrong reason. Marrying to solve a problem would be the wrong reason. Even if her heart did a funny little blip when Paul gazed into her eyes or smiled at her from across the room at church services, that did not mean marriage would be right for them. Even if marrying Paul absolutely, positively guaranteed that Mollie would remain with her, Rosanna couldn't do it. She wanted a marriage based on love, trust, and common beliefs.

She was pretty sure she and Paul held similar, if not identical, beliefs. She knew she could trust him with her life and with Mollie's. But did he love her? Did she love him? Life was too confusing for her poor, tired brain.

"Rosanna!"

Rosanna jerked awake. If Sarah's hand on her arm hadn't held her steady, she would have slid right out of the chair. She gasped. "Mamm! What time is it?" She reached up with her free hand to rub her eyes.

"A little after two in the morning. Are you all right?"

"Mollie!" Rosanna attempted to leap from the chair, but Sarah pressed her down.

"Mollie is sleeping peacefully. I checked before I came downstairs. What happened to you? Did Paul just leave?"

"*Nee.* He's been gone a long time. I sat here thinking and fell asleep." She moved her hand from her eyes to massage her aching neck. "I think my neck is broken."

"A wooden rocking chair, even one with a cushion, does not make the most comfortable bed."

"What are you doing up, Mamm?"

"I got up to use the bathroom, and I saw a flickering light downstairs. I feared the house was on fire."

"I'm sorry I worried you."

"That's okay. If I hadn't investigated, your poor neck would be broken for sure. Did Paul say or do something to upset you?"

"Of course not." Rosanna couldn't say she was upset. Perplexed or confused, but not upset. "I guess I should get to bed." She leaned over to pick up her knitting and almost toppled out of the chair. Again Sarah steadied her. "I guess I'm more tired than I thought." She attempted a smile.

"Rosanna, do you . . ."

"I'll put another piece of wood in the stove and be right upstairs."

"In other words, I should mind my own business and leave you alone."

Rosanna squeezed her *mamm*'s hand. "Of course not. I just don't have anything to say." Not now, anyway.

"Okay." Sarah's deep sigh sounded like pure exasperation. "We can talk tomorrow—well, make that later today."

Rosanna nodded. She doubted she'd reveal the details of Paul's visit later, either. She stuffed her knitting into its bag and stood on stiff legs. She raised one knee and then the other in an effort to work out the kinks. She laid her bag on the chair to use both hands to add a big chunk of wood to the stove. That should keep the fire going until she got up for the day in only a couple of hours.

What seemed only moments later, the fat, loud rooster announced the approach of dawn. Rosanna groaned as she flung off the covers. There wasn't any use lying there wishing she could stay in bed. She needed to help with breakfast and get ready to tend to Mollie. She had hoped the Lord Gott would have sent an angel to whisper in her ear as she catnapped. To her dismay, she awoke without an answer and without a single idea of what she should say to Paul the next time she saw him. Would he return for an answer today? *Ach!* There was one more worry to add to her growing list. She hurried to dress and stumbled down the stairs.

"You did get up. I thought you might sleep a bit later since you had such a rough night." Sarah glanced over her shoulder in the middle of flipping pancakes.

"I wouldn't do that. Do you want me to pack lunches or help with breakfast?"

"Lunches are ready. You can stir the oatmeal and make some orange juice."

"You must have gotten up extra early. You did go back to bed, didn't you, Mamm?" Rosanna knew her *mudder* was used to catching snatches of sleep here and there ever since she started tending to laboring women years ago. She seemed to have boundless energy, but then could drop off to sleep in an instant.

"I did, but I was restless, so I figured I'd get the day underway."

"Not at two in the morning."

Sarah chuckled. "Not quite that early, but I did manage to get out of bed before that old rooster woke up this morning. Did you hear any sound from your *schweschders*?"

"Not a peep."

"Would you holler for them, please? Daed and the *buwe* will be in by the time those two finish dawdling."

"Do you want to tell me what's troubling you?" Sarah dropped three plastic juice cups into the dishwater.

With silence reigning in the kitchen at last, this would be the perfect time to confide in her *mamm*. Everyone else had been sent off to school or work.

Mollie had been fed and now happily kicked and cooed in the playpen. Yet Rosanna couldn't bring herself to divulge her quandary. She watched the cups bob among the bubbles in the sink. "Nothing is troubling me."

"And I just dropped to the planet from outer space."

Rosanna smiled. "Nothing really different is bothering me. How's that?" She didn't dare look in Sarah's direction. Her *mudder* had the uncanny ability to read her like a book. She picked up a cup and swirled the dishrag in and over it. "Do you think we'll hear something from Kandi?"

"Only the Lord Gott knows that. We haven't heard anything yet, so maybe that's a *gut* sign."

"Do you think there is anything I can do to make sure Mollie stays with me other than hope and pray?"

"I think those are the best things to do."

Rosanna nodded. She rinsed the cup and set it in the drainer. She snagged the next floating cup and repeated the process. Her thoughts swam like the little cups. "You and Daed loved each other before you got married, ain't so? I mean, you didn't learn to love each other afterward."

"Our love has grown deeper and stronger over the years, but we did love each other before we took our vows."

"I know I've asked you before, but how did you know he was the one for you? Was it love at first sight?"

Sarah laughed. "We were *freinden* first, so we cared about each other in that way. Gradually we found ourselves pairing off more and more at the young folks' gatherings and realized our feelings had changed. Your *daed* was always considerate and kind. And he always made me laugh."

Paul had always been considerate and kind and totally selfless. He did make her smile, and he was *wunderbaar* with Mollie. Could he be the one for her? Could their feelings grow in time? Did she have to make a decision immediately, or could she take the time to let things take their course naturally?

"Is there a special reason you're asking these questions today?"

"Just curious, that's all."

Sarah cupped a hand under Rosanna's chin, forcing her to look up. "Are you sure?"

Rosanna met her *mamm*'s inquiring eyes briefly before dropping her gaze to the counter. "*Jah.*"

Sarah lowered her hand. "You aren't still thinking of Henry Zook, are you?" She lifted the heavy cast-iron skillet and handed it to Rosanna.

"Henry? *Nee.* He and I definitely were not right for each other." Rosanna plunged the skillet into the water.

"It's best to know that early on."

"For sure."

"Do you have your sights on someone else?"

Rosanna shook her head but felt heat creep into her cheeks. "Not yet." She focused on the skillet and scrubbed it with all her might.

Chapter Twenty-Seven

Rosanna laughed as she tried to capture Mollie's wiggling arms and legs to wrap her in a warm blanket. The *boppli* had sure grown. She constantly exhibited new skills that Rosanna marveled over. It hardly seemed possible that two weeks had passed and church day had rolled around again.

She hadn't heard a word from Kandi Kottyn but did not let down her guard. It could be that the woman was away on some acting or dancing job and would pursue custody when she returned. Rosanna still held her breath whenever she pulled the mail from the big metal box at the end of the driveway. Her heart pounded as she riffled through the envelopes in search of some official-looking one.

Rosanna hadn't heard from Paul during the past two weeks, either. She didn't know if he had been busy or if he'd been giving her time to think or if he had changed his mind altogether. That last thought brought a tinge of sadness. She would be disappointed if he'd decided taking on a girl with a *boppli* would be too hard, especially with a possible forthcoming legal battle. It wasn't their way to become involved in lawsuits and legal matters, but Rosanna would do whatever she had to in order to keep Mollie.

She finally succeeded in securing all four limbs in the blanket and gathered the bundled infant in her arms. "You're such a squirmy little thing. And you're growing up so fast." Rosanna had learned to make sure she was completely ready first so she wouldn't have to lay Mollie down and risk all her efforts coming undone. "We're ready." She was certain Mamm had Katie, Sadie, and James in presentable condition by now. She hurried through the house to meet up with the rest of the family near the back door.

Rosanna stopped short at the sight of Micah Zook, Henry's older *bruder*, standing in their kitchen. He twisted his black felt hat in his hands while talking to Sarah. From the snippet of conversation Rosanna overheard, she gathered Micah's *fraa*, Lydia, had gone into labor.

"Katie, run get my bag," Sarah ordered.

"I'll *kumm* with you, Mamm." Rosanna set the diaper bag on the table.

"It's a first *boppli*. It could be a false alarm."

"Sh-she's having a lot of pain. A-and the pains are happening faster."

Poor Micah. He was going to shred that hat. Rosanna wondered if Paul would be so nervous if she was about to give birth. Yikes! Where did that thought *kumm* from. "It doesn't sound like a false alarm, Mamm."

"What about Mollie?"

"I'll bring her. I'm sure there will be other women around. I just need to grab extra formula and a couple more diapers. I want to help." Rosanna glanced around. "Sadie, would you grab a few more diapers, please?" She shoved a whole can of powdered formula and an extra clean bottle into her already full diaper bag. Katie and Sadie nearly collided in their mad dash back to the kitchen.

"You girls go on to the buggy," Sarah said. "Rosanna and I will go with Micah."

"Who will we sit with?" Sadie tugged at her *mudder*'s arm.

"Your *daed* will decide. Behave yourselves." Sarah gave each one a hug. She looked over their heads and rolled her eyes at Rosanna, who smiled. Her *schweschders* could be a handful, but they would probably be on their best behavior under Daed's watchful eye.

Rosanna was eager to help her *mamm* bring a new life into the world. Yet, a pang of regret at not seeing Paul today shot through her.

Micah had *gut* reason to be nervous. Lydia was indeed in labor and progressing rapidly. She paced the entire upper floor of their house between contractions, and Rosanna trotted along beside her. When a pain hit, Lydia paused to grab Rosanna's hand. When each pain subsided, she apologized for squeezing the life out of Rosanna's fingers.

"It's okay," Rosanna assured her. "I'm tough." When Lydia wasn't looking, Rosanna flexed and straightened her fingers to make sure they still functioned properly.

Sarah bustled about transforming the bedroom into a birthing room. Usually Rosanna helped with that, but Lydia had latched onto Rosanna immediately and claimed Rosanna helped her relax. Rosanna did her best to distract the laboring woman by regaling her with Mollie's accomplishments or telling her funny stories about Katie and Sadie. "Do you and Micah have names picked out?" Rosanna mopped Lydia's brow with a cool cloth when they stopped pacing for a moment.

"Sort of. We have names we like, but I want to see the *boppli* first before I make a final decision."

"That makes sense." Rosanna had considered several names before deciding on "Mollie."

Suddenly Lydia sucked in a breath, held it, and grabbed Rosanna's hand.

"Don't hold your breath. Breathe through the contraction." Rosanna demonstrated. She wondered if she'd remember her own advice if she ever gave birth. "Let me know whenever you want to lie down."

Lydia nodded and squeezed harder. Rosanna hoped she'd have feeling left in her fingers later. Every few minutes, Micah hollered up the stairs, and every time Lydia replied she was fine.

"Mollie is such a *gut* little girl." Lydia paused in the pacing she had resumed to gaze at Mollie sleeping on a blanket in the corner of the room. "I hope my *boppli* is as sweet." She gritted her teeth. "You're lucky to have a *boppli* without going through this pain."

Rosanna laughed. "They say you forget about the pain once you hold your little one in your arms."

"I hope that's true."

"It must be, or women wouldn't long for more *kinner.*"

"I guess you're right. About now, I'm thinking this one will be our only one."

Rosanna laughed again. She heard Sarah stop

humming to chuckle, too. "I've heard that before, Lydia. It will be over soon."

"Not soon enough." Lydia clenched her teeth and grabbed Rosanna's hand again.

Rosanna clenched her own teeth. She had to figure out a way to maneuver herself to Lydia's other side without the girl's noticing. This poor hand needed a rest. With the pains occurring closer together and stronger, birth surely couldn't be far off. Maybe before the church service ended. Wouldn't it be a nice surprise to have the infant tucked in Lydia's arms by the time people arrived to check on them?

A change in Lydia's breathing sounded an alarm in Rosanna's brain. "Are you feeling pressure, Lydia, like you want to bear down?"

"I-I think so."

"It's time to let Mamm check you. Let's get you to the bed before the next contraction." Rosanna slipped an arm around Lydia's waist and guided her to the bedroom. She nodded in answer to Sarah's unspoken question.

Sarah hurried over to help Rosanna position Lydia on the bed. "Let's see if this wee one is getting anxious to put in an appearance." After a brief check she instructed Lydia to push with the next contraction.

"I don't know how." Lydia's breath came in little gasps.

"Your body knows what to do." Sarah patted Lydia's arm before making sure all her supplies were ready.

"We'll help you. Don't worry." Rosanna dipped her cloth in a bowl of water, wrung it out, and wiped Lydia's face.

"Have your parents returned from their trip to Ohio?"

"Not yet. W-we thought we had a few more weeks."

"I know. Sometimes *bopplin* have their own plans. That's okay, though. You're close enough."

"I'm here! What can I do to help?" Micah's *mudder* rushed into the room. "How are you doing, Lydia?"

"I-I'm okay."

Rosanna felt Lydia tense and wondered about the relationship between the two women. "Relax," she whispered as she pushed a damp strand of hair off Lydia's neck.

"She's doing just fine." Sarah took charge. "I don't think this infant wants to wait too long. Here, Miriam, you can help me over here."

Lydia's muscles relaxed when Miriam Zook hurried to do Sarah's bidding. Rosanna knew Miriam could be a bit overbearing. Lydia had always been a quiet girl, so Miriam's outspoken ways might very well be intimidating. And Rosanna doubted Micah stood up to his *mamm*. He seemed rather timid himself. From the traits Henry had displayed lately, Rosanna couldn't imagine him not standing up to Miriam, unless he behaved totally differently at home. Maybe he was more considerate of his *mamm* than he was of younger women. She was suddenly thankful she hadn't gotten any closer to joining the Zook family.

"I-I think I have to push." Lydia tensed, and a panic-stricken look crossed her face. "Help me."

"You can do this, girl. Buck up and bear down." Miriam's gruff voice traveled across the room.

Lydia's eyes filled with tears. She reached for Rosanna's hand again. "Breathe." Rosanna demonstrated regular breaths.

"Just do what *kumms* naturally, girl. Women have been giving birth since Eve. And she didn't have anybody to coach her through it." Miriam didn't seem to have a sympathetic bone in her body.

"Miriam, would you mind checking on Mollie? She's waking up, and I need Rosanna's help." Sarah nodded to the corner, where Mollie was gurgling.

Rosanna knew her *mamm* was trying to get Miriam away from the frightened young woman, but she wasn't sure she wanted the grumpy woman caring for Mollie. Miriam certainly didn't display any gentle, motherly traits.

"You probably got here just in time," Sarah called. Rosanna knew her *mudder* wanted to ask why the woman hadn't been here immediately for the birth of her first grandchild.

"First *bopplin* usually take a long time. I'm sure I don't have to tell you that," Miriam snapped.

Rosanna cringed when Miriam lifted Mollie none too gently. The poor little girl looked so startled that she puckered up her face. Miriam seemed not to notice or care. She ignored Mollie and continued her conversation. "Besides, how was I to know it wasn't a false alarm? Lydia wouldn't know if she was in labor or not."

"I told you it sure seemed like the real thing. Lydia would know how the pain felt." Micah must have heard the exchange and finally came to the defense of his *fraa*.

"Your *daed* is outside. Why don't you go out with him?" Miriam shouted back. Her tone and volume caused Mollie to whimper. Rosanna wanted to rush to her little girl, but Lydia needed her right now.

"I'm staying right here, Mamm." Micah stamped a foot and resumed his pacing.

Gut for you, Micah Zook. You stick up for yourself and your fraa!

"Hmpf!" Miriam sniffed and gave Mollie a little bounce.

Sarah wiggled her eyebrows at Rosanna, who smiled in return. She had a hard time keeping one eye on Mollie and one on Lydia. She hoped Lydia's little one arrived soon.

Chapter Twenty-Eight

"Hello!" a cheerful voice called out.

Rosanna sighed in relief. She could relax more now and focus on Lydia. Mary Hertzler had arrived. She would happily relieve Miriam of caring for Mollie. The *boppli* would be happier, too, for sure. Mollie knew Mary and was used to the woman's gentle ways. Miriam was a stranger to her and did not appear to be particularly gifted with youngsters. Maybe she communicated better with older *kinner*, but Rosanna had doubts about that.

"How's our soon-to-be new *mudder*?" Mary poked her head into the room.

"She's whining, like this one." Miriam shot a disgusted glance first at Lydia and then at Mollie.

"She's doing fine." Sarah's firm voice matched the look she turned on Miriam.

"Is there anything I can do for any of you?"

"I believe everything is under control here, Mary, but *danki*." Sarah turned her attention back to Lydia.

"Well, then, I'll just steal this beautiful little girl from you, Miriam." Mary didn't get any protest from Miriam when she reached to take Mollie into her arms. "I've missed you, precious one," Mary cooed.

She snatched the diaper bag off a chair and started for the door. She looked over her shoulder to smile and wink at Rosanna. "We'll go for a little walk and then I'll feed her. She'll be fine, Rosanna."

"*Danki.*" Rosanna wanted to say how relieved she was that Mary would care for Mollie, but she believed Mary already knew that.

"Well, if you don't need me in here, I'll go downstairs to prepare food for later. I hope Lydia has food in the house." Miriam spun about to leave the room.

"Don't you want to see . . ." Rosanna stopped in mid-sentence when she caught Sarah's subtle head shake.

"Let her go," Sarah whispered when Miriam was out of earshot. "She might feel more comfortable in the kitchen. I'm pretty sure Lydia will be more comfortable."

"I. Do. Have. Food. In. The. House!"

Rosanna patted Lydia's arm. If the girl hadn't been panting for breath, she would have probably shouted those words.

"I know you do, dear." Sarah's voice could soothe any ruffled feathers. "Don't concern yourself with her. Think of the little one you will hold very soon."

Lydia tried to nod but grunted instead. "I have to push!"

"Let's go to work, then!" Rosanna supported Lydia's head and shoulders so she could put all her effort into bearing down. This would be hard work for the young woman, but the end of the ordeal was now in sight.

Rosanna only vaguely heard footsteps and new voices downstairs. She didn't detect any crying so assumed Mollie was content with Mary. She focused on Lydia and the miracle of birth. Since she might never experience such an event firsthand, helping other women bring their infants into the world was the next best thing. And Mamm always taught her something new. Each birth was unique.

Miriam should have been here, Rosanna thought an unbelievably short time later. She would have gained a whole new respect for her son's *fraa*. Lydia faced and discarded her fears, summoned up all the power and strength she possessed, and gave birth after five mighty pushes. Rosanna's tears rivaled those of the new *mudder*.

"We did it! *Danki!*" Lydia squeezed Rosanna's hand, but not nearly as hard as she had done all morning.

"*You* did it, Lydia. You were totally amazing." Rosanna squeezed back.

Sarah smiled as she dried and swaddled the newborn. "Your *boppli* is just fine. Ten fingers and ten toes. A perfect little girl."

Lydia squealed and held out her arms. "A girl. I know most want a *bu* to carry on the name and such, but I'm ever so glad to have a girl."

An ally. Rosanna figured poor Lydia needed one with Miriam around. Who knows? Maybe a little girl would soften Miriam's gruffness.

Sarah tucked the red-faced infant into Lydia's arms. "Let's get you started nursing while your little one is wide awake. Pretty soon she'll be all tuckered out from this big transition she's made, and she'll sleep deeply."

Rosanna plumped up the pillows behind Lydia. "You need to get comfortable so you don't have to bend forward and get a crick in your neck."

"Okay, but I'm not sure what to do."

"I'll help you." Rosanna helped Lydia get started nursing, the same as she helped other women they attended. "Look, she knows what to do all on her own."

"I-it isn't very comfortable. Ow!"

"Here, let's adjust things a bit." Rosanna offered all the knowledge and pointers she had gleaned until Lydia and newborn were comfortable and happy. "That's *gut*. I think you've got the hang of this." Rosanna's eyes filled with tears. The sight of a new *mudder* nursing her *boppli* always filled her with awe and longing. Would she ever nurse an infant of her own? Thank the Lord she had Mollie.

Sarah had the room looking like a bedroom again in record time. Rosanna helped her remove soiled linens from the bed without disturbing Lydia and her little one. "I'll go fetch Micah and check on Mollie." Rosanna couldn't wait to gather her own *boppli* in her arms.

She bounded down the stairs with renewed energy. Micah sped around the corner and nearly collided with her. "*Ach*, Micah!" Rosanna grabbed the banister to keep her balance.

"Lydia?"

Rosanna grinned. "Lydia is fine. Go up and meet your *dochder*."

"A girl? I have a little girl? Great!" Micah took the stairs two at a time.

"Don't fall and break your neck, Micah. They aren't going anywhere." Rosanna chuckled as she went in search of Mary and Mollie. She needed to let Miriam know about the birth, too, but she wanted to give the new parents time alone with their newborn. Knowing Miriam, she'd charge up the stairs, offer some criticism, and totally destroy the new little family's happiness. Rosanna prayed Miriam would fall in love with the *boppli* and that love would sweeten her sour disposition.

Rosanna peeked into the living room to see if Mary had taken Mollie there. Her mouth opened in a surprised O at the sight of Paul rocking Mollie in the scarred old rocker next to the stove. Man and infant seemed totally absorbed in each other. Rosanna held her breath, afraid any sound would interrupt the sweet scene. Paul talked to Mollie, who watched his face as if she understood every word he said to her. When he sang a soft, slow melody in his rich, deep voice, Rosanna's eyes filled with tears. Her heart filled with . . . what? Joy? Peace? Love? *Nee*, not love. Well, love for Mollie, for sure. But love for Paul? Of that she wasn't sure.

She didn't know if she should back away quietly so Paul didn't see her or if she should make her presence known. If she scooted right around the corner, she would still be able to hear Paul's voice, but she wouldn't cause him any embarrassment at being discovered singing. She found herself wanting to sing along but didn't dare. Ever so slowly, she inched backward. The song broke off with the last notes suspended in the air.

"Rosanna? *Kumm* on in." Paul smiled. He didn't appear the least bit flustered or embarrassed.

"That was lovely." Why did *she* feel flustered? She hadn't been the one singing. As she drew a little closer, she could detect the rose-colored blush on Paul's cheeks.

"That was a song my *mamm* used to sing to us before bedtime or nap time. When I sat down to rock Mollie, the song came to me out of the blue."

"I liked it." She didn't add that she liked the sound of his voice. He could be singing a nonsense song in a foreign language and she would enjoy it. "Mollie liked the song, too." The little girl's gaze remained fixed on Paul's face. "I don't believe I know that song. You'll have to teach it to me."

Paul smiled at Mollie before looking into Rosanna's eyes. "I'd be happy to. I hope you don't mind my holding Mollie. I know you expected to find Mamm here."

"I don't mind at all. Did Mary leave?"

"*Nee.* Miriam was banging things around so much in the kitchen and mumbling so loud, Mamm decided she should make sure everything was all right in there. I got the privilege of tending to Mollie."

"Maybe Miriam is nervous or worried."

"Maybe she's just being Miriam," Paul whispered with a wink.

Rosanna giggled but put a hand over her mouth to muffle the sound.

"How is Lydia? I thought I heard a cry upstairs."

"You did indeed. The newest member of the Zook family is a precious little girl."

"*Wunderbaar!* That should cheer Miriam up, unless she had her heart set on a *bu.*"

"Lydia and Micah are certainly delighted with their *dochder.* When I gave Micah the news, his face lit up like a fireworks display on the Fourth of July. He couldn't race up the stairs fast enough."

Paul chuckled. "Everyone is all right?"

"They are fine." Rosanna reached down to gently stroke Mollie's soft pink cheek. She gasped when Paul grasped her hand and held on to it.

"I'm sorry I haven't been by to visit lately. Things have been hopping at the store. Eli has kept me plenty busy. By the time I could have gotten cleaned up after work, it would have been too late to visit." Paul tugged on Rosanna's hand, pulling her a little closer. His already hushed tone became even quieter. "I hope you've been thinking about our last talk."

I've thought of practically nothing else.

"I don't want to rush you or anything, I only want to know that you're considering my idea."

Idea? Plan? Deal? How about proposal? Was it silly of her to want a man to confess his undying love and to propose marriage instead of striking a deal? She knew Paul didn't mean to sound like he was negotiating a bargain. He was not a cold, calculating person. A man who had just sung so sweetly to a *boppli* had to be sincere. Now he patiently waited for her response. Maybe her dreams were foolish, anyway. "I-I've been thinking about it." *About you. About us. Lord, help me!*

Rosanna cleared her throat. She had to change the subject. "I guess I should tell Miriam about the *boppli.* I wanted to give Micah and Lydia a few minutes alone with her." She slipped her hand from his and was surprised to discover she missed the warmth and support the simple gesture provided.

"That was smart thinking. I'm sure the new parents appreciated that."

"I-I'll be right back. *Danki* for watching Mollie."

"It's been my pleasure. I'm happy to do so anytime."

As Rosanna left the room, she heard Paul's whisper. "All the time."

Chapter Twenty-Nine

"What's that you're humming?"

"Huh? Was I humming?" Rosanna glanced at her *mamm* before yanking open the door of the gas-powered refrigerator. She quickly stuck her head inside to rummage around for the potato salad and pickles. Maybe the cool air would douse the flames in her cheeks. She had been humming the song Paul sang to Mollie. It was a *gut* thing she didn't know the words or Mamm might have caught her belting them out.

"*Jah*, you were definitely humming."

Rosanna turned around quickly after backing away from the refrigerator. "I don't know what the song was." She scurried to the table to set out foods for a light supper. She and Sarah hadn't been home for too long, but the rest of the family had been home all afternoon and would soon be anxious for food.

"The tune sounded familiar, but I can't place it."

Rosanna shrugged and sought out a new topic. "Do you think Miriam Zook is glad to have a little girl in the family?"

Sarah chuckled. "It's hard to tell with Miriam, but I'm sure she'll be pleased with any *boppli*. I only hope she remembers that Micah and Lydia are the parents, not her."

"She does seem to rule the roost."

"Everyone's roost."

"Mamm!"

"I'm not trying to be mean. That's the way Miriam is. Bossiness and sometimes downright surliness seem to be her nature."

"I wanted to cheer when Micah stood up for Lydia."

"A man should stand up for his *fraa*. I'm sure that came as a shock to Miriam, though."

Rosanna wondered if Paul would stand up for her. He wouldn't need to as far as his *mamm* was concerned. Mary must be one of the sweetest people to walk the earth. *Ach!* What was she thinking?

"Rosanna?"

"I'm sorry, Mamm. Did you say something?"

"Are you woolgathering?"

"I guess I'm tired."

"Are you too tired to attend the singing tonight?"

"I'm not planning to go. I told Tobias he didn't have to worry about me tagging along with him. I told him he was free to take Emma home without having me sit beside them."

"Emma?"

"Oops! Don't mind me."

"Tobias is interested in Emma?"

"Could be." Rosanna pretended to zip her lips.

"You know, I think it would be fine for you to go. I doubt anyone would be monitoring your activities on a Sunday evening."

"I don't want to take any chances. Besides, I really am tired."

"It's up to you. I don't want you to pass up every opportunity to be among the young folks, though."

"Sometimes I don't feel so young anymore."

"With Mollie sleeping through the night now, you should start to perk up a bit."

Jah, *if I could turn my brain off at night so one thought didn't compete with another.* Images of Kandi snatching Mollie away from her pushed out memories of Paul holding Mollie and his talk of marriage. "Perking up would be a blessing, for sure and for certain."

"You sound like every other weary young *mudder*. Things do get easier."

"I suppose Lydia will be joining that club now. Do you think Miriam will stay and help her?"

"She might stay around, but I don't know how much help she will be."

"Mamm!" Rosanna pretended to be shocked but couldn't resist giggling.

Sarah sighed. "I must be tired, too."

Rosanna rocked Mollie as she fed her what she hoped was the last bottle of the evening. Only the soft squeak of the rocking chair and the occasional crackle of the fire broke the silence in the room. Mamm, Daed, and all the younger *kinner* had gone to bed. Tobias hadn't returned from the singing and probably wouldn't be home for a while if he decided to take a certain someone home.

The same tune that had played in Rosanna's head all evening seeped out in a hushed tone as she rocked. She'd have to get Paul to teach her the words. Paul. He had been in her thoughts all evening, too.

He would never pressure her. That did not appear to be his way. But he did ask her a question that deserved an answer. The only thing was that she didn't know what that answer should be. She liked Paul. Maybe she more than liked Paul. She certainly experienced a depth of emotions she hadn't encountered with Henry Zook. Henry never made goose bumps dance up her arms if his fingers happened to brush hers. Henry never caused her breath to catch. Henry never made her heart sing.

Did these things spell love? Rosanna set the empty bottle on the end table next to her and lifted the drowsy *boppli* to her shoulder. She gently patted the little back as she rocked and hummed. She sure loved this wee one. If she had to give Mollie up, there would be a hole in her heart that would never mend. She would not spoil this evening by letting that worry take over.

Mollie's head plunked down on Rosanna's shoulder and her tiny body went limp. Rosanna continued to rock even though the infant had succumbed to sleep. Holding Mollie close and thinking about Paul were pleasant ways to end the day. Thoughts of Paul had become more frequent and brought more and more pleasure. The next time she saw him she'd give him some sort of answer. She couldn't keep making him wait. Now, if she could ease herself out of the rocking chair, she'd tiptoe upstairs to tuck Mollie into her crib and crawl into her own bed.

A flash of light outside startled Rosanna out of her drowsy state. It was winter, so that couldn't have been lightning. Oh, they'd had thunderstorms in winter in Southern Maryland before, but the day had been much too cold and blustery for that. She rubbed her eyes. It must have been her tired eyes playing tricks on her, or maybe Tobias had returned and was swinging a flashlight as he walked from the barn to the house. Her humming and rocking must have kept her from hearing any outside sounds. She sat perfectly still and fixed her eyes on the window. She'd wait a moment longer before resuming her plan to go to bed.

There. The light shone again. Not lightning at all. Someone stood outside flashing a light. The light wasn't moving toward the door, so it must not be Tobias. It was stationary, shining in only one direction, and that was toward her window. A sound of something tapping against the house caused her to jump. The person had thrown something at the house. Pebbles?

He'd toss one more handful of pebbles and then give up. He didn't want to awaken the entire household. As it was, only a dim glow shone through the front room windows. He didn't want to draw that person outside, either. He mentally counted the upstairs windows. He didn't want to frighten the little girls, and he sure didn't want to be tossing pebbles at Tobias' window. Tobias should still be at the singing, unless he had come home early. *Jah*, that should be Rosanna's window he'd been shining his flashlight toward.

Paul wasn't exactly sure what he was doing here tonight. After all, he had seen Rosanna earlier, and she didn't have an answer for him. He didn't want to be a pest or seem demanding. But something had compelled him to hitch up his horse and drive to the Mast house tonight. He couldn't explain it even to himself.

Maybe Rosanna was busy with Mollie or wasn't even in her room at all. Or maybe she had been so exhausted she had dropped into a sleep so sound she wouldn't hear a dump truck crash against the side of the house. He had only wanted to see her for a few minutes, to hear her voice briefly before crawling into his bed and dreaming of her. He'd even enjoy rocking Mollie again and helping Rosanna put her to bed.

That sure was a special little girl! She tugged at his heartstrings as much as her *mudder* did. He'd do anything for either of them. Somehow he needed to make Rosanna understand that. He had certainly bungled his marriage offer. Rosanna probably thought he had suggested a business deal they could shake hands on instead of a commitment based on love and respect they could seal with a kiss. He drew back his arm to toss his final handful of pebbles.

"Paul?"

Rosanna had laid Mollie in the cradle in the living room so she could investigate whatever or whoever was causing the strange happenings outside. From the height of the silhouette, she assumed the perpetrator was Paul. The shadowy figure crossed the yard toward the front porch, where she leaned over the rail.

"That was you in the front room?"

"*Jah*. Everyone else has gone to bed. Well, everyone except Tobias. He hasn't gotten home yet. I was sitting by the stove rocking Mollie."

"I hope I didn't wake her."

"*Nee*. She dropped off to sleep after she finished her bottle. I just couldn't seem to get out of the chair and go to bed."

"I'm sorry. You're probably very tired."

"I was thinking and enjoying holding Mollie."

Rosanna didn't say she wanted to spend every second she could making memories to last a lifetime in case Mollie was taken from her. She gave a little laugh. "And I keep humming that song you sang to her. I need you to teach me the words."

"I can do that."

"Would you like to *kumm* inside? It is a bit nippy out here." She rubbed her hands up and down her arms to ward off the chill.

Paul climbed the steps and stopped beside her, nearly touching her. "Sure, if you don't mind. I promise not to stay long. I know you had a busy day, even if it was Sunday."

"*Jah*, who would have thought Lydia's *boppli* would pick the Lord's day, and a church day at that, to enter the world?"

"I'm no expert, but I guess when it's time, it's time."

Rosanna laughed. "You're right about that. And Lydia's little one was definitely ready. That was one of the quickest births I've seen." The warmth of the living room beckoned. Rosanna closed the door softly behind Paul and led the way to the stove. Why had he shown up tonight playing the role of suitor? "Would you like something hot to drink?"

"I'm fine." Paul tiptoed across the room to peek into the cradle. "She looks like a little angel."

"I think so, but I'm probably prejudiced. I just laid her in the cradle to investigate the strange goings-on outside." There. She had given him an opening to explain his actions.

"I hope I didn't scare you."

"I was more confused than scared. I saw a light and then heard scratchy sounds. At first I thought I'd fallen asleep and was dreaming."

Paul turned away from the cradle to look down at Rosanna. "If you'd known it was me outside, would it have been a *gut* dream or a nightmare?"

The lamplight flickering in Paul's hazel eyes mesmerized Rosanna. She thought Paul had asked her a question. She needed to reply if she could claw her way out of the deep well she'd tumbled into.

"Never mind."

An unidentifiable emotion crossed Paul's face before he averted his gaze. Was it pain, confusion, regret, or disappointment? Or was it a little of each? *Snap out of it, girl!* "I'm sorry, Paul. I heard you. My brain kind of took a hike or something. If I had been dreaming that you were outside, it definitely would not have been a nightmare."

His face brightened enough to rival the lamplight, and a grin spread from ear to ear. "Really?"

Rosanna smiled at his enthusiasm and obvious relief. Her earlier fatigue had vanished. "Why don't we sit down, unless you'd like a snack?"

"We can sit if you're sure you don't want to grab a few minutes of sleep while Mollie is asleep."

"I'm fine."

"Okay." Almost hesitantly, Paul reached out to take Rosanna's hand. He tugged her toward the sofa and waited for her to sit. When she was situated, he lowered himself to sit close but not touching, all except for the hand he reclaimed when he sat.

Rosanna would be picking her nails right now if one of her hands hadn't been intertwined with one of Paul's. She needed to ask him if he meant this visit to be the start of a courtship, yet she hesitated to ask. If he said that was his intention, what would she say? Her heart raced. Is that what she wanted? If he said courtship was not his intention, how would she feel? Relieved? Disappointed? Hurt? Her heart thumped harder. "Paul?"

"*Jah?*"

"You shined a light in my window tonight. Do you . . . is this . . . well, exactly what is on your mind?" Rosanna slumped back, her head bumping the wall behind her. She chomped on her tongue and wished she had chomped on it a few minutes earlier so it hadn't been able to ask that question. What must Paul think of her? What would he say? She held her breath.

He squeezed her hand and chuckled softly. "I suppose I was being impatient."

"You? I doubt it."

"I told you to take your time thinking about what I asked before, but I think I went about everything all wrong."

Fear wrung Rosanna's heart. Did Paul mean he made a mistake with his offer of marriage? Why did that thought make her feel incredibly sad? Her eyes and nose burned. She waited for him to continue, knowing her own voice would catch on a sob if she tried to speak.

"I didn't mean to sound like I only wanted to marry you to improve your chance of keeping Mollie." Paul squirmed. "I do want you to keep her, but I'd like you to consider me as someone you could spend your life with."

"What if I lose Mollie? Then you'd be stuck with me."

Paul laughed. "I wouldn't consider that a hardship. You see, Rosanna, I care about you. I've cared about you for a long time. Before Mollie, even. When I thought you planned to step out with Henry, I kicked myself every day for not having the nerve to tell you how I feel."

"You were interested months and months ago?" Either he had kept his feelings well hidden or she was not very astute. She supposed she had been pretty preoccupied with her thoughts of Henry. And then Mollie had *kumm* along and turned her world upside down—but in a *gut* way. A *wunderbaar* way.

"Even longer."

"Y-you never said anything."

"Like a *dummchen*, I hesitated. I almost lost you. I'm not hesitating any longer. Rosanna, could you possibly allow me to court you? We can take things as slow as you like. I only need to know if I can hope you might one day be my *fraa* and Mollie will be my *dochder*."

Tears streamed down Rosanna's cheeks. She swiped at them with the back of her free hand.

"*Ach*, Rosanna! I'm so sorry I upset you." He tried to pull away, but she tightened her grip on his hand.

"These are tears of joy, Paul. Sometimes women cry silly, happy tears. I would be honored to have you court me. I think it's safe to say that Mollie would agree. She adores you."

"I think she's pretty special, too."

"And if she's taken away?"

"We'll pray that never happens, but we will always have each other."

Chapter Thirty

Rosanna had tucked Mollie into her crib and crawled beneath the quilt on her own bed.

Tired as she was, her eyes refused to stay closed as the thoughts whirred through her brain. Had she really consented to a courtship with Paul? Not a business deal, but a real courtship?

Little tingles raced up her spine before shooting out in all directions throughout her body. Her heart beat out a new, joyful rhythm. Paul cared about her. He really cared. He wasn't merely suggesting a deal between them to try to ensure she kept custody of Mollie. How had she never noticed he cared about her?

When did her feelings for Paul change? Rosanna couldn't put her finger on a specific date or time, but at some point she had begun to see Paul in a whole new way. His ease and gentleness with and obvious affection for Mollie touched her deeply. She knew he would make a great *daed* someday. And he had been so supportive of her and so quick to offer his help. None of the other young men, nor most of the girls, ever gave Mollie more than a passing glance. Paul never hesitated to hold her, rock her, or feed her. He would probably even change her diaper without a single qualm. He had been a *gut freind* for sure.

Somewhere along the line Rosanna's feelings had deepened. Paul had become more than a *freind*. Much more. And to think she had wasted so much time trying to get Henry's attention while Paul already cared for her in a way Henry never would. *Thank You, Gott, that things didn't work out how I planned with Henry. You truly do know what is best for me.* And the best for her could only be Paul Hertzler. Rosanna smiled into the darkness. She couldn't be any happier. She had a *wunderbaar* man who loved her and whose love she was ready to return and a precious little girl they both adored.

Paul whistled the song he'd sung to Mollie earlier in the day as he plodded toward home. He hadn't gotten around to teaching Rosanna the words tonight, but now there wasn't any rush. He would have plenty of time to teach her during their courtship. He could scarcely believe Rosanna had agreed to that. One day soon, he hoped, she would become his *fraa*. The woman he had feared would always remain simply a fixture in his dreams had agreed to be a part of his life. *Gut* things do *kumm* to those who wait. And he had waited a long time for Rosanna Mast.

He didn't believe Rosanna had consented to their courtship only to give Mollie a *daed*, since she didn't jump at that chance when he first mentioned it. *Nee,* she truly seemed to care. She had slipped her tiny hand into his as they walked to the door moments ago. Did she have any idea how very much he wanted to kiss her? *Ach!* There would be time for that later.

He shook the reins but really didn't need to encourage the horse to trot faster. He seemed to want to get home to his warm stall as much as Paul wanted to sink into his dreams of Rosanna.

Rosanna happily settled into a pattern of caring for Mollie, helping her *mamm* with household chores, assisting with births, and strengthening her relationship with Paul. He visited one or two evenings during the week. On Saturdays or Sundays, they often bundled Mollie up and took her for rides with them.

"I don't imagine many courting couples take a *boppli* along with them on outings." Rosanna laughed as she threw an extra blanket over Mollie.

"I don't mind one bit, Rosanna." Paul reached over to squeeze her hand. "It's like we're already a family."

"That's a very nice thing to say."

"It's the truth. Don't you feel that way, too?"

"I do." Rosanna squeezed his hand in return. She counted her blessings every day. She stole a quick glance at the handsome young man beside her. She couldn't have asked for a more caring, supportive, dependable man. And he had been there all along. Waiting. *Thank You, Lord, that Paul waited for me to* kumm *to my senses.*

With the extended cold spell St. Mary's County had been experiencing, the ground stayed frozen as hard as concrete, so any snow that fell stayed around. Better yet, the pond had frozen. Young folks could haul out the ice skates they didn't always get to use in the unpredictable winters and glide across the ice for hours. Paul and Rosanna had taken Mollie with them to watch the skaters twirl and zoom around the pond.

When the nip in the air turned into a snarl, they decided to head for Rosanna's house. The sudden strong wind snatched Rosanna's breath away and nearly yanked the black bonnet off her head. She hugged Mollie tighter. "Where did this wind *kumm* from?"

"I think we were more protected down in the woods by the pond. Out here in the open, there's nothing to block the wind."

Rosanna shivered and picked up her pace. She wanted to hurry and get Mollie inside the buggy. The wind had become so strong it almost knocked her to the ground.

"Do you want me to take Mollie?"

"I've got her. I think we're keeping each other warm, if only I can stay on my feet." The wind tugged at her again. Paul wrapped an arm around her shoulders and pulled her and Mollie closer to him. She leaned into him and let him help her battle the wind.

"There." Paul slid close to Rosanna on the buggy seat. He tucked the blanket in around Rosanna and Mollie. "Feel better?"

"Much. Just getting out of that ferocious wind makes me feel one hundred percent warmer."

Paul shook the reins and started the horse moving. "It was fun watching the skaters, though."

"It was, but I think I'm ready for some hot chocolate now."

"Sounds great. And cookies, too?"

Rosanna elbowed him. "Of course."

"Chocolate chip?"

"Definitely. I baked them yesterday with you in mind. There are probably some oatmeal and peanut butter cookies left, too, if my *bruders* didn't eat them all."

"I like that."

"What? That there are other kinds of cookies?"

"*Nee.* That I was in your thoughts."

"You are always in my thoughts."

Paul leaned over and lightly pressed his lips to Rosanna's cheek, sending her heart tumbling over itself.

Rosanna reached to the back of the big metal mailbox to slide the envelopes forward. Something sure felt thick. With her heart thundering, she separated the fat letter from the rest. *It can't be. Please, Lord Gott, don't let this be the correspondence I've been dreading.* Tears pooled in her eyes, making the return address blurry, but the bold print shouted out the name of the law firm anyway. The other mail dropped to the ground as she ripped the envelope open and drew out the contents. She scanned the message and moaned when she really wanted to scream. *Calm down. Breathe.* She tried to obey her brain's commands but instead scooped up the mail and raced to the house.

"What does this mean, Mamm?" Rosanna's lower lip began to tremble as much as her hands did as she shook the letter in Sarah's face.

"What is it?" Sarah jerked back from the paper under her nose. She gave the meat loaf she'd just shaped a final pat, then rinsed her hands and dried them on a paper towel. "Who is that from?"

"A-a lawyer." A huge tear slid down Rosanna's cheek.

Sarah snatched the paper from Rosanna's hand and began to read. Rosanna watched her *mamm*'s eyes travel down the page and then return to the top to repeat the process more slowly. She gasped and fixed wide eyes on Rosanna.

"D-does this mean what I think, Mamm?"

"It looks to me like Kandi is filing for custody of Mollie."

"*Ach*, Mamm!" Rosanna threw her hands over her face and sobbed into them. She felt Sarah pull her into an embrace and pat her back.

"It doesn't say she's been given custody, just that she's going to file."

"How can she?"

"I believe she feels it is her duty since Mollie is her niece."

"But Mamm, she won't even feed her or change a diaper!" Rosanna knew her voice came out in a pitiful whine, but she couldn't help it. Whining had to be slightly better than wailing, which is what she really wanted to do.

"She would have to learn to do that."

"She wouldn't mix the formula. She didn't want to feed Mollie. She didn't want to risk getting spit up on. She couldn't even soothe Mollie when she cried."

"She will have a lot to learn, then."

"She hasn't even visited in a while. Mollie doesn't know who she is. And what will she do with Mollie while she's acting or dancing or whatever it is that she does? Being shifted around from place to place and handed off to one person after another is not a *gut* thing for a *boppli*."

"I know that, dear. You don't have to convince me."

"Do you really think they'll allow her to take my *boppli*? Jane wanted me to have Mollie. She had it all planned out and written up legally."

"I know that, too. I'm not sure how the *Englisch* court system makes a decision. We need to keep taking the best care of Mollie that we can, like we've always done. And pray."

Rosanna sniffed. "But what if—"

"Stop! Don't borrow trouble. We will trust Gott. He knows what is best."

"We're what is best for Mollie, ain't so, Mamm?"

"Rosanna, you have been a *wunderbaar mudder* for Mollie. We all love her dearly. We must try not to worry. Now, dry those tears before that dear little one wakes up. She will want to see your happy face."

Chapter Thirty-One

Rosanna did her best to carry on as usual. The fear of losing Mollie hovered in the back of her mind when it wasn't front and center. Every bump or thump caused her heart to leap into her throat until she assured herself Kandi had not arrived for a cursory visit or to whisk Mollie away. She shared her fears and doubts with Paul, who did everything he could think of to bolster Rosanna's spirits. Together they played with Mollie, cared for her, and took her on outings. Rosanna prayed they weren't storing up memories for a time when Mollie was no longer with them.

Saturday afternoon had been beautiful. Though the calendar said it was still winter, the air hinted at spring. Of course, they could have snow the next day. That's the way the fickle weather behaved in Southern Maryland. Rosanna and Paul had taken advantage of the lovely day. Since he had worked extra hours during the week to complete a big order, Eli had let him off early. They had taken Mollie to watch the skaters again. Another day or two like today and the ice would thaw too much for skating.

"I'm sure you could borrow Emma's skates and

take a twirl or two around the pond," Paul said. "I'll watch Mollie."

"I'm fine watching, but you can skate if you want. It looks like Tobias is off early, and I'm sure he would loan you his skates."

"I'll settle for watching, too. It seems like everyone has the idea that this might be the last opportunity to skate this year. Most people who usually work on Saturdays have shown up."

Rosanna nodded and sniffed the air. Pine wood smoke from the crackling bonfire drifted over to where they sat on a log. Mollie perched on Rosanna's lap, biting on a teething ring. She was sitting now and even trying to crawl. When Rosanna placed her on her tummy on the floor, she could push up to her hands and knees and rock back and forth. Rosanna knew the little girl would soon figure out how to propel herself either forward or backward.

Rosanna gradually breathed a little easier when each day's mail contained only the usual letters or junk mail, not a single legal document. The notice she had previously received had not yet been followed up by a court summons or any other official papers. The doubts and fears didn't dissipate, but she was able to push them farther back in her mind. She concentrated on enjoying every moment with Mollie.

She watched a few people poke sticks with marshmallows on the ends into the fire. She laughed when some lost their treats to the flames. When Paul nudged her, she looked where he pointed. Tobias and Emma skated side by side, seemingly oblivious to everything around them. "I knew it! I knew he was interested in Emma!"

"They make a nice couple," Paul observed. "Like us."

"Like us." Rosanna beamed at him. She hoped things worked out for Emma and Tobias, as they had for her and Paul. Her *bruder* and her best *freind* were perfect for each other. Maybe she would visit Emma soon for a little chat. She'd never get any information out of Tobias.

"Do you want some marshmallows? I can try my hand at toasting some. I can't do any worse than the folks over there."

Rosanna glanced at the people gathered around the bonfire. Some held up sticks with charred marshmallows. Others held empty sticks, since their marshmallows had slid off. Only a few popped gooey masses into their mouths. She laughed and shook her head. "Maybe later."

"You just want to keep an eye on your *bruder*," Paul teased.

"It is kind of fun watching them."

"What do you think?"

"I think they are great together. Emma would certainly be able to hold her own with Tobias' teasing."

"They certainly look like they're enjoying themselves."

"They look oblivious to the universe."

Paul laughed. He scooped Mollie off Rosanna's lap and held her high in the air. Mollie's blue eyes opened wide before she let out a squeal of delight.

After they had mingled with the other young folks who had finished skating and had eaten marshmallows Paul had toasted to perfection, Rosanna decided they should head for home. The sky had turned mostly gray, and the temperature had dropped. Mollie's little cheeks glowed bright pink.

Rosanna and Paul sang silly songs to Mollie all the

way home and laughed when she babbled along with them. All merriment died when they rolled up the Mast driveway. A battered green car sat close to the house.

"Did you know she was visiting today?"

"I didn't have any idea. I haven't heard from Kandi in ages. I only got that letter from a lawyer." Goose bumps unrelated to the temperature marched up and down Rosanna's arms. Her breath came in short gasps.

"Calm down." Paul reached for Rosanna's hand. "She can't take Mollie today."

"I-I hope not." Rosanna gripped Paul's hand like a drowning man grabbed a rope.

"It will be all right."

Rosanna nodded and prayed he was right.

Paul hopped out of the buggy as soon as it stopped rolling and jogged around to help Rosanna and Mollie out. "Do you want me to *kumm* inside with you?"

"Please." She clutched Mollie tighter. Together they climbed the steps to enter the front door, since Rosanna figured Sarah had probably parked Kandi in the living room.

"There you are!" Kandi called out as soon as the threesome crossed the threshold into the room.

"I wasn't expecting you." Rosanna held her head high. She would not let this woman think she intimidated her, even if her insides had turned to jelly.

"I can't call to make arrangements."

"You could write when you plan to visit."

"I could if I had a set schedule."

Kinner need a set schedule. They need someone they can depend on. Rosanna fought to keep those words inside. "Oh" was all she said.

"My lawyer said I should visit more often if I plan to get custody. You did get the lawyer's letter, didn't you?"

"*Jah*." Rosanna paused a moment to think but had to get an answer to the question burning in her brain. "Don't you want to visit her, Kandi?"

"Oh, sure. It's just so hard with my crazy hours and all. I've been so busy lately. I've had a lot of gigs, which is a real boost to my career."

"I see." Rosanna didn't see at all. It sounded to her like Kandi was visiting only because it would look *gut* to do so, not because she really wanted to visit her niece.

"Man, she's really grown."

"She seems to get bigger and learn something new every day."

"Is this your boyfriend?"

Heat crept up Rosanna's neck and face like mercury rising in a thermometer at noon in the middle of August. "I think you already met Paul Hertzler."

"Hello." Paul nodded at Kandi.

"Nice to see you." Kandi stuck out her hand.

Surprised, Paul extended his hand and allowed Kandi to pump it up and down. "Would you like me to wait in the kitchen, Rosanna?"

She cast a sideways glance at Kandi. Rosanna could really use Paul's support right now. Would Kandi mind if he stayed?

"You don't have to leave on my account. The more, the merrier." Kandi's laugh sounded forced. She batted at a wisp of platinum hair.

Rosanna could have wept with relief. She sank down on the edge of the rocking chair and began unwrapping Mollie from her warm layers of clothing.

"She's a beauty. She still has her blonde hair." Kandi leaned forward slightly. "Hi, Mollie."

Rosanna had wondered when Kandi would ever address her niece. She had seemed almost hesitant to do so. "Would you like to hold her?" Rosanna wanted to hug Mollie close and never let her go, but she knew she had to give Kandi a chance to know her. After all, the woman was Mollie's *aenti*.

"I . . . well, sure."

Rosanna stood and dropped the blankets and outerwear onto the chair behind her. She took the three steps toward Kandi's chair since the other woman didn't make any effort to move. She lowered Mollie onto Kandi's lap.

"Oh my, you seem heavier than last time." Kandi threw awkward arms around Mollie to keep her from sliding off onto the floor.

"She's been gaining weight well. She's very healthy."

"So it seems. I really wouldn't have any way to gauge that, so I'll take your word for it."

"Do you help with your coworkers' *kinner*, uh, children?"

"My what? Oh, you mean the other dancers. I see their kids sometimes. I don't really help out with them. They have other babysitters if they need them."

Rosanna almost asked who Kandi had lined up to care for Mollie but couldn't bring herself to do so. She certainly wouldn't know the people anyway, and it might be better if she didn't know anything about them. That would only add to her fears.

"Ahhh! Oh! Oh my!"

Rosanna jumped up from the chair she'd just perched on. The empty rocking chair thumped crazily behind her. "What's wrong?"

"Something feels warm, damp." She yanked Mollie off her lap and held her out at arm's length. "Eww!

I think she just wet on me." Kandi wrinkled her nose and looked totally disgusted. "How gross! Here, take her!"

The sudden movement and shrieking caused Mollie to let out a howl. Her arms and legs flailed, and she nearly elbowed Kandi's chin. Rosanna gathered the frightened little girl to her in a fierce hug. She kissed the top of her head and tried to hide the smile that tugged at her lips. What a comical sight! A grown woman afraid of a leaky diaper! "I'll go change her, unless you'd like the practice, Kandi."

"No! No, thank you. You go right ahead."

Rosanna bit her tongue and didn't dare look at Paul. She could tell he, too, was struggling not to laugh. "I can change her right here in the cradle, and you can watch."

"You really should give it a try, Kandi." Sarah's voice came from the doorway.

Rosanna glanced in her direction and couldn't miss the crinkles surrounding her *mamm*'s eyes and the twitch of her lips. She obviously found the situation as comical as Rosanna did.

"That's okay." Kandi's nose was still wrinkled.

"If you plan to care for Mollie, as your lawyer's letter stated, you'll have to change diapers. Mollie can't very well do that for herself." Sarah's foot tapped on the floor.

"I-I'll watch, then. It can't be that hard, right?" Kandi used her hands to push herself off the chair, mumbling as she did so, "Maybe she'll be potty trained early."

Rosanna let the comment slide, but Sarah pounced on it. "Don't count on that. They potty train at all different ages. They have to be ready."

Kandi shrugged but kept quiet.

Rosanna laid Mollie in the cradle while she pulled diapers and wipes from underneath it. Immediately four little limbs batted and kicked.

"It must be a challenge to change a squirming baby. Is she always so rambunctious?"

"She's stretching and working those little muscles." Rosanna had the next diaper ready before unfastening the one Mollie wore. "You're in luck, Kandi. She's only wet. Do you want to try?"

"I'm good right here where I am."

"Okay." Rosanna talked to Mollie to distract her. She handed the little girl a small toy to hold while she captured the bicycling legs and expertly changed the diaper. "There. All done. She's clean and dry. Do you want to pick her up?"

Kandi shrugged again and leaned over the cradle. She moved her hands one way and then another as if trying to decide how to best lift Mollie out of the cradle.

"She's much stronger now. She can hold her head up and everything, so you don't have to worry how to pick her up." Rosanna couldn't decide whether she should let Kandi figure out how to pick up the wiggling little girl for herself or simply pluck her from the cradle and hand her to her *aenti*. "I'm going to get rid of this diaper and wash my hands. I'll be right back."

Rosanna noticed Kandi's look of distress. Sarah had already moved from the doorway or Rosanna would have somehow silently asked her opinion. But Mamm was right. If Kandi wanted custody of Mollie, she had to be able to properly care for her. Rosanna dashed back into the room in time to see Paul lift Mollie from the cradle, kiss her cheek, and hand her to Kandi. She couldn't help but feel sorry for the woman. Kandi stood stiff as a statue, not even swaying as most people did when holding an infant. "You can sit with her, if you like."

"I can't stay much longer. I have to work tonight."

"When do you sleep if you work at night?" Paul asked.

"I don't work *all* night. I'm usually finished by one or two. I can't go right to sleep, but I generally get into bed around three or so."

"In the morning?"

Rosanna had to smile. Paul sounded horrified. She knew he was thinking he would be weaving his last few dreams of the night when Kandi was just going to bed. Who would keep Mollie all night, and how would Kandi care for her during the day if that's when she slept?

"Well, if I had Mollie, I'd probably try to sleep for a little while when I got home. I'd get up when she did and take a nap when she took hers. That should work out fine." When Mollie began to squirm to change positions, Kandi panicked. "Someone take her quick before I drop her! Quick!"

Rosanna rushed forward. "It's okay." She wasn't sure if the reassurance was directed toward Kandi or Mollie or herself. She held out her arms as Mollie's tiny hands reached for her. "You know, Kandi, you could always visit Mollie if you decide—"

"If I decided to give up the custody suit? No way, sister. This is my niece. She belongs with family."

"But do you really want to care for a little one now at this point in your career?"

"Well, it certainly isn't convenient, but I'll figure it out." Kandi spun around on those high-heeled boots and fled from the room. The front door banged behind her.

Rosanna stared openmouthed and patted Mollie's back.

"She'd better figure out how to change a diaper, then," Sarah called.

Rosanna laughed almost hysterically, releasing the tension that had mounted to an almost unbearable level.

"I'm sorry, Rosanna." Paul left his chair in the corner and crossed the room to stand beside her. He tickled Mollie's chin. "I know you wanted Kandi to figure out how to lift Mollie from the cradle, but I couldn't stand it any longer. I was afraid she'd hover over the cradle until sunset trying to do such a simple thing. It was pitiful, and I couldn't bear to watch."

"That's okay." Rosanna giggled. "The whole situation could be comical if it wasn't so serious."

"It was rather comical anyway." Sarah entered the room, drying her hands on a dish towel. "I don't think that woman has a maternal bone in her body." She clucked her tongue and shook her head. "I don't think you'll have a thing to worry about, Rosanna. Mollie will stay here with us."

Chapter Thirty-Two

Every day Rosanna prayed her *mamm* was right. Apparently the wheels of the *Englisch* court system turned as slowly as molasses running uphill in February. Or maybe Kandi had decided not to pursue custody at all. At any rate, Rosanna had not received any new correspondence from either lawyers or Kandi. Still, she held her breath every time she plunged her hand into the big metal box to withdraw the day's mail. And each evening she thanked Gott for allowing her to have Mollie for one more day.

Almost a month had passed since Kandi's last visit. It was possible she had gotten an acting job out of the area. Would it be too much to hope that she had decided a *boppli* would hinder her career too much? Rosanna would hope anyway.

Spring had been whispering to Southern Maryland more and more. Daylight hung around a bit longer in the evening, and the morning frost disappeared. Even a few brave robins had returned to the area.

Mollie was becoming more and more interested in the world around her. She cooed and laughed at each new discovery. She figured out that rocking on her hands and knees didn't get her anywhere, but that with a bit more effort, crawling could propel her to wherever she wanted to go. She even produced two additional little teeth and showed real interest in everyone else's plate at the table.

The fact that Paul celebrated Mollie's achievements just as enthusiastically as she did would have made Rosanna fall in love with him if she hadn't already done so. And that was another marvel. Her love for Paul had blossomed into such strong feelings, she now knew for sure he was the one for her.

On a particularly warm off-Sunday afternoon, Rosanna and Paul took Mollie outside to watch Katie, Sadie, and James play. Rosanna smiled and Mollie squealed as Paul chased Rosanna's shrieking younger siblings around the front yard. The ground was still too cold to spread out a blanket for Mollie to play on, so she squirmed in Rosanna's arms, acting as if she wanted to play with the others.

To amuse the little girl, Rosanna sat in the wooden swing suspended by a thick rope from a sturdy oak limb. She pushed off with her toes and sent the swing gently swaying. She had always loved swinging when she was younger. She would pump her legs and soar so high she believed her feet would brush the clouds. "It won't be long before I can push you in the swing, ain't so? And you'll try to grab one of those puffy, white clouds up there just like I did." Rosanna watched the billowy clouds slide across the bright blue sky for a moment and then looked back at Mollie's sweet face.

She could look into that angelic face with the big blue eyes forever. The only thing that rivaled that pleasure was gazing into Paul's ever-changing hazel eyes. Every night she thanked Gott for both of these people

who meant the world to her. She also thanked Him for
Jane's courage and determination to seek a proper
home for her infant. Jane's selfless decision had forever altered Rosanna's life and gave her the greatest
gift she had received in her twenty-one years.

A flash of green caught Rosanna's eye. She dug her
toes into the dirt to bring the swing to an abrupt halt.
The song she'd been singing to Mollie died on her
lips. Her heart crawled halfway up her throat and sat
there. After weeks without any word whatsoever, what
was Kandi doing here now?

Paul must have seen the green car inching up the
driveway, too. In an instant, he appeared beside
Rosanna and Mollie. He dropped a hand to Rosanna's
shoulder and gave a gentle squeeze. "It will be all right.
Hold on and I'll give you a little push."

Instead, Rosanna started to slide from the swing.
"I should . . ."

"You should relax." He patted her shoulder and
tickled Mollie's chin. "Relax. Act normal. You don't
have to be afraid."

Somehow his words soothed her. Tension drained
from Rosanna's stiff shoulders. She wiggled on the
wooden seat to get comfortable and held on as Paul
had instructed. "Hang on, Mollie. We're about to fly."

Paul drew the swing back a little way and let it go.
His gentle touch on her back whenever the swing
reached him gave Rosanna the reassurance she so
needed.

Katie and James continued to chase each other.
Sadie ran to the swing, excited to show Mollie a pine
cone she'd picked up at the edge of the yard. The
eight-year-old chattered away as though the infant

understood her every word. Paul stopped the swing's motion so Mollie could look at the perfectly formed pine cone. Her little face lit up at Sadie's excitement. Rosanna looked up at Paul, and they shared a smile, as any other parents did over their *boppli*'s actions.

"See, Mollie?" Sadie held the pine cone out for Mollie to touch. "This pine cone is perfect. Just like you."

"What a nice thing to say, Sadie." Rosanna reached out to pat her *schweschder*'s arm.

"I-I'm sorry to interrupt."

For that brief, tender moment, Rosanna had forgotten about Kandi's arrival. Reality crashed back on her. "H-hello, Kandi."

"You all look so happy."

"We are." Rosanna straightened the tiny bonnet on Mollie's head.

Katie and James ran over to stand near the swing, as if forming a shield around Mollie. Katie ventured close enough to plant a kiss on Mollie's cheek.

"You all can go back to playing." Rosanna wasn't sure she wanted her younger siblings to witness whatever Kandi had come to say. She didn't want to hear Kandi's words, either. James, Katie, and Sadie reluctantly drifted away.

"I'm going to look for more pine cones to show Mollie." Sadie trotted back to drop her pine cone into Mollie's lap before running to catch up with James and Katie.

"I have a feeling they're always attentive to Mollie, that this isn't just a show for me." Kandi nodded toward the *kinner* searching the edge of the yard for more treasures.

"They are sincere," Rosanna replied. "I don't think

they know how to be otherwise. And they dote on Mollie."

"I figured." Kandi twirled a strand of brittle-looking hair around an index finger. The nail was violet today instead of bright red.

"We haven't heard from you in a while." Rosanna hoped that didn't sound judgmental. She hadn't meant to criticize.

"Yeah, well, I've been busy." Kandi twisted the hair tighter. "I got a part in a play." Kandi's eyes sparkled, and her whole face brightened, even through the layers of makeup. "It's a big part, too, almost the lead."

"Congratulations. You must be so excited." Rosanna thought those were the appropriate remarks to make.

"I am. It's what I've always wanted. A dream come true. It's one step closer to making it big."

"I-I'm happy for you, then." Rosanna had never been to a play other than the Christmas reenactments at school. She couldn't begin to imagine what it would be like to prance around on a stage with hundreds of strangers gawking at you.

"Thanks."

The silence that filled the air caused no small amount of trepidation. Was Kandi about to say she had arranged a babysitter and was ready to take Mollie? Rosanna hadn't received any legal correspondence and hadn't had any visits from Social Services or whoever handled such matters.

Kandi coughed and looked toward the laughing *kinner* picking up and discarding pine cones. Rosanna couldn't help but notice the brief sad expression that raced across Kandi's face. Was she about to say words

Rosanna didn't want to hear? Kandi coughed again and cleared her throat.

"Would you like something to drink?"

"No thanks. I'm good." She twiddled that same poor lock of hair and looked at Mollie, who was completely fascinated by Sadie's gift. A tiny smile tugged at Kandi's lips. "She is happy here, isn't she?"

"She's a very happy little girl. She wakes up in a pleasant mood and doesn't fuss or cry much at all. She got a little cranky when she cut her first couple of teeth but was nowhere near as fussy as Katie was when she was cutting her first one." Rosanna clamped her lips together. She was rambling, but talking about Mollie came easily, and it delayed hearing whatever Kandi planned to say.

"I can tell she's loved. By all of you."

"That's for sure."

"And she loves you, too. I can tell."

Rosanna hoped so but hadn't really thought about that. Didn't all *kinner* love their parents?

"Do you want to hold her?" Rosanna didn't want to relinquish Mollie for even a moment but felt compelled to make the offer.

"Rosanna, I need to tell you something." Kandi looked down at her pointy-toed black boots.

Here it comes! Rosanna braced herself for bad news. Her grip on Mollie tightened. Her heartbeat pounded like thunder in her ears. If she hadn't been holding Mollie, she'd have clapped her hands over her ears like she had when she was little to block out Tobias' teasing. Paul must have sensed her rising panic. He moved closer and touched her shoulder as if he could transfer courage to her.

Rosanna willed Kandi to look at her and to deliver her news. Why was Kandi drawing this out? Rosanna needed to hear the words so she could begin to deal with the pain.

After what seemed like eons, Kandi lifted her eyes from her boots and looked at Mollie. When she shifted her gaze to Rosanna, Rosanna was surprised to see tears in the woman's eyes. Did she feel that bad about tearing Mollie away from the only family she'd known?

"Rosanna?" Kandi's voice cracked. She cleared her throat and tried again. "I've decided not to pursue custody."

"Excuse me? I don't think I heard you correctly."

"I'm sure you did."

"Wh-why?"

"I thought I should be responsible for my sister's child. I wasn't there for Jane, so I thought I could make amends by taking her child." Kandi sighed deep and loud. "Do you know I sometimes resented Jane when we were kids? When she was sick, she took all of our mother's attention. I felt like Mom had no time for me."

"I'm sorry." Rosanna had an urge to comfort the other woman.

Kandi waved her hand and sniffed. "Oh, it's okay now. I understand. I know mothers love all their children. I'm pretty sure I could offer Mollie love, but I could never take care of her properly and live the kind of life I lead. I've worked hard to reach my dreams, and though I'm sure it sounds selfish, I don't want to give them up. Being raised by babysitters would be worse than my childhood with a preoccupied mother."

Mollie squirmed and Paul silently lifted her from

Rosanna's arms. He bounced her and whispered to Mollie but didn't stray far away from Rosanna.

"You have a good man there." Kandi nodded toward Paul.

"*Jah,* I do."

"You are both so good with Mollie. And you're good for her, too. I can see how much you love each other and Mollie."

Rosanna knew her cheeks glowed. She smiled but couldn't force out any comment. Her brain grappled with Kandi's words. Was she really going to drop the whole lawsuit? Her attention snapped back to Kandi.

"Jane was right. She picked the best person to raise her baby." Kandi ran a finger under each eye. She sniffed again. "I thought a baby belonged with her own family. I thought she needed to be raised in the same world as her family. Jane was a lot smarter. She saw the love, faith, and stability in your world, in your family. Jane picked the right mother for her baby." Kandi's shoulders slumped. Her gaze returned to the ground.

Rosanna couldn't stop herself. She slid off the swing and stepped forward. Before she could rethink her plan, she pulled Kandi into a hug. "I'm sure this is very hard for you. I'm happy to be Mollie's *mudder.* I love her as my own. We all do." Rosanna paused. Her eyes locked with Paul's. He nodded and smiled. "It took a lot of courage for you to *kumm* here today to tell me this."

"I didn't want you to get another letter from the lawyer. I wanted to explain. I'm sorry for all the trouble I caused."

"I don't hold any grudges."

"You really don't, do you?"

"Of course not. All is forgiven." Rosanna flicked

away a tear that escaped from her own eye. "I want you to know I will be the best possible *mamm* I can be."

"I know you will. Thank you for being here for Jane and for Mollie." Kandi's voice cracked again. "C-can I visit Mollie sometimes? I'll try to make arrangements with you before I come."

"Of course you can visit. Did you want to hold her or play with her now?" Rosanna signaled for Paul to bring Mollie closer.

"I'll talk to her for a few minutes, but then I need to get back for a rehearsal."

"They have rehearsals on Sundays?" Rosanna mentally smacked her forehead. *Englischers* shopped and worked and did everything else on Sundays, so why wouldn't Kandi have a rehearsal? She much preferred their way of keeping Sundays special days, set apart for Gott and family. They only did necessary chores, like feeding the animals or putting wood in the stove. It would never occur to an Amish person to hitch up and drive to the grocery store. They might take a ride to visit or even go on an outing to the river, but Sundays were reserved for worship and fellowship.

Kandi ran a hand through her bristly hair. "The closer we get to opening night of the play, the more rehearsals we have, even on Sundays."

Rosanna bobbed her head as if she understood. Poor Kandi. She rushed from place to place and never seemed to take time to enjoy where she actually was. "You must get very tired."

"Yeah, but I try not to think about that." She laughed. "It's the life I chose, so I really can't complain."

Rosanna was glad she chose to join the Amish church. Her life was pretty much mapped out for her, and she liked it that way. "I'm sure you are very *gut* at what you do, Kandi."

"I'm trying. It's taken me a long time to get this far, but this play is a big step in the right direction. I don't want to dance in clubs all my life."

Rosanna suppressed a shiver. She would hate that herself.

"Do you want to hold her?" Paul held Mollie closer to Kandi.

"Well, okay." She took Mollie into her arms but didn't look terribly comfortable. "Hi, Mollie." She jiggled the little girl up and down. "Sorry, my experience with babies is practically zero."

"You're doing fine." Rosanna could afford to be more encouraging now that she knew Mollie would be staying with her.

Kandi babbled to Mollie for a few minutes before handing her to Rosanna. "I have to go. Be good, Mollie." Kandi kissed Mollie's pink cheek. When she looked, Rosanna saw the tears in her eyes. "The lawyer knows I've changed my mind. I know I would make a terrible mother. And I don't have the kind of life that leaves much room for kids." Kandi brushed at the tears that smeared the dark makeup. "Y-you can go ahead with the adoption, Rosanna. You are a great mother. Bye." Kandi whipped around and strutted to the car without a backward glance.

Rosanna hugged Mollie tight. Could she be dreaming? She searched Paul's face. His expression mirrored her own astonishment. "D-did she really say Mollie is mine?"

"*Jah*, Rosanna. She gave up her plan for custody. She gave Mollie to you."

Rosanna smiled through her tears. "To us."

Paul pulled Rosanna and Mollie into his arms. He kissed the top of each of their heads even though they were standing in the yard in broad daylight with Rosanna's younger siblings running around. "*Jah,* to us."

"The Lord Gott is so *gut.*" Rosanna pulled back only far enough to look into Paul's loving eyes. "He has given me you and Mollie—the most *wunderbaar* gifts ever."

Epilogue

"Are you nervous?" Emma whispered as she squeezed Rosanna's hand.

"Not in the least. I am absolutely certain I am doing the right thing." Rosanna raised a hand to make sure her *kapp* was straight. She ran her hands down her sides to smooth any nonexistent wrinkles from her royal blue wedding dress. The nip in the November air, the smell of wood smoke curling from the chimney, the assorted *freinden* and family members who had arrived in a parade of gray buggies all imprinted themselves in Rosanna's memory. But her most cherished memory had yet to be made—joining hands with the most *wunderbaar* man ever and taking vows to love and care for each other for the rest of their lives.

Rosanna thanked the Lord Gott daily that Paul Hertzler had patiently waited for her to *kumm* to her senses. He offered friendship, hope, help, and even love when she needed it. He loved her *boppli* as much as she did. She couldn't have found a better man anywhere. Thank goodness she had abandoned any notion that Henry Zook would be a match for her. Even Frannie Hostetler had wised up and figured out Henry would never do for a husband. Rosanna hadn't had to say a word about that awful conversation she and Henry had had in the store. Frannie had faced that reality all on her own.

Rosanna couldn't suppress a smile when she followed Emma's gaze straight to Tobias. Her *bruder* couldn't possibly do better than Emma Kurtz, and vice versa. She would be as happy to add Emma to their family as she was to join Paul's family. She already loved Mary Hertzler as a second *mudder* and wouldn't mind one bit living in the Hertzler home while their own house was being built on the back of the family's property. Rosanna squeezed Emma's hand and winked. "You're perfect for each other."

Emma's pale cheeks took on a rosy hue. "I don't have any idea what you're talking about."

"Certainly you don't expect me to believe that."

Muffled giggling captured Rosanna's attention. Frannie and some of the other unmarried girls stood in the distance chattering and looking toward a group of eligible young men. Henry, she noticed, was not among that gathering. Rosanna hoped Frannie found a nice fellow who could endure her idiosyncrasies, like infernally fiddling with the glasses that crept down her nose.

At the bishop's nod, Rosanna slipped away from Emma and followed the church leader toward the room where she and Paul would meet with him and the ministers before the service. The guests would take their seats in the big, clean-as-a-whistle barn and sing until the service began, the same as they did on church days. From the corner of her eye, she caught her *mamm*'s big smile and nod. Even little Mollie looked excited, as if she knew she was about to acquire a *daed*.

Paul and Rosanna had visited the lawyer several

times to make sure all the paperwork was in order so they could drive to the courthouse tomorrow to officially become Mollie's parents. Rosanna pinched herself several times to ensure she wasn't dreaming. On this lovely fall Thursday, she and Paul would become husband and wife. On an equally happy Friday, they would legally adopt Mollie. Rosanna had been blessed indeed. Tears welled in her eyes. Happy tears. Just the same, she blinked hard to keep them in check. There would not be any tears on this joyous day.

A sputtering engine and tires crunching on gravel caused Rosanna to whip around to identify who could possibly be speeding up the driveway on her wedding day. *Please, Lord Gott, don't let there be some legal hitch that will prevent finalization of the adoption.* She held her breath, heart pounding like thunder booming during a July thunderstorm. She sighed with relief when she recognized the wheezing little green car.

The vehicle squealed to a halt. The driver leaped out before the engine died. Wild, platinum blonde hair, whipped by a sudden gust of wind, wrapped around the woman's face. Rosanna was sure she heard the snap of chewing gum.

"I'm. Not. Too. Late. Am. I?" A gasp punctuated each word.

Rosanna smiled and shook her head. Kandi had made it after all. She didn't think the aspiring actress would be able to fit a humble Amish wedding into her busy schedule, but somehow she managed to do so. Since Kandi didn't present a threat to the adoption plans any longer but, rather, embraced the idea, Rosanna could rejoice that Mollie's *aenti* was able to share this happy day with them. Kandi would probably leave as soon as she could, as usual, but Rosanna was touched by her effort. She smiled. Kandi wouldn't be leaving too soon, though, since Amish weddings lasted three hours, the same as a church service.

Kandi gave a thumbs-up sign and wobbled across the uneven ground in her black, pointy-toed, high-heeled boots. Rosanna nearly chuckled when she saw Kandi tug at her too-short skirt as she headed into the barn. She turned away from the other woman and hurried to catch up with the bishop.

Rosanna feared her mouth would be forever set in a wide smile. She couldn't force her lips downward even if she wanted to. Here she stood in the crook of her new husband's arm and hugging her little girl to her breast.

"I'd take a picture of you if I could, but I read you folks didn't go for that." Kandi somehow got the words out between crackles of her gum.

"We'll remember and cherish the day even without pictures," Rosanna assured her. "I'm glad you were able to attend our wedding."

"I wouldn't have missed it for anything—actually, I almost did miss it, didn't I?" Kandi laughed at herself. "That has to be the longest wedding service I've ever been to. Whew! I thought my backside had grown to that hard, wooden bench."

Rosanna smiled. "Our church services are the same."

"You don't have to invite me to one of those, then." Kandi massaged her lower back with a red-nailed hand. "Well, I have to run. Rehearsals, you know."

Rosanna nodded. She'd figured as much. Kandi didn't ask to hold Mollie, but she didn't flinch and pull away when the little girl tugged at a strand of her

326 *Susan Lantz Simpson*

coarse hair as she leaned close to greet her niece. That was some progress, anyway. Kandi hobbled back to her car, waved, and exited in a cloud of dust.

Paul leaned down to brush his lips across first Mollie's cheek and then Rosanna's. "What are you thinking, Fraa?"

"I'm thinking that must be the sweetest word in all the world and that the Lord Gott couldn't have given me a more *wunderbaar* husband and *dochder*."

Paul's arm tightened around Rosanna and Mollie. "He always gives us the best gifts, ain't so?"

"For sure and for certain."

Connect with U s

Visit us online at
KensingtonBooks.com
to read more from your favorite authors, see books
by series, view reading group guides, and more.

Join us on social media

for sneak peeks, chances to win books and prize packs,
and to share your thoughts with other readers.

facebook.com/kensingtonpublishing
twitter.com/kensingtonbooks

Tell us what you think!

To share your thoughts, submit a review,
or sign up for our eNewsletters, please visit:
KensingtonBooks.com/TellUs.

More by Bestselling Author
Hannah Howell